I would like to dedicate this book to James, who always believed in me and my writing and never gave up on helping me achieve my dream. I would also like to dedicate this to my father, Michael, who inspired me to fall in love with the written word.

Shannon Whittall

A WARRIOR'S BLUSH

AUSTIN MACAULEY PUBLISHERS™

LONDON • CAMBRIDGE • NEW YORK • SHARJAH

A CIP catalogue record for this title is available from the British Library.

ISBN 9781788788076 (Paperback)
ISBN 9781788788083 (Kindle e-book)
ISBN 9781528956130 (ePub e-book)

www.austinmacauley.com

First Published (2019)
Austin Macauley Publishers Ltd
25 Canada Square
Canary Wharf
London
E14 5LQ

Prologue

Why am I here?

I don't deserve to be here. I have not deserved to be here for three years of my life. And yet, I take solace in the fact that most people do not even last one year in this pit of torment.

But after all… the Forge Camp of Golnar is designed to kill us. To kill all those who threaten Aneya. To kill me.

Aneya is our continent. Or at least it was until Myrna Verena murdered our faithful King Adrian Maddox, the ruler of Aneya's capital city, Eradan. These morbid events took place four years ago. Myrna was a servant girl in the Palace who made an oath to serve with relentless loyalty… but clearly, she had other intentions. It turns out she was in fact the Dark Queen of Vangar; a place of darkness and cruelty in the eastern lands.

Adrian's daughter, Jocelyn, is said to be enslaved while his son Jasper remains within the Palace walls to become Myrna's own heir as she is rumoured to be barren herself; I dread to think what the siblings have endured these past years. But, would it be so different to what I have suffered?

Three years I have spent here. Three years of beatings, lashings, sweltering summers and unforgiving winters. But in this time, my past lays forgotten, my reputation has evolved into something new, my identity morphing into someone new.

I am feared.

I am loved.

I am Golnar's Ghost.

Chapter 1

Tomorrow is the day.

The day I have planned for so long.

I tell myself that it will work, but I know better. My plan holds host to doubt, uncertainty and sure death should I fail.

Tomorrow is the day that I escape.

As I squeeze myself into the foetal position one last time, I try to think about what freedom was like. But, I can hardly remember. All I can do is feel the familiar tension and ache of my muscles from being confined into a cell with no room to stretch. I can feel the damp soil of the floor and walls of my quarters soaking into the thin grey rag we are forced to wear. I can feel my toes tingling with the beginnings of numbness from being cramped against the steel bars that hold me captive.

I find myself smirking at that thought. Those bars have not held me inside these walls for a year and a half now. I look at the thin hole I fashioned at the edge of my cell and think about the lives it has allowed me to save, including my own. The hole is just big enough to slip through, but small enough to remain concealed when I choose to use it.

I clutch the jagged rock I used to fashion my salvation in my fist. Rocks are a common hazard around here. But, I seem to be the only one to recognise its dual purpose as a make-shift shovel. Since then, I had sharpened its edges along the bars of the cell to form my trusted weapon; you can never be too careful around Golnar. And the irony of that fact is that we are imprisoned as we are considered a danger to society and yet we prisoners do not fear each other. We fear the guards.

As a women's facility, the guards here seem to think that we are their rightful property; that we are expendable. That being a slave of Golnar ultimately means that we are slaves to their lust also. Except… I have come to be known as the repelling force against it.

My thoughts are interrupted as the sound of soft sobbing reaches my ears. I instantly straighten, eyes darting back and forth in the darkness to distinguish the source of the noise. The eternal darkness of Golnar no longer hinders my sight and so my eyes zero-in on a door across the way as it slams shut. The Cupboard. It used to be where residential essentials could be found such as freshly sharpened shackles or newly thinned rags for the new arrivals. But, now it remains a once popular place for the guard's to exercise their indiscretions that has since been abandoned since my last tirade there. And for good reason.

With wrath flushing my skin, I squeeze through the gap I made, my shoulders cramping in pain from having to bend so much so that I may fit. I feel the eyes on me from the thousands of cells stretching beyond the darkness. One could spend a century wandering Golnar and still not figure out its true expanse. I can almost feel the anticipation brewing in the air from the other prisoners.

I stalk to the door and creep inside with expert skill. The familiar rows and columns of shelves tower before me, brimming with the everyday essentials to make our lives a living hell. I hear their voices before I see them. I clutch my weapon tighter in my hand, bracing myself for the events to come.

"Now is not the time to be shy, darling." A man growls. I hear a sharp smack and a cry of pain. Gritting my teeth and blood boiling in my veins, I edge closer so that I can see my target.

Through a gap between a stack of silver buckets and piled rags, I see them. A young girl maybe fourteen, sobbing her heart out. A guard I do not recognise, a new recruit, licks his lips at the sight.

"Please, I'll do whatever you want, just—" she begins to plea but with a sharp cackle, he slams her face-first into the wall and slides his own body against hers like a feral snake. I grip the rock so tight that the sharp edges dig into my palm.

"That is precisely what I am counting on." He pulls her by her long auburn hair to tilt her head back and then licks the expanse of the pale skin of her neck. She emits a terrified scream. He then grabs her by the neck and throws her to the ground and laughs while she attempts to hide in the corner, scrunching herself up as if it will create an unbreakable barrier.

"Make another sound, love, and this will not be painless," he threatens her and she cries even more.

But I have had enough.

Just as he begins to undo his trousers, I sneak up behind him with lightning speed. I grab him by the neck and throw him into the adjacent wall with so much force that the wall even cracks. I can hear the girl screaming in terror, but it does not compute. I focus on my target like a hawk to its prey.

Almost unconscious and bleeding profusely, I saunter my way over to the guard whose eyes widen in fear. He tries to speak but only splutters out blood. I lean down, grab him by the throat and lift him up against the wall so that he can look into my merciless eyes.

"Let me tell you about the way things work around here," I offer, my hand straining not to rip out his throat right now. "The guards think that they are the only ones prowling around these cells at night. They could not be more wrong." I dig my nails deeper into his skin and blood trickles from his mouth and onto my hand.

"Please… I don't want any trouble," he begs, desperately trying to claw my hand off him but getting nowhere. The rock in my other hand is aching to strike and my arm shakes with the restraint.

"You got yourself into trouble the moment you set eyes on that girl."

"No, I—" he begins, but I squeeze tighter to silence him.

"Too late." And with that I unleash my weapon across his throat in one swift motion and he sags to the floor, lifeless and bleeding. I can tell that my face is splattered with blood although I choose to ignore it.

For a while, I just stare at the guard's body, the wrath in my veins taking longer to leave than usual. But slowly and surely, I can feel it draining from me. A soft whimper alerts me to the fact that the girl is still present. I turn my gaze towards her and she flinches, but slowly rises and stares at me with haunted eyes, auburn hair tangled with the remnants of the guard's last touch.

I grab two buckets and two rags from the shelves and bring them to the rusted tap on the edge of the room. I fill the buckets up with water and leave one there and then bring the other to where the girl stands still and set it and the rag before her. She just stares at me as I back away from her. I return to my bucket and quickly wash the blood off my skin in one fluid motion. When I look at her, she is still staring.

"I would not want the shadows of his touch clinging to my skin. Wash. Rid yourself of him," I say to her curtly. She stares at me a little longer and then slowly dips the rag into the water and begins to wash. Soon enough, her once mild movements turn into a wild frenzy and she starts sobbing more before throwing the rag to the ground and thrashing the bucket to the side.

She cries harder than ever as she stares daggers into the already-dead body of her attacker. I surge forward and grab her wrist to stifle her turmoil and stare deep into her pale eyes; the unyielding force to her terror.

"Take my strength," I command her, gripping her wrist harder as she still cries. "Take my strength," I repeat and as this unknown girl stares at me, her muscles begin to relax. "He cannot hurt you anymore. He is gone. So, do not waste your fear on someone who does not deserve it." She takes a deep breath and I can see the resolve steadying her face. "Take my strength," I repeat more softly.

Once I can see that she has calmed down, I smile weakly at her and head for the door.

"Wait, what about the guard?" she asks tentatively.

"The others will find him. In the meantime, go back to your cell. That way you will not be implicated." I begin to leave again, but her voice stops me.

"I arrived here a week ago," she calls to me, "I heard stories of a prisoner who killed guards who sought to conquer women. A prisoner who protects the women bound here at no expense for herself. What is your true name?"

As I look at her frail form, with her arms wrapped around herself in insecurity, I think about how young she is. How young she is to endure this place.

"Golnar's Ghost has no name."

Chapter 2

I am awoken by shouts of terror from the guards who found their not-so-new recruit lying dead in the Cupboard. I smirk as I straighten and take in the scene before me.

Guards run frantically along the cells in a desperate attempt to figure out which one of us is the infamous Ghost. They have never suspected it is me. How could they? The only people who see the act is a dead man and a woman who will never tell. That is solidarity for you.

The guard's slack body gets carried away to the mechanical lift at the centre of the prison. Exactly as I want it to.

Golnar is a very complex structure. After all, it is ultimately a slave-camp for women and our male equivalent is Canaan, the Forge Camp at the southern border of Zatria, the desert lands. Golnar holds a cylindrical shape and has three levels. Level One is the entrance, forbidden to all prisoners and heavily guarded. Level Two is the residential quarters meaning the alcove of dirt we are forced to live in. Level Three is the Forge... Golnar is nothing, if not sadistic.

The Forge is our manual labour although it is a death sentence all on its own. There is only one vent down in the forge for air to get through so when working in the stifling conditions, many women here die of dehydration let alone exhaustion. When actually making the weapons, everything must be perfect. If it is not... you get beaten. If you fight back, you get branded. And if you continue to disobey, then it is the whip for you. Why resist working in the forge? The weapons we make here are the ones used to slaughter our families in the name of Eradan.

Since Eradan was seized by Myrna, it has been alienated into something dark that even Vangar will not participate in. Aneya is built up of men and mages. Some of us are born with natural powers of this world, a magic of sorts. And some are not. And under Adrian's rule, there was always equality within the races. But with Myrna, a sinister wielder of darkness, she believes that all those who best her are worth eliminating which unfortunately means most of Aneya.

Many of the prisoners here at Golnar are mages and it is always easy to tell who they are through the two irons dots on each of their wrists; it almost looks like they have been bitten by a snake. Iron is a known absorber of magical energy; it stops them from using their powers within Golnar. When I was first sent here, I was incised to have these iron rods in my wrist also but I think Myrna just wanted to cause me as much pain as possible for my crimes.

Nonetheless at the centre of this cylinder of torture is the mechanical lift that can only be accessed by the guards so that they can manoeuvre between levels. We on the other hand have to use the spiralling steep staircase set around the lift. By the time you reach your quarters, you are expected to be too dizzy and weak to fight back. The stairs stop at the residential level because naturally we are exempt from tasting real oxygen or have the possibility of escape.

I have not killed for three months for a very particular reason. The last time I had killed involved a set of three guards who were holding down a middle-aged brunette when I found them. It was quick. It was bloody. And it was that day that I realised the bodies of the guards get collected by a courier from Eradan. Which means a mode of transportation will be waiting for me at the entrance.

But first I need to get there.

It is dawn. I stand before the steel bars, waiting to be released for duty. As my personal guard comes forth with a wary gaze, I smirk almost violently at him and he gulps.

"You're a little eager today, aren't you?" he asks with suspicious eyes. I shrug in a relaxed manner.

"There is just something incredibly exhilarating about the demise of authority. Wouldn't you say so, Marcus?" I continue to look at him like a lioness admiring her next prey and he gulps again, unlocking the padlock to my door and cuffing my hands and feet efficiently.

Across from and next to me, all the other women are being released and cuffed as well, ready for our day's work. I cannot help but notice that every time Golnar's Ghost strikes, the air is almost euphoric and this is imminent in the smug grins of the prisoners. I smirk knowing that these women have taken my strength to better this day, and yet... as I make my way to the steep staircase and become invisible in the swarm of unwashed bodies, I find that this time I take my strength from them.

There are many duties in the Forge: those who load the barrel with heavy metal ingots, those who pour the contents of the barrel into the various weapon casts, those who create the casts for each weapon, those who pour water on the casts and endure the steam, those who temper the steel once it has been cooled and those who transport the steel to the residential level for the guard's inspection. All tasks are gruelling and cruel and meant to break you.

As I stand at my post at the tempering station, I observe my surroundings. It is almost like the forge has no colour except that of the flame. The hundreds of bodies down here make it almost too cramped to work. Cries and grunts of pain echo in these tin walls and each one is a stab to my chest. I look to the steep staircase and find the women there carrying obscene loads of forged weapons up and down them. One woman looks ready to faint and stumbles, dropping a couple of fresh daggers; when she gets back up, she is slapped so hard across the face that she falls down to the bottom of the stairs. I wince. But there is nothing I can do to help them today.

I grab another freshly cooled longsword, heat the steel until it glows effervescently, and begin hammering away at the blade. I am tolerated by the guards purely for the blades I produce. I am the most natural temperer in this place but am also the best. I temper the steel so often, it creates a thin and light blade but maximises sharpness; I have earned the name Iron-Will because of it. It hurts to know that I am the best at making the weapons that destroy so many innocent lives.

Tempering has become a mindless art for me now and this gives me time to watch the mechanical lift. The guard patrol has doubled so there is a turnover every half hour now. The doors keep opening and closing and with each motion, my heart thunders more loudly in my chest. Two guards have just rotated and Marcus is on this shift. Good. He is no stranger to my tones of persuasion. He edges near me, putting me under his suspicion, as I hammer through another blade.

"See something you like?" I ask him, rolling my eyes in fake annoyance. He chokes on a bitter laugh.

"I would not touch you if my life depended on it." I turn to face him and place my hand on my hip, emphasising my curvaceous figure.

"Afraid I might bite, Marcus?" I purr but he just stares at me with hungry eyes. I try my best not to look nauseous. "Or are you afraid you might want me to?" I amend and he gulps before shaking his head and looking away.

"I don't know what you mean," he replies evasively.

"That guard is dead, right?" I move closer to him, using my feminine whiles.

"Yes." He steps back from me warily.

"It's a terrible shame to lose such a fine man, don't you think?"

"Y—yes," he stammers and I flash him a winning smile.

"His family must have been distraught with the news. Are they coming to retrieve him?" I ask innocently.

"No… they… they are waiting in Eradan for the Zatrian ship to deliver it."

"That's odd," I say, frowning while I stroke his shoulder absent-mindedly. He smiles dreamily.

"Well, it's standard procedure. An Eradan soldier is coming at midday to take the body to the ship and inspect the crime scene."

"That seems like an awful inconvenience." I continue to stroke him and I can see he is staring at my mouth. He rolls his eyes.

"We don't need a babysitter." He sneers and I hold in my glee. The guards will all be on edge when this soldier arrives.

"No, I trust you can handle yourself pretty well." He shivers under my touch and I return to my station and start hammering away at a longsword.

"Maybe you'll find out just how well." I stiffen at those words but turn around and smile nonetheless.

"We'll see about that," I reply almost robotically although he does not hear the threat underlying my words, only a promise of pleasure. He walks off grinning and I find myself hammering the sword with more force with each blow.

A soldier is coming at midday. That's four hours from now. He is surely travelling by horse from the docks… that is a means of transportation. A means of escape. What use is escaping with nowhere to go and no means to get there?

I look back at the elevator and I know how hard it will be to gain access. But I will do it. I have to. There is only so much of this place I can stand. I took it for three years. Accepted my punishment. Paid my dues in labour and flesh. Sure, there have been a few homicides on the way but what is life without a little bloodshed?

As the heat in Golnar increases, I can tell that noon is fast approaching. My muscles ache from the innumerable amount of weapons to have crossed my path. As I hammer another blade, my eyes never leave the elevator. Open. Close. Open. Close. The rhythm overtakes my racing heartbeat. The guards are looking frantic, scrambling to get everyone in their places and positively sweating with the effort. I smirk at the fact that they are sweating profusely from a task involving minimal effort and yet as a woman who spends most of her days with her face over a furnace, only a slight sheen glistens on my skin. I have even grown accustomed to the persistent burns which are customary in this line of slavery. I do not feel their sting. I do not even notice their existence.

Nonetheless, I need a distraction. A distraction to attract the attention of the guards stationed at the elevator. The elevator so crucial to my freedom. A distraction. A distraction... ah, I know just the man for it. I spy around the forge and find Marcus surveying a couple of new prisoners at the back of the room. The air is aglow with embers and swirling with steam... I need to be stealthy if I am to cause the desired reaction. I look to the guards again and they are wiping their brows anxiously. Now is my chance.

I swipe my hand under the desk and pull off the fine dagger I had attached to it in my hours of overtime. Swift. Light. Sharp. I managed to gain some silver from another girl who had worked here maybe a year ago now. She had worn silver hairpins and so had given them to me as payment for killing her first attacker. How she managed to smuggle them in here, I have no idea. She was my friend. Her name was Elyra Dior, the High Priestess of Delphor. Fate had taken her too soon.

And still it haunts me.

Still, I have the nightmares.

So in her honour, I melted the silver down and it now gleams in beautiful strands across the golden pommel of my blade. I hide this blade in the folds of my rags so that it may be concealed.

I notice a woman next to me is desperately trying to temper a sword. I silently go to her workbench and inspect the weapons in her tray that have been completed. I pick one up and give her such a sneer of disgust that she cowers away from me.

With the blade in hand and a puzzled expression forced upon my face, I make my way over to Marcus. Hunched shoulders, a slight tremble to the hands... everything a guard wants to see in an inmate. Vulnerability. His eyebrows rise as he takes me in. I smile seductively and the two other prisoners start murmuring to themselves before inspecting their trays.

The sound of a whip cracks in the air and every woman flinches at the sound and the young girl's scream that follows. I clench my teeth so as to steel myself to not run after the source of the noise. This is Golnar. This happens.

"You are not supposed to leave your station, Iron-Will," he says sternly.

"Well… I wanted your opinion on this blade. Do you have a moment?" I angle my arms in a very specific way to amplify my ample cleavage and this, combined with my shy voice, has him smiling. He clears his throat and gestures for me to head behind the steep staircase. Alarm-bells ring in my head, but I smile and go there anyway. Shadows encase us and I hate how much Marcus is enjoying it.

"You wish for me to inspect this blade?" he asks mockingly while I try to ignore the whips slicing into the backs of women above me.

"Yes, sir."

"Iron-Will is in need of *my* opinion?" To this, I nod and his grin broadens. "I know why you wanted to see me." I smirk only to entertain his arrogance.

"You do?"

"Yes…" he strokes my hair playfully, "You just could not wait for our encounter, could you?" He tugs my hair to expose my neck and inhales deeply. My heart quickens.

"So, you refuse to inspect my wares?" I reply huskily. He chuckles against my skin and goosebumps arise there; not out of pleasure, but of fear. He stands before me, fingertips caressing my neck and slowly reaching lower than I would like.

"Oh, I will inspect your wares, Iron-Will. Just more intimately than you expect." He leans in toward my neck but just before he can kiss me, or worse, I press my lips to his ear.

"Goodbye, Marcus." With that, I plunge the pommel of the second-rate blade against his head and he falls to the floor unconscious. I take the small access-key from the inside of his jacket and tuck it under my dress with the dagger. I drop the blade next to him and use his sleeve to smear off any lingering evidence of myself.

Peering through the slats of the staircase, I find that everyone is going about their normal tasks. Still, I have to uphold the ruse just in case. I cannot afford to make any mistakes. Not today. I ruffle my hair slightly and emerge from the shadows with a lazy smile and wobbly legs. Some women roll their eyes, some smirk. The guards are too busy to notice my little escapade. I head back to my workstation and realise that when someone finds Marcus, I have to act quickly.

As I mindlessly temper more items, my skin prickles in anticipation for the outcry. But it never comes. I look behind me and Marcus remains unnoticed. I guess the guards are really taking this inspection seriously. I will just have to do it myself then.

I slowly stride over to where Marcus lays unconscious, pretending to transport a new blade over for inspection. I drop the blade with a shriek and the noise instantly attracts the two officers guarding the elevator. Naturally, many other prisoners crowd around the stairwell to sneer or cheer at the fallen guard. While the other two push through the sea of steaming bodies, I duck my head and swerve my way out of the throng with ease. I dare not turn back at the commotion for fear that someone will notice my disappearance.

Heart pounding in my chest, I step into the elevator and use Marcus' access key to shut the doors and begin my assent to Level One. The shaft is surprisingly hot on my bare feet and the surrounding heat is almost suffocating. A small amount of relief enters my mind but it quickly vanishes as the elevator begins to decelerate. I curse myself colourfully. How did I not consider that others may use the elevator while I am stuck inside it? The odds of that are phenomenal, a shift-change has already occurred... but I should have foreseen this. I am losing time.

By the sounds of the gruff muffled voices, there are six guards in the residential quarters on Level Two. Why is there that many? They travel in pairs. Never any more than that. I do not have time to ponder the patterns of guards as I slow my breathing and brace myself yet again for another impromptu performance.

The doors open and I will myself to look frantic. Bursting through the doors, my voice is positively shrill.

"Please, you have to help me!" six guards stand before me as I had predicted, their black standard uniforms manifesting like shadows would in shade. Their faces are foreign to me but all are wide-eyed with surprise although their eyes soon narrow in rage.

"What are you doing up here, prisoner?" the one nearest to me exclaims.

"A guard has been assaulted on Level Three. He is unconscious behind the stairwell!"

"And they sent *you* to tell us?" another sneers.

"The others are—" I begin but my gaze strays to the officer at the back of the group.

His eyes constantly glance to his side. He is perspiring. I note that all of the guards have their hands hovering over the pommels of the daggers strapped to their sides. They are standing wide-legged, broad-shouldered and tense. A defensive position.

They were not wide-eyed in surprise to see me up here. They were wide-eyed at being caught.

Something is not right here.

"Something to say, Iron-Will?" a third guard snarls. Oh, we will see if I have something to say when I find out what is going on here. I side-step and angle my head towards the last guard and my breath catches in my throat.

A young girl. Maybe eleven. Head bowed, shoulders hunched, arms folded protectively over her chest. Rage instantly flows through my veins as if like wildfire passing through a dry forest. Her dark brown hair has been cropped short in a brutal way as if scissors have been there moments ago. Her thin legs are trembling beneath her. She refuses to look up.

"What has happened here?" I ask steadily, hand inching towards the blade hiding in my dress. The guards all stand fast in front of the girl. An effort to cast my eye away no doubt. The leader places his hand on his weapon as his sardonic face turns to mine.

"I don't believe you have the right to know. Now back off." His threat summons a reaction in me that sends my body into a stance ready for battle.

"Did you harm her?" I can barely get the words out through my clenched teeth, but he gets the message. The fact the guards begin to laugh mockingly raises my hackles even further.

"Playing with filth is not a crime." Another guard to the leader's left smirks. I unsheathe my dagger in one fluid motion, poised to strike. My dagger is met with that of the leader's.

"You think that I am afraid of a filthy little slave?" his growl lifts my heart with the promise of violence and my answering sadistic grin tells him so.

"No. But tell me men… are you afraid of Ghosts?" I don't take the time to breathe in their expressions of fear.

My blade reaches flesh instantly as I slit his throat and in one quick turn swipe the blade across the other on his left, I dodge a blow by another and plunge the dagger into his stomach, whirling to push my pommel against another's head whilst landing a kick to the abdomen of the one coming to his aid before stabbing him in the chest. Only the final guard remains. His own dagger poised against the girl's throat. Her warm brown eyes full of terror, her pale skin flushed with her impending doom.

"Step away or I will kill her," he demands. I only stare at him, blood sprayed across my face and body, dagger dripping crimson.

He presses the blade into her throat and her own blood swells there. Without thinking, I throw my dagger swiftly and surely and watch with pure gratification as it lands within the guard's face. The girl swerves from his grasp and clutches her bleeding neck with a sob.

I stride over the bleeding corpses, feeling their gore squelch between my toes. With utter lack of empathy, I pull my dagger out of the skull of the final guard and hear his limp head thud on the floor. I wipe my blade clean along the edge of my dress and then turn to the young girl beside me, still in complete shock.

"Are you okay?" I ask as I grab her by the shoulders. She's so young… so young to be in a place like this. Her eyes continue to stare at the bodies around her until I shake her for her gaze to lock with mine.

"Are you all right?" I ask her again albeit more sternly. Her frightened face allows a small smile to turn-up the corners of her delicate lips.

Suddenly, an alarm sounds from beneath us. Loud and unyielding. I quickly look at the elevator and it has not locked itself up yet but I am afraid it may not be for long. I stride away from the girl but her soft whimper has me turning back. The fear in her small face plunges my stomach deeper than I would like it. She hugs herself again as her eyes scan for a safe place to hide. If the guards find her up here… she will be punished.

I make the decision with ease.

"Come, quickly!" the girl rushes towards me and I wrap an arm around her waist as we step into the elevator. I try to use the access key, but the door does not close. I try again and it fails once more. With a huff of exasperation I throw the key out of the door. The alarm booms overhead. They must have locked the elevator from use. Staring up at the vast expanse of tube left, I know that I have no choice. I hear shouts and cries from this level and the one below. I am out of time. I scoop the girl into my arms.

"Wrap your legs around me and bury your head into my neck. Do not look up. Do not look down. Stay tight around me. Do you understand?" she nods and does what I ask.

With her body tightly wrapped around my chest, I place my palms on each side of the shaft and I hiss in pain while I retract my hands from it. It burns. Looking above me, there is twenty feet of pure space between me and the final stretch to freedom. I hear doors

18

slamming in the residential quarters as well as orders being barked. I do not have a choice.

I place my hands on either side the shaft and try to ignore the burning sensation there. I haul myself upwards and use my feet for leverage, placing them on either side also. The girl whimpers into my neck but she holds firm. Good girl. I push myself up and up and up. Even, when I feel my skin sliding from my body onto the smooth searing metal, I carry on.

Fifteen feet.

Ten feet.

Five feet.

I clamp my teeth shut to avoid screaming and it takes everything I have. The opening to Level One looms above me and I almost moan with the relief. The pain will stop soon. We will be free soon. I quickly peer over the ledge of the opening and find that it is mainly empty. The entrance is primarily empty, no doubt most of the guards on their way down the steep staircase to see what the commotion is about. Three guards is all there is. I am sure I can take them.

"I am going throw you out into this open space so that I may leap out after you," I whisper in the girl's ear. She only clutches me tighter.

"No." She sobs.

"Trust me. I will be right there with you. They will not harm you."

"*No*," she says again but I use one hand to push her backwards away from my neck so that I may stare into those terror-filled eyes.

"Take my strength," I command her, the searing of my hands and feet merciless as I hold this conversation.

"What?" her brows furrow in confusion.

"Take my strength," I repeat with hardness in my eyes. She stares at me and then slowly, that same resolve hardens her gaze. She nods with a slight smile.

Without warning, I shove her with all my strength over the threshold and she shrieks. Naturally it attracts the guards on station here. I haul myself up one more step and then I too leap into the open space and quickly bound over to the girl, dagger already in hand, and take a defensive stance over her.

The guards come at me from the North, East and West. I throw my dagger into the eastern guard to eliminate the threat furthest away. It lands in his chest and he does not get up from the blow. I charge towards the western guard who is surprised at the aggression and I clamp my hands on his head and rip it sideways so fast that the snap of his neck is barely audible. The northern guard changes direction to the entrance station where I am sure he plans to alert the others to my existence. I run to him with all my might and manage to slam him into the wall of the station before he can enter. The fury in my eyes shivers at the fear in his.

"You cannot escape here, Iron-Will." His mask of defiance makes me laugh.

"I can once I eliminate all witnesses." I slam him into the wall again and blood seeps from the back of his head.

"Roran Maar is here." He chokes out from between my nails digging into his throat.

I halt myself right there.

That name is like poison to me, corrosive and relentless.

"Excuse me?"

"Maar is here. He is inspecting Golnar and for any evidence pertaining to Golnar's Ghost. You will not get out of this place alive." The man laughs and his teeth are coated in red.

"I can try," I spit at him before smashing his head against the wall with such force that his head explodes upon impact.

I ignore the blood all over me while I stride toward the girl who seems to have slipped into shock again. I haul her over my shoulder and run towards the open doors.

The roaring sunlight has me shielding my eyes for fear of blindness. It has been so long since I have seen daylight. So long since I have felt the warmth of the sun upon my skin. The stark brightness of the Zatrian desert momentarily has me shell-shocked. Golden sand and large dunes as far as the eye can see. The sand surely absorbing the sun's might in each of its grains. The hot air does nothing to quench my thirst for easy breathing after a lifetime of it being laboured.

Nonetheless, next to me and tied to the visitor's post is a large blonde stallion. Roran Maar's stallion, Codax. I know him well. I lift the girl onto Codax's saddle and I stroke the long snout of him with my index finger. His large brown eyes hold recognition of my face no matter how starved or beaten.

Roran Maar is here; the General of the Sentillian Army in Eradan.

What I would give to go back down into the depths of Golnar and repay his betrayal with my dagger embedded into his heart.

I steel my hands into fists but hiss again at the burning sensation that lurks there still. I dare not look as my hands and my feet sting with the grains of sand coming into contact with raw flesh.

One day. Roran will feel my revenge.

But today, my priorities are elsewhere.

Lucky for him.

I pull myself onto the saddle and grab the reigns from around her. I can hear the yells of guards shrieking for my capture but I use my dagger to sever the line from Codax to the post and kick my heel into his side. Codax surges forward with ultimate speed, prized for being the fastest horse Eradan has to offer.

Arrows fly past me from all directions and I know that getting away will only be on a fool's chance. Even so, my faith in Codax remains true as he outruns all of the arrows. Riding away across the dunes, I have never felt more alive.

An arrow slices into my shoulder and I yell in pain. The girl shrieks in surprise but Codax does not falter. If anything, he speeds up. I can feel the blood trickling down my chest but I choose not to look at the arrowhead protruding there.

I look behind me to see my attacker and despite the long-distance stretching before us, Roran stares back at me, bow still in hand. He looks just as I remember him. Shoulder-length blonde hair, light blue eyes, broad chest and strong muscles. A truly honed warrior. Even from this distance, I see him drop the bow to the sand in shock and step forward as recognition dawns on his face at the sight of mine.

A moment is all I give him before returning my gaze back onto the path ahead.

Before I let the dunes engulf me.

Chapter 3

My vision remains in and out darkness. Even in times of consciousness, my sight is blurry. The girl has remained silent across the expanse of the desert, no doubt as exhausted as I am.

The sun is never forgiving in Zatria. It will either kill you, or relish in your torment. And I think in regards to us, the sun enjoys both. My muscles ache with fatigue and my mouth is fresh with the tang of dehydration.

I cannot tell how long we have been riding. The days morph into one. I cannot even remember when gold turned emerald as Codax enters us into the Broxen Woods, North of the Zatrian desert.

Even the striking green of nature's gifts is not enough to keep me awake. The sting on my hands and feet is relentless. The wound in my shoulder becoming ever a hindrance. In a consciousness bound by pain and marred with exhaustion, I feel myself slipping from Codax's back and I thud to the ground, the arrow pressing deeper upon impact. I do not have enough voice in my throat to emit a scream, only a strangled cry comes out.

I vaguely sense the girl falling beside me. Without my weight to hold her up, I suppose she would have dropped days ago. My breathing becomes laboured and despite the oncoming footsteps, I do not have the strength to defend myself or the vulnerable girl lying next to me.

Darkness greets me.

My body remains immobile, as if made of a substance so strong that not even I can make it adhere to my command. I am inside. That much I can tell. My eyes cannot catch up to my alert mind and so voices are all I can take in.

"I found her in the heart of Broxen Woods. The girl was in her company," says a deep, husky voice.

"Strange. Very strange. They both show sure signs of…" another male voice trails off in thought. Not as deep as the first but definitely older.

"What, sir?" a deep sigh ensues from the other, almost sad.

"Well, they both seem to appear to… have come from Golnar."
A silence from his companion.

"That is not possible."

"It must be possible Elijah; we have the sheer proof lying before us now. The circumstances of which this has occurred remain to be discovered."

"You truly believe that this… *girl*…"

"I would not judge her just yet, Prince. For all we know, she is a very powerful mage. We must not underestimate her."

I can feel unconsciousness dragging me under again and despite all of the strength in me… I let it.

***

I drift towards consciousness yet again. I can feel strength returning to my bones. I can feel the movement beckoning in my limbs.

I can feel a pain in my wrist. So sharp and so intense that it must have awakened me from my slumber. The sharp pain only intensifies and I feel warm blood seeping across my open palms. Someone is cutting me.

Without thinking, I leap up from whatever table I am on and grab the stranger by the neck and use all the force I can to shove them into the wall. I stare at the man with such pure wrath that I see a flicker of fear there. But it is only for a moment before his rage replaces it. I can feel the blood continuing to drip down my arms but I dare not look.

"What are you doing to me?" I snarl in his face. My voice is not as hoarse as I thought it would be… they must have fed me water in the days that I have been here.

I cannot take in his features just yet; my gaze only sees red as I watch the growl rippling across his lips. His strong hands grip at the wound on my wrist and I hiss in pain but hold my position. I slam his head into the wall and his anger only grows.

"Where is my companion?" he does not answer, only defiance lurks in his eyes. "*Where is she*?" I shout surprised at the protective instinct I have for a girl that I have known for five minutes.

With a surprising cry of rage, the man uses superior strength to throw me off of him and instantly takes the opportunity to twist my arm behind my back and plant me face-first into the stone wall. I writhe and thrash as hard as I can but with hardly enough time to recuperate, I am useless against his well-rested muscles.

"Calm down!" he orders but I refuse to acknowledge it. "I said calm down!" he uses his elbow to land a blow to the small of my back and my legs give way from beneath me. He continues to hold me against the wall but I let myself go still.

"Why am I bleeding?" I demand.

"Do you want those iron rods out or not?" the viciousness in his voice is both compelling and terrifying. "Because to do so, a little blood must be shed but if you cannot handle that then I have no qualms in sending you and your poor excuse of combat skills back into Broxen to die. Do you understand me?"

"Where is my companion?" I say through clenched teeth.

"She is getting her rods removed as we speak. And if you stop *fighting* me then I promise to not accidentally rip through an artery while I remove yours. Got it?"

I silently nod and he releases me from his grip. I turn around and the first thing I notice is that I am in an infirmary. The room is made of stone and candles gently cast an amber glow across the grey walls. I was lying across a small wooden bed and next to it is a table with an array of bottles and flasks full of various healing remedies. Numerous utensils line the walls ranging from small pairs of tweezers to large saws that could no doubt cut bone.

Against my better judgement, I switch my gaze to that of my attacker. His shoulder-length dark brown hair has the sides pinned back to accentuate his face. His hair almost looks bronze in the candlelight and his golden tan skin emanates that too. His broad chest and large shoulders indicate vast amounts of strength and skill; strapped to him is a large steel machete and something tells me that he is well trained in using it. His eyes are a striking emerald green that could rival the leaves of Broxen itself. High cheekbones give rise to a full pink mouth and he would be extremely handsome, if it were not for the hardness and sheer brutality pulsating from every inch of him.

He sits onto the stool next to the bed gracefully and I cannot fathom how such an obvious warrior can be so elegant. Still, my blood boils with my dislike for him.

"Are you going to sit down or am I going to have to make you?" he asks in a tiresome way.

I look to my hands and feet and realise that white bandages are wrapped around them tightly. Their sting is only minimal now. The wound in my shoulder has been stitched closed. I look at my wrists and find that only one rod out of the four has been removed and sure enough, blood cascades along my skin.

I suppose he has healed me this far. He must not want to kill me just yet.

"Are you always this charming?" my mocking tone sets him into a harsh scowl and I show my palms to him in a placating gesture, a smirk on my lips.

I sit on the table and hold out my wrists for him, mindless of the crimson now staining the floor. He grabs my wrist harshly and begins soaking up a sponge and dabbing at the wound. I do not give him the satisfaction of wincing. His hands are calloused but his touch is gentle. He silently clears the blood from my skin and then grabs tweezers to take out the iron rods. It is silent the entire time. That is... until I cannot bear it any longer. He is taking the final rod out as I open my mouth.

"Where am I?" my voice is soft so as not to startle him out of his healing calm. His intense green eyes scowl up at me and a hint of a snigger plays on his mouth.

"You do not know?"

"Forgive me, that being unconscious for two days, has not allowed me to take in my surroundings." My sarcasm sends him digging his finger into the final puncture and I grimace at the pain.

"Three days. You have been unconscious for three days."

"Your precision is noted now may I know where in fact I am?" I am surprised that I am not shaking with my frustration of him but he sighs deeply.

"You are in Drodal's Keep," he replies simply.

Drodal's Keep... the home of the mages. A refuge for all those with magical abilities under the safety of its King, Breccan Saltmist. Breccan is a water-wielder. A very powerful man. I had heard of his legends bustling through Eradan all those years ago. A kind and strong ruler to rival that of Myrna Verena. Only those who can manage to navigate Broxen may reach the Keep at the North end of the wood without being killed.

"How did I get here?"

"I found you unconscious and severely wounded." It is obvious that this man is not much of a speaker. It is strange to think that this brutal warrior had carried me here... shown mercy. Not just warrior, I remember from the conversation I had overheard, but a Prince; that is something I could care less for in this instant. I am not a fan of royalty.

"And you did not kill me on sight?" The smirk on my mouth vanishes as he looks into my eyes with steel.

"You had a child with you." That girl is the only thing that kept this warrior from killing me. I must thank her for that.

"How is she?" I find myself yearning to know if she is safe.

"Weak. She is asleep for the moment." I nod at his words as he finishes up and cleans my wrists once more.

He stands up swiftly and places the waste in a nearby steel bucket. He does not even look at me as he heads for the door and then halts.

"You are required to go into the adjoining room where you will find a bathing suite. A warm bath has been drawn and new clothes have been left for you to adorn. Make yourself presentable."

"Why?" I grit my teeth at the demand.

"You are to meet Master Saltmist in an hour."

"Will you be there?" I question, hoping that this will be the last time I see his emotionless self.

"Unfortunately."

"Can't wait," I mumble, letting my annoyance show. He just slams the wooden door behind him as he leaves. Good riddance.

Looking to my right, I see another wooden door which must lead to the bathing suite. I try not to sag with relief at the thought. Pushing the door wide open, my heart flutters at the sight of the space within. A long-mirror stands at the back of the room with a red velvet and wooden chair next to it, holding clean clothes. In the middle of the room is the medium-sized bathtub that has me, sighing in contentment.

Heading over to the bath, I dip my finger in the fragrant waters and marvel at the heat touching my fingers. The aromas of lily and lavender fill my nose and despite not being my favourite scent, it is the most perfect smell I have ever come across. Looking at the various bottles next to the bath, I instantly pick the scents for my next bath; orange blossom and rose water. Oh how I have missed that perfect concoction.

In pure eagerness I strip myself out of the rags and relieve myself of the bandages along my body. My hands and feet contain some scarring but they should heal fully in a matter of days. I place the dagger I had forged softly on top of the pile of clothes on the chair; a symbol of my time in slavery. I wish Elyra could have been here.

Steeling myself, I enter the warm waters and a soft moan escapes my lips. Three years. Three years without this joy. And I wonder how I had ever survived.

Submerging my head beneath the water, my muscles truly relax in what seems like centuries of tension. I pick the lily scented soap rather than the lavender and lather it across my body and atop my head. The amount of filth that I scrub away amazes me. I wash three times to ensure that every scrap of Golnar is ripped away from my skin.

When I reluctantly decide to leave the bath's warm waters, cold air kisses my skin but before I manage to reach for the towel, I am struck by the mirror's reflection.

Almost as if in a trance, I stand before the mirror, water dripping from every inch of me and let what I see truly sink in.

My black hair flows silken just beyond my ample chest. Such a change from the matted, dirty look I have grown used to. My grey eyes are stark against the dark satin of my hair and I can see the ghosts hiding in their irises. My skin, once golden from the sun, now is as pale as moonlight from not having seen daylight in years. My curvaceous figure holds true, but starvation has made my bones more visible.

The scars that pepper my body almost make me cringe. Only a few jagged scars spread along my stomach and abdomen. Brutal scars of war. And as I turn around and arch my head so that I may see my back, I am not prepared to see the evidence of my time at Golnar lurking there. Long white scars drape themselves along the expanse of my back, too many overlapping to count how many lashings I had been given. One for each sarcastic comment I made to the guards. I will not miss the whip. Countless strips of mottled skin join those marks made by the whip. One for each punch I gave a guard in public. I will not miss being branded.

Tears almost threaten to flow from my eyes but I hold them back. I am stronger than Golnar. I just wish others could follow suit. The thought of having left all those women suffering as Elyra had… I must not let the guilt consume me.

I will serve them better as a free woman.

I will serve them better as the woman that I once was.

Turning away from the mirror, I inspect the clothes that I have been given to wear. Tight black trousers, a white flowing undershirt, a black basque for over the top and black leather boots to match. Well… the warrior may be a brute but he has good taste.

I slip them on with ease, surprised at how well they fit and it feels good to be fully clothed for once. I strap the dagger to my hip and the outfit is complete. Looking in the mirror again, I look more like the woman I once was. A warrior. A shield. An unrelenting force.

I know that I must soon meet with Breccan so I leave the suite and the infirmary and find that a labyrinth of stone walls awaits me. Drodal's Keep is a beautiful simple structure. Walking through the numerous hallways, casual glimpses of what lurks beneath the stone take me by surprise. Some rooms are adorned with lavish furniture and fireplaces and some rooms remain simple in a sea of riches. I suppose that each room has a purpose.

Passing by a young man walking with a bushel of fresh apples, I decide to halt him in my frustration.

"Excuse me, you don't happen to know where the Master of this Keep dwells, do you?" My voice is kind but his brown eyes still widen in surprise. Surprise for me or surprise at the conversation? He does not answer me although the blonde shaggy hair lapping at his forehead is drenched with sweat.

"How about I help you with those in exchange for the information?" I smile, trying to make it seem as if I am not late for a crucial meeting. He just stares at me again, his lean form almost shaking.

Without warning, I take the bushel from his arms and a strangled string of words try to escape him but fail miserably. The bushel is light to me. But for a man who may have been working since dawn, this bushel might as well have weighed a thousand tonnes.

"Are you going to show me where you were heading?"

"Y—yes," he stammers and he begins to lead me down the stone hallway, bronze braziers lighting our path and plush deep red carpet softening our footfalls.

"What is your name?"

"Lukas. My name is Lukas," his young voice replies.

"Are you afraid of me, Lukas?" I enquire softly, boring my eyes into his. He looks scared as I do so.

"No, ma'am."

"And yet something has made you tense."

"Being wary is strikingly different to that of fear, miss." He does not look at me but something about him intrigues me. He is afraid and yet he chooses to rise above that fear. Something that I admire.

"And do you have a just reason to be wary of me?" he pauses for a moment as he regards me, pure contemplativeness etched into his face.

"You escaped from Golnar." I stop in my tracks and stare at him, shocked at how fast news travels.

"What else do you know of me?" I ask sternly. I cannot afford for anyone to delve too deep into my past.

"I know of the girl you travelled with. Nothing more." The corner of his mouth turns up a little but his face is unreadable. I clear my throat to rid myself of the tension.

"Are all those who dwell here mages?"

"Not at all. Drodal's Keep is a safe-haven for all those who have caught Myrna's eye."

"Her eye catches even those who believe themselves invisible," I murmur, my dislike for Myrna shining through my tone.

"Including you, ma'am?" stopping outside of what appears to be the kitchen at the far end of the hall, he surveys me. I can tell that Lukas notices more than he chooses to admit.

"I fight those whose eyes roam too far for their own safety."

"And what awaits those who do?"

Smirking, I hand him over the bushel again and grab one of the apples from it. I gently toss it into the air before catching it and savouring a precious bite from its juicy flesh. I am surprised at the ravenous hunger curdling my stomach as the bite lands there.

"Master Saltmist?" I remind him, refusing to answer his question. The boy smirks in return, eyes aglow.

"Next floor up, end of the hall."

I nod my appreciation and begin my journey to the next floor, my meeting with Lukas sparking my curiosity about him. As expected, I see the warrior lurking outside the wooden door that must lead to Breccan. For his pure annoyance, I saunter over to him, throwing the apple-core into a bucket at the side of the hallway, a lazy smile on my face. His answering grimace makes it worth it.

"You're late," he states with a growl.

"And you are irritable." I walk around and place my hand on the brass handle but he grips my arm so tightly that I can barely move it.

"I don't think that you realise how important this is."

"I did not realise that my presence here means so much to you. I'm flattered."

"This is not a game." The sheer violence in his voice sends a shiver down my spine but I refuse to let him know.

"And I am not some weakling that you can push around at your leisure."

"Do you not understand that—"

"What?" I snap, "That you are a boorish brute who favours fists over wit? Forgive me if I think that there is not much to understand."

He lets himself tower over me, his fists shaking in rage and emerald eyes positively searing. I choose to ignore him and waltz through the door and find that a smiling man with twinkling eyes awaits me.

Breccan Saltmist. For a man halfway through his life, he is rather handsome. His black hair is tied back behind his neck, his short beard giving him a rugged air. His sea-blue eyes twinkle in the light of the candles and the crinkles lining their sides prove that he is a happy man. Lean muscles line his figure and his simple white shirt and brown trousers may not look much, but I can see that they were not cheap.

He stands behind his large ebony desk, a matching chair set aside. His back faces the large window that oversees a paved courtyard and Broxen beyond. Numerous papers and stationary pepper his desk and books line the shelves around the perimeter of the room. He chooses simplicity over extravagance. Interesting for such a rich man.

"You must not be so hard on him. You barely know him." His rich voice wraps around me like silk.

"I know enough," the warrior snarls beside me, no doubt wishing he had that machete embedded in my neck. Breccan only chuckles.

"I do not think that my most trusted warrior matches your description of a boorish brute who knows no wit." I refuse to let myself blush at the fact that he had heard me.

"You have obviously had more favourable experiences than I have, Master Saltmist."

"Indeed." Those eyes never stop sparkling. It is as if they have a life of their own itching to see the world as he does.

"Why am I here?" I keep it blunt and I keep it short. Breccan holds up his palm towards the warrior and I can tell that the man must have made a threatening move towards me. I hold my stance.

"You were wounded."

"And now I am not," I counter and his tanned skin stretches over his grin.

"Well observed." I roll my eyes at that.

"What of my companion?"

"She is enjoying the orchards. I will have Ayla bring her to you shortly."

"And what of myself?" Breccan merely holds his hand out towards the chair opposite his own. A motion for me to sit. I take it warily. He sits down in front of me and interlocks his fingers in thought.

"I wish to know... how you came to be inside my borders."

"Didn't Captain Sunshine bring me here?" I jerk a thumb over my shoulder and Breccan grins as if trying not to laugh.

"Choose your next words wisely," the warrior warns.

"Or what? You'll scowl me into oblivion? Not likely." He does not get a chance to reply as Breccan seeks to diffuse the violence.

"Where did you come from and how did you end up in Broxen?"

"That would be a very long story."

"If I get bored, I'll let you know." The warrior's snide remark grates against my ears and I find myself glaring at his amused expression as he leans against a shelf.

"Calm yourself, Elijah," Breccan warns and I realise that this brute was in my room with Breccan during my first moment of consciousness. Breccan sees my curiosity and decides to placate it.

"Elijah Warren. A wielder of the earth and all its spoils. My most loyal, skilled and trusted warrior." I recall the word 'Prince' being used earlier but I choose not to ask.

"What do you wish of me, Breccan?" I ask, desperate to get to the point.

"I shall start with your name."

The request startles me. My identity is sacred. Something I cannot reveal to those who are neither friend nor foe thus far. They could alert Eradan of my existence quickly enough that I would not last two days in Broxen without an enemy on my tail. Being labelled as a traitor tends to make one be more careful as to who she considers friends.

"Elyra," I reply quickly. "Call me Elyra." I do not know why I choose her name or if it is any dishonour to her. But I know that as I say it, it just feels right to do so.

"And the girl?"

"I do not know," I answer truthfully.

"You are so anxious for the welfare of your companion and yet you do not even know her name?" Elijah asks incredulously from the side.

"I was too busy killing the bastards who hurt her to ask for the details." The venom in my words is unmistakeable but the news sets Elijah's mouth into a hard line. He should not judge so quickly.

31

"We mean you no harm, Elyra," Breccan says softly. "How did you escape?" I choose not to answer him and he sighs. "You must understand that your injuries were grave… and we have no clue as to how they were ascertained. You were covered in so much blood."

"The blood came from the nine guards I had to kill to fight my way out of there. My hands and feet got burned when I had to press them against the elevator shaft to haul us up to the final level. The girl was latched onto my chest. The arrow came from Eradan's General who saw me fleeing on his horse." Another debt I will pay to Roran's flesh.

"That is Maar's horse?" the only expression Elijah shows is his raised eyebrows.

"Why, are you impressed?" He soon shrinks back into his sneer.

"I think it is safe to say that we are all impressed, Elyra. You are the only person to have ever escaped Golnar in its entire existence."

"Lucky me." I shrug. Breccan leans back in his chair and I can tell that my mood is irritating him, even if it is only a little.

"How long were you in there for?"

"Three years."

"Bullshit." Elijah scoffs and I have had about enough of him. I stand up out of the chair.

"This conversation is over," I spit at Breccan, Master of Drodal or not. His eyes are still wide from the duration of my time at the forge. I head to the door and his voice reaches me again.

"You will train with Elijah at dawn."

"What?" both mine and Elijah's voices boom.

"You don't understand. I'm just passing through," I tell him, my jaw almost throbbing.

"As far as I can tell, Elyra, you are in my kingdom now. And so you must abide by my rules."

"I did not escape Golnar so that I could be imprisoned once more."

"You are not a prisoner, Elyra, you are but a guest."

"My training is quite extensive. I have no need for your lessons."

"You will need these ones, I assure you." Breccan sets his eyes upon mine and I can feel the chill tingle along my spine.

"I have duties that I need to fulfil elsewhere." I pray that he is honourable enough to understand this at least. I have obligations in Eradan. Oaths I must not break.

"And what might they be?" when I refuse to answer him, he grins in triumph. "The only duty you have here is to arise before dawn." It takes a lot of my willpower to keep my fists from shaking. As if I would tell him my secrets. He is a fool to have even asked.

"Master, if I may interject—" Elijah begins, horrified as much at this idea as I am.

"There is no-one I trust more than you to get this done," he tells him. "So get it done," he adds with a smile, one that Elijah does not reciprocate.

"I will not agree to this." I sneer at Breccan.

"You will. Goodbye, Elyra." He then waves me out of his quarters but I storm out before he can even finish it. The rage in my veins threatens to boil over but Elijah's presence only adds to it. He slams the door behind him and sets his wrathful face an inch away from mine.

"Miss *one* morning and I will gut you where you stand."

"And here was me thinking that you were just beginning to like me." He huffs through his nose as he inches back, roving his eyes down my defiant stance. He nods to himself with a slight smile.

"I am going to enjoy this" are his final words and then he walks in the opposite direction to me, the casual wanderers instantly parting from him as they sense his frustration.

"Bastard," I say to myself.

"Excuse me, miss?"

"What?" I almost yell but my voice is stifled at the site of the girl next to the woman who spoke to me. She is cleaner. Happier. Clothed in a simple white dress, her short brown hair spiking up at odd angles.

"Hello," I say to her softly.

"My name is Ayla," says the woman accompanying her. Her straight mousy hair frames her heart-shaped face perfectly; her faded blue eyes are aware of my rage.

"Elyra," I reply. I must get used to using this name. I must learn to not allow my heart to break every time I hear it. She nods in acknowledgement and smiles at the girl next to her.

"I will give you two a moment." Ayla walks off but her eyes send a warning to me as she does. As if I would hurt the girl. The girl who is barely looking at me now, one hand clutching her other arm. So vulnerable.

"I did what you said," she murmurs, her young voice cutting through to my bone.

"Excuse me?"

"I did what you said," she repeats, her warm gaze slowly lifting to mine, "I took your strength." My heart flutters at the words.

"You were very brave." She smiles a little.

"I had never seen someone killed before."

"I am sorry for that." And I mean it. I was brutal. And she saw every last bit of it.

"I'm not. You saved my life." I do not answer her. I do not know what to say. And so she steps forward, holding out her small hand.

"My name is Maer." I take her hand and almost balk at the frailty of it.

"Where is your family, Maer?" I motion for her to walk alongside me and she does with a smile. How she can manage to smile just sets her aglow with resilience. She is strong.

"They live in Eradan. We are…" I let her trail off to save her the agony of revealing that her family are poor. I know that hesitation well.

"We all come from somewhere." She nods at that and she does not utter a word for a while.

"You are the one they all talked about, aren't you?" I cock my head at her and her eyes are alight.

"I'm sorry?"

"You are Golnar's Ghost." What a smart girl.

"Aren't you a little old to believe in ghost stories?" Despite my attempts at shrugging it away, she persists.

"You hated the guards. When you saw the ones who…" she trails off again and I do not have it in me to ask her to explain, "You unleashed hell."

"I am not the only one who loathed the guards."

"You're right… but you are the only one who hated them enough to do something about it." The way she makes it sound allows for a small amount of guilt to seep into my mind. And then I think of the things I saw them do. Of the atrocities they were allowed to perform. The guilt disappears.

"I suppose you are right." I smirk and a triumphant flush rushes to her cheeks.

"Elyra?"

"Yes?"

"Can I stay with you?" the request stumps me and my reaction instantly has her balked. "I mean… I just… You are…" she gives up, "I feel safe with you." She shrugs. My heart swells and I

34

interlock my fingers with hers. Maer is surprised at the contact but I can tell that she is warming to it.

"You are not leaving my sight."

Chapter 4

"Courtyard and training ground, who would have known."

"Shut up," Elijah snaps.

The flickers of dawn paint the indigo sky and a chill breeze whips through my clothes. I wish I had been given a coat. The fact that the fountain emitting spouts in the centre has not yet frozen astounds me.

Maer soundly sleeps in the room I had been given, hopefully in calm so thorough that nightmares are unable to reach her. The plush bed was enough for two and she was scared to sleep alone. I had no qualms with it.

Ayla had taken us to our room yesterday evening after we had gorged ourselves at the feast that was prepared for dinner; I had never eaten so much in my life. The room was fit for a queen almost. A large four-poster bed with ebony trimmings and matching furniture. A separate bathroom large enough to make its own furnishings seem small. A huge window allows Maer to absorb the beauty of Drodal's landscape whilst keeping away from prying eyes.

And I am stuck out here with Aneya's friendliest soul in the freezing hours of early morning.

I cannot shake the thought that I have exchanged one prison for another.

The square expanse of the courtyard is lined by pink blossom trees that catch my breath with their beauty. A water fountain lies in the centre of it, a round marble basin with various majestic spouts filling it. Guards adorned in deep green are stationed at every corner of the courtyard as well as on every balcony, including the watchtower. This Keep is heavily guarded.

Elijah stops ahead and faces me with his arms crossed. I just observe how his hair now looks as black as mine under the indigo sky. His appearance is shaggy just enough to let me know that he probably slept in his green shirt, brown trousers and boots. I turn away when I realise that the top of his shirt is unbuttoned to reveal a smooth chest. Today he carries his machete as well as a quiver full of arrows and a long curved wooden bow with a string so tense I wonder how a normal man would fare drawing it.

"Do you know why you are here?" his voice booms across the empty courtyard. I am sure that the servants aren't even beginning breakfast yet. In reaction to the thought, my stomach grumbles.

"For your sadistic purposes?" I offer and he scowls, an animalistic sound emitting from him.

"To train. You must learn to use your magic safely and in control."

"Excuse me?" I step forward in disbelief, thinking that my ears must be clogged.

"Do not tell me that you thought those rods were in your arm purely for decoration?"

"I am no mage."

"Then what are you?" I simply glare at him. "What are you?"

"A warrior," I answer instinctively and I know that there is amusement in his eyes before looking at him. Wisely for him, he does not mock my answer.

"Those rods would not have been placed if you were not magically involved."

"I have no magic. I have never *had* any magic. Now cut the bullshit and teach me something worthwhile." Something about Elijah gets under my skin too easily. It is not something that I am used to.

He laughs without feeling and perches atop the ledge of the fountain, unstrapping a husk from his belt and swigging from it generously. He wipes his mouth and his eyes pierce mine.

"Just stand there."

"Excuse me?"

"Stand there," he repeats as he draws out his machete and starts sharpening it against a whetstone. The sound scratches against my eardrums. I take a step forward and he points the machete at me.

"I said stand." The thrill on his face lets me know that he is enjoying this way too much. Just as he promised.

"This is ridiculous."

I make a move to step forward and roots suddenly burst through the paved slabs of the courtyard and start tangling their way over my feet and up my calves. I try to wiggle free but the roots do not give way. I am stuck here. I look back at Elijah and he is still mindlessly sharpening his blade. I cannot help but wonder how much power he truly possesses.

"Nice trick," I say mockingly and he does not react. I place my hands on my hips and resort to looking at the sky.

As the sound of metal scraping against stone starts to unravel me, I do not know how long I have been here, only that people begin to wander the yard and they do not seem surprised to see me out here. Elijah has done this before then.

Without warning, he gets up from his perch and sheaths his blade, instead pulling out his bow.

"You are permitted to stay here until midday, when the sun is at its apex. I will come for you then." What sort of game is this?

He starts striding towards the wrought iron entrance gates, towards Broxen. I do not even bother calling for him. His roots hold me in place further and I can feel my legs beginning to shake under the strain. I do not have time for this. I have places that I need to be.

I cannot move so I do not move. My eyes dart around for distraction from my aching muscles and so I watch the lives of those who live here. Servants carry produce to the kitchens, others chat amicably in the courtyard, soldiers train with their blades in shady corners. The one thing that they all have in common is that they all pay me no head. It is as if I am invisible. Whether this is because of me or just standard procedure, I suppose I will never know.

The sun reaches higher in the sky and my muscles almost throb with the threat of cramping. My calves buckle from beneath the roots and I am sweating beyond belief. This is ridiculous. How long has it been? Five hours? Six?

Without warning, the roots suddenly shrink away and my legs sag with the relief. I can barely stand without their security. My legs continue to shake uncontrollably and the sweat along my brow drips down my face. Maybe Elijah's power does not stretch this far.

With a smirk, I take one step forward and I see it before I hear it. An arrow so large and so swift lands an inch from where my foot had fallen. The brown feathers at its top quiver in the slight breeze and the shaft of the arrow ebbs back and forth from its secure stance within the concrete slab.

I whirl behind me and do not see Elijah anywhere in sight. I scan the stone balconies along the fortress and see nothing. I dart my eyes across the various apex points in Drodal's structure and find nothing. So I resort to stretching my gaze amidst the tall foreboding trees that laden Broxen Woods and even though I cannot see him, I can sense his presence among the nature.

Despite myself, I smirk at the arrow swaying in front of me. Elijah may be a bastard. But he has great aim. I am not a fool to try to move again. No doubt he will not miss next time. I stay where I am. There cannot be long to go.

After another hour, I can see Elijah's strong form surging for me from the entrance gates. He is emotionless. As usual. But I have not moved from my stance since he had placed me here at dawn. The anticipation for this to be over fills every aching bone inside me.

"Are we done here?" I ask him, voice hoarse from dehydration.

"No. Now, we run." Shock turns my aching muscles tense.

"Are you joking?"

"Do I look like I make jokes?"

"Fair enough." He merely starts stripping himself of his weapons and laying them before the fountain.

"You will part with your weapons here," he demands and I immediately feel for the dagger at my side.

"Afraid I might go for the kill, Elijah?" I tease, hoping that this is the only reason for his request.

"You will have no use for it" is his only reply and my hands begin to get clammy at the thought of parting with it. I do not wish to part with her.

"I will not be separated from this dagger." I challenge him and he cocks his head in surprise, eyes scorching. He places his face so close to mine that I can taste his breath on my tongue.

"You will do what I ask of you, Elyra. Now place it on the damn fountain." Little does he know that Elyra is the reason why I will not leave this weapon.

I know that I will not win this battle so I unstrap the dagger from my side, the gold and silver hilt glinting beneath the sunlight. I hand it to him with hurt in my heart and he snatches it away and throws it to where his lie on the fountain-side. The flinch of my body is completely involuntary. He notices straight away.

"This dagger is special to you. Why?" he asks, not as harshly as he would if I had not flinched.

"What is a warrior without the blade that helped them become one?" I counter and he softens then but only for a moment and then the hardness sets in again.

"We run. Now."

I do not have the chance to say anything else as he runs ahead of me, graceful and strong. I run after him although the fatigue has me slower than I would like. Nonetheless I keep behind him as he drags me up murderous hills and through endless bracken. But I am not entirely bored.

Elijah is at home in this forest. That much is true. I suppose as a man of the earth, it is only natural for him to enjoy being in Broxen. A place where most cannot survive but I have no doubt that Elijah can. He is swift and true as he vaults over logs and uses branches to swing over large spaces. He reminds me of a wolf, a true predator with his cutting strides but he also strikes me as a deer, graceful and elegant in his leaps.

Studying Elijah makes me feel as if the more I learn about him, the more at an advantage I will be. I can barely keep up with him but I do not care. Golnar did not have a training facility so naturally the stamina and endurance I have built my entire life has dwindled dramatically. So I take this training as a blessing, no matter if I am with Aneya's most irritating man or that this run is almost killing me.

I need to be strong for when I reach Eradan to uphold my oath.

And Elijah is going to help me.

Sitting with Maer and Lukas in the kitchen, I feel a small amount of contentment that I have not felt in a long while. I find this a lot better than having to sit in a hall full of revellers where I can barely hear myself think. The other servants in the kitchen have gone to the feast and so it is just us three in the large kitchen; Lukas happens to be one of the chief cooks at Drodal.

Darkness looms outside and the candles supply a warm glow that soothes the sore muscles of my body with their heat. Even the gentle browns of the wooden structures in the kitchen provide a relaxation that vibrancy does not allow for.

Sitting on the concrete floor cross-legged and eating a bowl of warm stew, I find myself observing the boy who is making it his mission to make Maer laugh. And his attempts make me smile. He soon catches my gaze and blushes.

"What?"

"You are at ease with children and yet barely an adult yourself." I note and he nods in acknowledgement.

"My family was large and we all had our duties. Mine was to look after my siblings while my older brothers hunted game with my father." I try not to let the thought of duties sting me. I should be accomplishing mine. And yet as I look at Maer, I know that she has now become one of them.

"Where are they now?" she asks and Lukas pats her knee.

"They remain lost to me. Scattered to the four corners of this world and everything in between. Myrna has her ways of tearing

40

families apart." My heart breaks for him but all I can offer is a reassuring smile.

"Yes… I know," Maer agrees and I am surprised at the implications it holds; I do not push it further. She will confide in me when she wishes to.

"I just wish someone could stop her… stand up to her. Show her that bullies don't have a place in Aneya." She casts a wary glance at me.

"Has she ever bullied you?" I ask seriously and Lukas goes tight-lipped at my side. Maer does not answer me for a while but soon smiles.

"Doesn't she bully us all?" she offers and I cannot help but feel that there is more to Maer than meets the eye.

"What about you, Elyra? What are your experiences with the Dark Queen?" Lukas looks to me with an inquisitorial gaze.

"The Dark Queen and I…" I do not know how to finish this sentence, there are too many options, so I simply settle for, "Have never had the pleasure of meeting. But I am sure that if that were to change, safety would not be on her side."

The lie catches the eye of Maer and it as if she can see right through it to the truth beneath, except I know that she could not possibly know my history and so it must be a trick of the eye. The second part is true enough. When I see Myrna again, I will unravel the flesh from her bones for what she had done to Adrian, to his children, to me.

"That would be a sight I would like to see for sure." Lukas grins and I cock my head at him.

"To what sight are you referring?"

"You and Myrna in the same kingdom." His brown eyes shine with laughter and I cannot fathom why it would be such a joyous moment. In my eyes, it would be a tragedy.

"You do not know enough about me to make that assumption," I counter and he shrugs amicably.

"But I do. I have seen what you can do, Elyra. I would love to see Myrna tremble before your blade." Maer does not look at me as she says this but plays with her spoon, scraping it against the sides of her empty bowl.

"And I happened to see you in the courtyard today with Elijah." Lukas lifts his brow higher than expected and I chuckle at his suspicious expression.

"And?"

"You two were ready to kill each other." He giggles, "Quite something to behold in my opinion."

"How so?" Maer asks quietly.

"Elijah is the most feared and respected warrior in Northern Zatria. Perhaps in all of Aneya. We have never seen him rattled. But something about you certainly sets his bones on edge." It appears that Elijah has quite the reputation. Somehow, it does not surprise me.

"Is he always so…" Lukas's eyes shine at my impending question. "Friendly?" I complete in a tone of dislike.

"Elijah keeps to himself and likes it that way. That much remains true. But I know that he would risk his life for the sake of everyone here at Drodal; servant, soldier and noble alike. And I know that he would be a wondrous friend, if only he allowed himself to become one."

"You speak as though you know him well." I chew the last remainder of my stew and set my bowl aside, eager for the story when Lukas nods his head.

"He saved my life. He did not have to. It would have compromised his mission to do so but he had risked it anyway, for me. And I owe him that debt for as long as I am here."

"He saved you from Myrna's soldiers, didn't he? And then he brought you here to Breccan's refuge," I murmur and he nods again.

I find it strange how Lukas and I have had the same meetings with Elijah. Both stranded, both injured. And he had taken us here. To safety. What was Elijah even doing in Broxen in the first place?

"He sounds selfless. For such a brute." I laugh at Maer's choice of words and how similar they are to mine.

"You two should probably go. I would hate for you to get into trouble for spending supper with me," Lukas announces and I place my hand on his knee.

"Any trouble is well deserved." But I get up anyway and pull Maer up beside me. She brushes the dust off of herself and gives Lukas a warm smile.

"Same time tomorrow?" She asks shyly and Lukas stands up and gives her a nonchalant bow.

"Milady, you are welcome here at all times. But alas, at the end of this week is the annual bonfire to commemorate lives lost to this Keep. I am bound to serve the valiant feast and enjoy the revelry afterwards; dances will be performed and stories will be told and it shall be, as ever, a beautiful evening. But it means that I must slave away to uncover dangerous recipes to ensnare all those who taste my food." His noble air sends sparks of laughter through Maer.

"Are we invited to the celebration?" her voice is shrill with excitement and I pat her shoulder.

"Who am I to object to two lovely ladies attending the occasion?" he kisses Maer's hand and she blushes profusely.

"We could help you prepare if you like?" she offers and he beams at us both.

"Only if you are able." Maer immediately looks to me with pure enthusiasm.

"Can we, Elyra? Please?"

"Fine." I roll my eyes and then lead her bouncing form away and turn my head over to Lukas.

"Thank you," I mouth to him and his answering grin mimics mine as I lead Maer back to our quarters.

Maer is asleep within a few minutes on the large bed and I run my fingers through her short brown hair. The slow rise and fall of her chest tells me that she is at peace and the small smile on her relaxed mouth only proves it more so. I plant a kiss to her forehead, realising that I am in no mood for sleeping.

Grabbing the dagger from the bedside table, I take it with me through the dark corridors of the abandoned keep and into the empty courtyard. Shadows loom as far as the eye can see and the fountain's trickle is eerie in the darkness. The chill air has me hugging my shoulders.

When I reach the centre of the courtyard, I hold the dagger out before me in a defensive position. I start lunging and thrusting and manoeuvring by myself in the bare space, practicing the movements that have felt lost to me since arriving at Golnar. It is as if the actions had never left me. All those years training under Adrian's guidance... all those years spent upon battlefields for Aneya... I should have known that all of those lessons would not fade from my memory.

With the moonlight as my guardian, I continue to train in solitude. My already barking muscles seem to yell for a relief that I cannot give them. Lukas' words of Myrna have risen the anger buried deep inside my soul, the futile desire for revenge as searing as the sun's first light. The burden of my identity continues to drown me while I am not fulfilling my oath; to destroy Myrna and release her hold on this kingdom to the rightful heirs of Eradan, Jocelyn and Jasper.

Striking with my dagger, I allow myself to believe that it is Myrna's heart on the end of it. And as I plunge to the left, I am surprised to hear a clash of metal before I see the man whose blade has met my own.

Breccan.

The glare I give him makes him smile as he retracts his rapier from my dagger, offering up his palms in surrender. I stuff the dagger into the top of my trousers and wait for him to speak.

"You fight with a skill that makes me believe that you are no stranger to war." He notices, his deep voice rippling through the darkness.

"Are you always in the habit of sneaking up on newcomers?" I ask, angry at the intrusion. He stabs his rapier into a crack beside a slab and leans upon the hilt, assessing me without being delicate.

"I'd like to know who it is that I am allowing to live under my roof."

"Have I not already told you who I am?"

"I fear that you have not been totally honest with me." I do not say anything to him and so he begins to circle me in slow strides.

"Honesty is a luxury that I cannot afford."

"I know of only one person," he holds up his index finger to illustrate his point, "Who would have the gall to have even attempted to escape Golnar. And only duty would have made her want to attempt it, as failure would have had her accept the punishment that she was forced to endure." My breathing quickens at his obvious knowledge and I purse my lips in an effort to hold in my distress.

"You have no right—"

"I will not reveal your true self, Elyra. I know that it would be unwise to do so. But I had wished that you would be honest with me." He looks to me with pleading eyes and as a man who bounds himself by honour, I know that to have been lied to is of great pain to him.

"There is too much at stake here, Breccan. You of all people know that this war between Aneya and Myrna relies solely upon my shoulders. I could not risk being implicated." I stand defiant before him in an effort to amplify my words.

"I understand the dangers. Do not doubt that." I relax at his words.

Breccan goes to sit upon the fountain's ledge and he pats the space beside him for me to do the same. Sitting next to him, I feel as if I have known him for years while he gazes at the tree line of Broxen as if he can see directly into Golnar beyond them.

"You have been faced with much more than you should have in your young age."

"I am not the worse for it," I state and he smiles at me.

"I suppose that you are the cause for the legends that have been seeping out from Golnar?" his mouth twitches in amusement and I notice that despite being quite old, youth still clings to Breccan's being.

"Legends?"

"Your feats have not gone unheard, you realise. Tales of Golnar's Ghost and Iron-Will have stretched throughout the realm of Aneya. I have no doubt that these titles will be a permanent fixture upon your name."

"I did not wish for glory when I killed those men, only justice. I did not expect it to evolve." I study the dagger in my hand with my fingertips, so gentle that it as if I am touching Elyra's soul.

"She means something to you, doesn't she?" his words startle me from the blade.

"Excuse me?"

"Elyra. The alias you have used." I grit my teeth, starting to get angry at how much he notices.

"She is not involved in this conversation." The finality in my voice turns him silent and after what seems like hours, he opens his mouth once more.

"I know that you believe that you are not magically endowed. But I have reason to believe otherwise. I hope that you will proceed with your training." He stands up and begins walking back to the large arched wooden door to the keep.

"What reason?" I call to him and he stops in his tracks, turning his head slightly to the side in acknowledgement of my question.

"Just an inkling," he murmurs loud enough for me here. And then Breccan Saltmist disappears within the folds of his stone fortress.

Sitting along the fountain's edge, I know that Breccan will keep my secret. But now, the solitude of being completely alone in such a vast space has me wary. Getting up, I trudge through the corridors of Drodal, thankful that no one can hear the sound of my tears as they roll down my face.

Chapter 5

Elijah's training this morning is the same as yesterday. Stand in the same spot from dawn to midday. And then run for hours through Broxen until I am near enough ready to collapse. I know that I did better today than yesterday but Elijah's silence is not reassuring. Somehow I doubt that he ever offers praise.

The training continues like this all week. Stand. Run. Stand. Run. On days where I feel particularly like being a nuisance, I will step out of line a couple times just to see if he does continue to fire the warning arrows and if he will ever hit me. An arrow never lands into my flesh and I have a feeling that no matter how far I move, he will not kill me.

As to what these training sessions are supposed to do, I am at a loss. What is the point in standing in the middle of a courtyard when I could be sparring with Zatria's supposed greatest warrior? But I do as he says only to make the time go faster.

And as the days go on, I find myself getting more patient. I find myself ignoring the aches in my muscles and becoming more aware of how I can cease them. I find that I am running faster and becoming stronger. I manage to catch up to Elijah most days in Broxen but again, he is silent. He barely even snarls at me anymore. And always after our training, he heads into Broxen with purpose in his strides. He never tells me why he goes despite my asking.

My days are spent exhausting myself physically, my evenings are in the stables tending to Codax and my nights are spent with Lukas and Maer in the kitchens, desperately trying to figure out what food to prepare for the feast that is now tomorrow night. We have prepared recipe after recipe and my mouth salivates at the very thought of the courses Lukas will be creating tomorrow.

After all of our hard work this week, we decide that tonight shall be where we sit and relax together without having to worry about how many cups of flour are needed to create a six-layer cake. Once we finish eating the vegetable soup and bread that Lukas had kindly made for us, we sit in contentment.

"I look forward to this night every year. And every year I cannot wait for it to be over." Lukas chuckles, wiping his brow with the back of his hand.

"I think it will be lovely." Maer smiles, hugging her knees against her chest, eyes looking severely drained.

"What exactly is this festival called, Lukas?" I ask.

"It is the Festival of Light where we summon the light of fire and bask in the light of the moon to honour those who have passed. The contrast of light signifies life and death and that there cannot be one without the other. So we pay our respects to those who have greeted both without fear."

"I have never heard of this tradition."

"That is because you have never come to Drodal before now. Our traditions are not universal."

"No kidding," I murmur under my breath and he gently pushes my shoulder in fake annoyance, warm eyes positively glistening.

"Any signs of magic yet?" he counters and my scowl only furthers his amusement. Lukas does not have any magic and I know that he wishes he did.

"No and there never will be. I am just grateful for the training. I need all the strength I can get."

"For what?" Maer asks, a yawn escaping her lips. While I am training every morning, Maer seems to wonder off somewhere too. And no matter who I ask, they never know her whereabouts until she shows up at noon.

"A warrior needs her strength." I smile and she does too. She is noticing a lot more lately… possibly a trait she is picking up from Lukas. Breccan has held true to his word and not spoken about our last discussion, either to me or anyone else, so I know that it is not under his influence.

I notice how late it has gotten and I know that I need to get Maer to bed soon seeming as she is falling asleep on the spot, so I arise from the floor and pull Maer up as well, much to her dislike.

"Time for you to get some sleep."

"But I am not tired," she argues as she rubs her eyes shamelessly. I only grin at her while she laughs and looks about ready to collapse.

It seems that getting up has made her realise how fatigued she is. She starts to sway and I catch her in my arms as she falls unconscious. Scooping her up, her head lolls against my chest.

Lukas comes beside me and strokes a finger along Maer's flushed cheek.

"She is lucky to have you," he mumbles so as not to disturb her.

"I would not say that."

"I dread to think what would have happened to her if you hadn't have got her out of there." I know that he is referring to Golnar but I would rather not talk about it. Maer still won't open up about her small time there but I am being patient.

"She *is* out of there. That is all that matters." I give him a small smile before heading towards the door.

"Elyra?" Lukas calls to me and I turn around, careful to not catch Maer's head on the frame. He runs a hand gingerly through his long blonde locks and does not look at me for a while.

"I was wondering if, maybe, you would like to—"

"INTRUDER!" someone shouts from the watchtower at the South of the keep and Lukas and I practically jump from the sudden outburst. Luckily, Maer does not awaken.

Without hesitation, I run as fast I can with Maer in my arms and lay her down on the bed in our quarters before running out to the courtyard. Soldiers armed with iron-tipped spears surround someone who had entered the gates, aggression marring their features without question.

Lukas is beside me as we watch the goings on, both curious as to who dares to enter Drodal's Keep without permission and who would make Breccan question whether he should give it. Someone has made his soldiers angry and willing to kill.

Breccan himself and Elijah burst into the night and both look ready to murder. They are a sight to behold as they storm over to where the commotion lies. I choose to hang back with Lukas, biding my time until I decide if I am needed. Something makes me incredibly cautious to approach… like a constant chill with no cause for it.

Breccan takes one look at the inside of the soldier's circle, whispers something to Elijah who then breaks through the soldier's lines and becomes his normal violent self as he reads the man the riot act of trespassing in Breccan's kingdom. I cannot catch what he is saying to the intruder as Breccan storms towards me; as if the young warrior has replaced the aged ruler. I catch a glimpse of fear in his eyes as he breathes in my curiosity and then quickly glances over his shoulder back at the unknown male.

I take a slow step forward but Breccan reaches me, grabbing my arm in a steel grip and turning me away. I push out of his hold and stare him down, fire in my eyes. He only looks pleading.

"Please, Elyra." He outstretches his leathery palm again but I do not take it.

Breccan's eyes betray the secret.

There is only one man that Breccan would intentionally steer me away from.

I know who is enduring Elijah's wrath.

I sneer at the outstretched hand as pure rage seeps into my veins.

I look over to the commotion and the guards have dispersed just enough to allow me to glimpse a mane of blonde hair.

I start to sprint before the King of Drodal can even comprehend my actions.

Breaking through the soldier's ranks, none of them even try to restrain me while I begin to throw violent punches in Roran Maar's face. I do not take the time to confirm that it is in fact Roran whose face is being impounded with my knuckles. Blood splashes against my skin but I barely notice it. Roran does not even try to defend himself against me. His hands are splayed against the cold stone floor in surrender. It does not douse the fire in my blood.

"I'm sorry!" he cries from beneath my impacts. I only snarl at him and draw my dagger above his chest.

But before I can strike, strong arms wrap around my chest and pull me off of Roran.

"Calm down, Elyra. You must calm down," Elijah spits into my ear.

I thrash against him more and more and his tightening grip only makes me angrier. Without thinking, I grab the dagger and turn around quickly enough that Elijah barely misses the blow when I strike down with my dagger towards his chest. The blade slices along his arm but he catches it before it can cause any serious damage. His arm versus mine. Our arms shake uncontrollably with the effort of our force. Elijah grits his teeth, his jaw throbbing, as his green eyes stare right into my grey ones.

"He is under the protection of Drodal now. Only Breccan can decide his fate."

"You don't know what he did to me." I snarl a vicious sound that surprises even me. His eyes soften then; the harsh green dulling to a serene emerald.

"I have no doubt that he deserves your wrath, Elyra. But save the blow for when it counts. Let Drodal destroy his soul before you destroy his body."

"*No.*" The hate flows like darkness through my veins, corrupting the scarlet blood already lurking there. His eyes then turn

49

sad and his grip on my arm loosens. The sight of him looking so vulnerable makes me do the same.

"Killing him will not make the pain go away, Elyra. Killing him will only add to our list of bloodshed. And you may just find… that the circumstances are far from what they first appear."

I turn my head to look back at Roran who is still on the floor, now wiping the blood spurting from his mouth and nose. *I'm sorry.* That is what he had cried during my assault. No cries for help, no words of vengeance. He did not fight it. He *accepted* it.

I release myself from Elijah and sheath the dagger at my side. Elijah only stands upright, his expression soulless and hardened once more. Behind me, I hear Roran being dragged to his feet by a couple of soldiers. I turn to look at him, the anger a constant ebb in my heart. I point at him and his bloody face is sad as he takes me in, body sagging in the arms of the soldiers on either side of him.

"You will not come near me," I demand, the pure force in my words enough to startle all those around me. "You will not speak to me nor will you seek me out. I will come to you when I am ready to do so and may the Aerix help you should I decide that your life is forfeit to my vengeance."

"I accept those terms," he says gravely, the blood from his ruined face drips onto the stone slabs as if in sacrament of this contract.

Without another word to anyone, including Lukas, I storm back into the walls of Drodal so that I may wash the Eradanian General's blood off of my fists.

Standing atop the watchtower in solitude, I gaze thoughtfully into the blackened skyline. I had dismissed the guards stationed here hours ago. I did not say when they could come back. They did not ask.

My knuckles are raw and red as I clench and unclench them on the tower's ornate railing. I have not been able to calm down since my attack on Roran.

Roran is here.

My friend.

My comrade in arms.

My betrayer.

Marvelling at the stars, I consider if I should have killed Roran where he stood. How did he find me? How did he muster the audacity to walk through Drodal's front gates? He is Myrna's toy now. She has assumed many rights since she had killed King

Adrian, not least of which was her leash on Roran which he so willingly adopted.

I will never forget his face when he had led Myrna's forces right to my doorstep. When they had shackled me and beat me. When they had taken me to Golnar.

I still do not know why he had done it. He was working with me to establish Jocelyn and Jasper to the throne of Eradan though their whereabouts were unknown. I do not even know how the young heirs are faring... I dread to even think about it for fear of what atrocities my mind would have me believe.

"Rumours of your brutality are spreading like wildfire across Drodal." Maer's small voice echoes across the barren winds of Zatria. I sigh deeply and smirk as I cock my head towards her tiny form.

"You should be sleeping."

"The excitement woke me." She shrugs. I nod at her and return my gaze to the skyline, indigo with night. I hear her shuffle forward, the fabric of her simple dress brushing her ankles.

"Why didn't you kill him?" she asks me and it startles me that she would be so forward. Nonetheless, I take a deep breath, trying to decide what to tell her. What should I tell her?

"Sometimes... brutality is measured not by our actions, but by our omissions," I say simply.

"You would have me believe that you failed to kill Roran by way of punishment? All I see is a blessing." It is strange to see her so worked up about something, even more strange that she is wiser beyond her years.

"He is being kept in the bowels of Drodal. I trust that he is being punished enough for now."

"Did he not hurt you?" Her voice rises to that of incredulity, "Did he not do something so terrible that you would consider killing him?"

"Yes. He did," I reply bluntly, still refusing to look at her. All I can feel are the scars and burns along my back, almost as if they are being seared into my flesh again.

"Did you not kill those men in Golnar who had hurt the women inside? Did you not murder the men who had sought me as a prize?" her words sting me as I hear the quiver in her voice.

"Yes."

"Then why does he still breathe?" she demands loudly. I whirl quickly to face her, hands balled into fists.

51

"He still breathes because I allow him to do so." I snarl. "He eats and he drinks what I choose to give him. He is alive because I simply wish for him to be. He lives knowing that every breath is numbered by my vengeance. So who are you to question my methods?"

Maer shrinks back into herself, the arms once folded defiantly against her chest now hugging herself loosely. I soften at the sight and loose a deep breath.

"I am sorry if I have scared you. But this is more complicated than a matter of life and death." I hold out my hand for her to take and she does so gingerly.

"How so?" I am relieved when she takes my hand and stands beside me on the balcony.

"This is a matter of my past which is more complex than you could possibly imagine."

"Won't you tell me who you really are?" I look down at her and run my hand through her short hair, her brown eyes pleading with me.

"I cannot risk your life, Maer. And to tell you would surely end what years you still have to live. I cannot bear that to happen."

A tightness in my chest leads to a stinging in my eyes. Maer reaches up on her tiptoes and strokes my cheek with her tiny hand, adoration glassing her own eyes. But before I can stop her, she retracts her hand and starts wringing them both nervously.

"Do you think sins can be forgiven?" she murmurs, not looking at me. It has me curious but I will not pry.

"I think that would depend on the sin." I smirk but it does nothing to calm her pursed lips. "What is it, Maer?" I ask, concerned for her.

"I should try and get some sleep." She smiles but it does not reach her eyes. She leaves the watchtower and I leave her to her own devices. Whatever is troubling Maer is serious and so it is a conversation to be had another day.

A dark speck catches my eye in the courtyard and I focus in on it instantly. A man, holding his chest and limping, walks through the gates. I cannot tell who it is from this distance and so I get ready to raise the alarm. But as a sharp growl reaches my ears, I instantly know that it is Elijah struggling across the courtyard.

I do not hesitate as I run from the watchtower, down the spiralling staircase and out the large double-doors into the courtyard beyond. The fountain trickles eerily against my eardrums while my feet pound the concrete slabs.

When I reach Elijah, I realise with shock that an arrow protrudes from his chest and from his heel. Blood stains the bulk of his emerald shirt and the back of his brown trousers. His mahogany hair is wet and matted against his forehead, strands loosening from their tie.

"By the Aerix, what has happened to you?" I murmur, placing my hand upon his shoulder but he shrugs me off.

"Get away from me." His voice is raspy from dehydration but the anger is obvious.

"Let me help you," I insist but I am annoyed when he shrugs me off again, smacking away my hand with such force that I hear something crack inside it. I purse my lips in pain but that is all I can afford to give him.

"I said *no*, Elyra." He growls with a certainty of death should I persist. My grey eyes glare into his green ones and it is a silent battle.

"Elijah, I know that you are not the wisest of all warriors but you are injured and I am the only one who knows of it. Now, unless you want me to wake up the entire citadel, I suggest that you stop whining and let me help you." Each word comes out more feral than the last.

"Fine," he snarls. "But tell anyone and I will—"

"Gut me where I stand." I finish for him in a bored tone, "I know the procedure by now, Warren. You should really come up with a new threat." His answering snarl has me chuckling but even so, I lift his arm around my shoulders and take his weight while I assist him down to the infirmary.

It is silent as we walk down candlelit corridors and shadowed halls. Slowly but surely, we are down onto the final floor of Drodal to where Elijah and I had first met. I nudge open the wooden door into the first infirmary room and I lead him over to the small white bed against the wall.

With a cry of pain, Elijah sits down and unstraps his bow and machete; muscles tense and sweat beading on his forehead. I quickly rummage through the healing-station and fill a bowl with water, sprinkle some salt through it and pick up a white rag.

"Take off your shirt," I call to him as I swirl the salt thoroughly through the water and I can hear that he does it without question.

Heading over to where Elijah sits, head bowed and breathing laboured, I pull over a wooden chair to sit in front of him. His sculpted tan chest catches me off guard for a moment but I pull myself together quickly.

"Are you still breathing?" I ask mockingly, desperate to keep him talking.

"Enough to keep you in line, Elyra," he rasps in an authoritative way. I laugh a little at that.

"No-one can keep me in line. But I appreciate your efforts." He smirks a little at my response.

Without announcing it, I snap the arrow protruding from his chest and he winces in pain. I then begin to pull it through his chest much to his detriment. The veins in his arms are protruding with the force he is tensing with to control the pain.

I put the arrow on the floor and then I quickly dip the rag into the salted water and start dabbing at his wound quickly. I know that I need to seal the wound so I grab the candle from the station and the metal tweezers.

"What are you doing?" Elijah pants. I sit down again and place the tweezers into the flame of the candle. His wound begins to trickle blood and I know that I do not have much time before it starts spurting.

"I leave for two seconds and you are already pining for me."

"That mouth is going to get you into a lot of trouble one day," he retorts but as he says it, I catch him glimpsing at my full mouth and I shy away from his gaze, an odd sensation appearing in my stomach.

"I do not doubt it," I answer. The tweezers begin to glow orange under the heat of the candle and I know that they are ready.

Again, without warning, I press the flat edge of the hot tweezers against the wound in his chest and he cries out, stifling the sound with his fist. Sweat drips down his face and his chest heaves with shallow breaths.

Once the wound is sealed over, I dab it again with the salted water just to make sure that it will not get infected.

"You have experience in healing?" he asks me and I begin to repeat the process with the arrow protruding from his ankle. I decide that keeping him talking is probably the best thing to do right now; I do not know how much blood he has already lost.

"I have developed my methods over the years." I smirk at him and the corners of his mouth turn up slightly but then he frowns.

"You have been wounded many times?"

"More often than I dare to admit," I murmur and his frown only deepens. At this point I am searing the wound again.

"You were really inside Golnar for three years?" his question catches me off guard and as I am on my knees, dabbing the seared wound on his ankle, the scars on my back seem to stretch.

"Yes," I whisper. I stand up and use the damp cloth to wipe the sweat from his forehead. He places his hand gently on my forearm.

"I'm sorry," he mumbles his eyes intense as they stare into mine. I almost want to look away but I cannot.

"What is life without some character building?" I shrug, trying to make a mockery of it but he only cocks his head to the side in sympathy. I have never seen Elijah look so soft.

"Enslavement is not something one should take lightly." His eyes take on a shadow that I have not seen in him before. I step away from him; the healing process is done.

"When you have been through as many trials in life as I have, one learns to turn them into an advantage."

"It is one thing to accept those trials but another thing entirely to ignore them."

"I ignore nothing," I tell him, that familiar agitation around Elijah dousing the new calmness I have experienced with him in this room.

"But you do not accept it either." He looks at me with an understanding that I cannot bear to share with him.

"Where were you, Elijah?" I ask, eyes narrowing. He simply begins to put his shirt back on before standing up and strapping his weapons back on. I stand an inch before his hardened face.

"Who injured you?" I demand of him but he heads toward the door in silence until he cocks his head towards me.

"Goodbye, Elyra."

Leaving me alone in the infirmary, I find myself staring at the arrows dropped onto the floor. I recognise those sharp edges. The black feathers on the stem. I remember how they felt slicing into the flesh of my shoulder.

Only one question comes to mind.

What was Elijah doing at Golnar?

Chapter 6

A brief note, stabbed into the door of my bedroom with a dagger, leads me to believe that there will be no training at dawn today:

No training today.
Do with it what you wish.
—Elijah

I suppose that Elijah remains blunt even in writing.

Would this have anything to do with the controversial events of last night?

Perhaps.

Even so, I am up now. This is my routine and I am not about to change it now. With Maer still asleep, I head out to the courtyard that now seems to be my home. Standing in my usual spot, I am ready to begin my vigil.

Until I hear the sound of pounding metal faintly on the breeze.

It is so faint that only by myself in the complete solitude of dawn would I be able to hear it. It almost sends me into a trance.

I know that noise.

I have grown used to it.

My hands react to the noises instinctively and I find myself mimicking those movements that I will probably remember for the rest of my life.

Walking around the back of the keep, the noise only gets louder. The clang reverberates off of my very bones. I move slowly, robotically. As if I am not in control of my limbs.

Nestled at the back of Drodal is an enchanting garden full of vibrant flowers. Roses, lilies, tulips, daisies, snowdrops and even bluebells. The smell is intoxicating but it is not the source of the clanging.

The source of the clanging is coming from an ivy-ridden concrete shack buried within the lovely garden surrounded by a ring of bluebells. I recognise the orange glow before I fully understand what it is I am looking at.

A forge.

Drodal has its own forge. Of course it would. Who else would supply its armoury? I try not to let the memories of Golnar consume me except my muscles cannot seem to forget.

A man is stationed here, bald with a red beard and biceps so huge that I can tell why he was chosen for this position. He is hammering upon a molten longsword, sweat dripping from his brow. His grey shirt is rolled up against the bulging muscles of his arms which I can tell could crush a man's skull in a second.

He looks at the longsword he was forging and cools it in a bucket of water ready to place with the other completed weapons. Except, this one is not completed. It is way too thick. All of my natural instincts arise out of me then. He is concentrating so much that I fear what will happen when I disturb him.

"Excuse me?" my voice is small and I find myself looking as vulnerable as Maer.

The man drops his hammer with a thud, before he could pick up another weapon, and glares at me, one of his eyebrows raised in question. But as he takes me in, he relaxes, if not a little sympathetically.

"Yes, miss?" his voice is as gruff as you would expect it to be but he does not have the wrathful air about him like Elijah does.

"That sword is not finished," I tell him and he laughs albeit a little condescendingly.

"And what would you know about forging?" he eyeballs me again and it is as if a guard is once again undermining me and my work.

"I have a method that could make your weapons the best in all of Aneya," I answer, trying to look strong but not feeling it.

"The best steel is forged for Eradan," he replies gruffly, "you would be a fool to challenge it." He picks up his hammer again and begins to pound on a small dagger.

"Perhaps." I find myself smirking, "Except I was the one who forged it." He drops the hammer yet again and stares at me in shock, blue eyes wide for only a moment until they crinkle with amusement.

"You are Iron-Will of Golnar." He grins. The man rushes forward, wiping his ashen hands on his trousers and handing one out to me. "My name is Brogan Stone."

"Pleasure." I shake his hand and admire the strength in his wrist. His cocky smirk has me smiling.

I am surprised at how he does not give me sympathy for enduring the forge-camps. He only admires my skills. It is a breath of fresh air. One that I will gladly take.

"So, you have some skills to teach me?"

"To maximise the material you wield, Brogan, you need to temper the steel." He looks at me blankly and I sigh with a laugh.

Heading over to his station, I take back the longsword that he thought was finished and begin heating it over the fire-pit. Brogan is twiddling his beard around a finger as he watches me. Once the steel glows red-hot, I pick up the hammer and start hammering away at the metal to make it flat. My muscles react easily as if I am in the humid forge-camp right now.

I then fold the molten-steel over and hammer it together before cooling it in the water-bath next to me. Steam erupts into my face and I repeat the process over and over. Brogan watches every technique, ever-silent.

Halfway through the process, a movement catches my eye from across the garden but I do not see what it is. Nothing or no-one comes out to greet me so I suppose it must be nothing.

Brushing the wet hair from my face, my hand is slick with sweat from my forehead. I find it strange that I have almost missed this feeling, performing this task. I have failed for so long in my quest and forging is something that I succeed in.

Once I cool the weapon for the last time, daylight already blooms across the charming garden. Brogan picks up the polished longsword and twirls it between his hands as a trained warrior would do. He balances it across his palm and his mouth twitches with admiration. He looks at me with amusement.

"It's light." He grins.

"It's stronger too." I counter, "Folding the steel allows the layers to become more compact. The repeated cooling allows for a purer blade."

"Indeed." He studies the sword again and places it within a pile of its own.

"Are you a blacksmith, Brogan? Or are you a warrior?" I find myself asking him. He stills at my question and so I feel a need to justify myself. "The skill with which you handled the blade is quite experienced. I could not help but notice."

"I originate from Ceylon. I have not revisited in years."

I catch my breath.

Ceylon. The realm of warriors as brutal as the weapons they carry. Bred from birth and skilled beyond belief, the warriors of Ceylon are not to be underestimated in the Eastern lands. This explains his incredible muscle and his ever-observant eye.

Brogan's eye glances behind me to where two medium-sized war-axes lay attached to the wall in the formation of an X. They are quite beautiful. Their stems are embroidered with swirls of black ink and their sharp silver edges glow like moonlight.

"When was the last time you used them?" I murmur and he sighs.

"I used to wield them across Aneya, from the deserts of Zatria to the slums of Vangar. Now, I only wield them in my mind." The sadness in his voice wrenches at my heart. Ceylon warriors are extremely attached to their weapons. Only something stronger could have parted him from them, forbidden among their race.

"Who is she?" I ask delicately and he smiles knowingly at my leap in knowledge. Ceylon warriors can only mate with their own race. To disobey this rule means immediate exile.

"She is exquisite. A work of art in the flesh."

"Where is she?" he turns away from me then and starts hammering away at another weapon.

"I have not heard from her for a long while. I fear the worst but I choose not to believe it."

Before I can ask anymore, Lukas comes running around the corner, eyes frantic.

"There you are, I—" his mouth gapes open when he sees Brogan standing next to me. Brogan simply glares at him and Lukas shuts his mouth. I giggle.

"What is it Lukas?"

"Would you…" he trails off as he looks from a chuckling me to a glaring Brogan, "mind coming with me for a moment. It is urgent."

"Define urgent." I smirk, expecting it to be something to do with his meal plan for the festival tonight. Brogan smiles cheekily at me and I can tell that he and I will get along just fine.

"Maer," Lukas replies and my smiles vanishes completely.

"Take me to her," I demand and without saying goodbye to Brogan, I charge with Lukas into the depths of Drodal.

"What happened?" I know that I have turned into a woman of business, trying to restrain my anger.

"She came back not too long ago from her usual voyages every morning. Except…"

"Except what?" I glare at him as we reach the basement-level, the air suddenly chilling my bones more than usual.

"She did not return in the same state as when we she left," he says evasively, his eyes betraying his sadness.

He halts in front of the infirmary door and I tense.

"You do not understand… she refused for me to alert you," he tells me and I do not even wait as I burst through the door and find Maer sitting on the wooden bed and Ayla dabbing a damp cloth upon her mouth. Maer flinches at my entrance.

"What is it that I am not supposed to see, Maer?" I fold my arms across my chest in an authoritative way and her shoulders sag as she surrenders. Ayla turns her golden head away from me as Maer turns hers to face me.

A murderous rage surges through my veins.

Maer's young face is now marred with an eye as black as my hair, a purple bruise staining her cheek and a split lip of which dried blood now crusts along it.

"I will kill them," I say through clenched teeth.

"Is that your answer to everything? Kill all those who harm people? If you were to do that, I am afraid Aneya will have no population left," Ayla says hatefully, her annoyingly beautiful face twisting into a sneer.

Ayla and I have never really spoken this past week but in whatever brief exchanges we have had, they have been short and somewhat brutal.

"Good riddance," I snarl back and she shakes her head in annoyance.

"It wasn't her fault, Elyra," Maer cries, her voice wobbling with incoming tears. I immediately crouch down in front of her and place my hands on her shaking shoulders as she sobs.

"Maer…" I say softly, stroking her cheek with my thumb. "I am not angry with you." She looks back to the door with daggers at a vulnerable Lukas, an expression I have never seen her perform.

"You promised she wouldn't know!" she cries again, hurt at his betrayal. "I can't trust anyone." The tears start flowing down her cheeks and I wipe them away as gently as I can so as not to hurt her wounds.

"You can trust *me*, Maer," I tell her, hurt that she would hide such a thing from me. "All I have ever done is protect you and you were going to lie to me."

"She has the right to keep secrets," Ayla snaps at me.

"Not from her guardian," I bite back, not even bothering to look at her.

"And when exactly did you earn that right?"

"I assumed the role when I rescued her from a terrible fate. Something you lack both knowledge and experience of so your opinion is no longer valid in this conversation." My anger keeps her silent then.

"Ayla, we should go. This is between Elyra and Maer." Lukas announces softly and with a huff she does as he asks. When the door slams and we are completely alone, Maer's tears turn into loud sobs.

"What has got you so worked up?" I sit on the bed next to her, place my arm around her shoulders and let her rest her head on my chest as she cries.

"Everything is so complicated," she answers.

"It does not have to be."

"You don't understand."

"Then help me to, Maer. I cannot protect you if you do not tell me what is going on." I try to ingrain into her. Her sobs stifle then and she lifts her head off of my chest and wipes her tears away, calming down.

"Telling you would do more harm than good."

"Let me be the judge of that." She sighs and looks to me with pleading eyes.

"I was sought out in Eradan by bad people. They wanted me to do something. They want me to do it still," she sums up for me. I nod.

"This is where you go every morning, isn't it?" I murmur and she nods, her face screwing up in guilt. "And they are the ones that hurt you this morning?"

"Yes," she mumbles, touching her fingertips delicately on her bruised cheek, "They hurt me."

"Why?"

"I wanted to stop." Her voice shakes with the threat of more tears but she manages to restrain herself. "But they won't let me."

"Oh, Maer..." I cup my hand to her face and she clasps it with her own tiny hand, "What have you gotten yourself into?"

"I can't say. You will hate me."

"I could never hate you." I try to console but my words seem worthless while she is so emotional. She looks away from me in denial and so I kneel before her again and take her hands, she looks at me with so much sadness... a sadness a young girl should never know.

"I made a vow to myself to protect you, Maer. I love you as if you were my own and I will defend you as such. Tell me who troubles you."

"No. If they found out—"

"They will not get the chance to find out anything once I discover their names," I threaten and I can see that she believes me but she shakes her head anyway.

"I will not say. For your safety and my own."

"Maer—"

"I see you as a sister, Elyra. As a mother." That term alone has me melting, "I cannot lose you."

"Nor will I lose you," I tell her, my voice cracking with emotion that I have never felt before, "I will not force you to tell me what you refuse to share. But I must ask that you do not meet those people again. You will not go anywhere unattended; you must always be accompanied, even within Drodal's walls. Am I understood?"

"I am sorry," she whispers, more tears streaking her flushed cheeks. I just smile and take her in my arms. She hugs me so tightly that I fear she will be stuck to me forever. I do not mind that idea.

"Take my strength, Maer." She sobs into my ear at the words I told her at Golnar.

"I love you," she says quietly and I clutch her tighter.

"I love you too," I tell her and am surprised at how much I mean it.

After a while, she releases herself from me, wiping her tears with a shaky laugh. I stand up from my kneeling position on the floor and take her hand in mine.

"Come on, we have a festival to prepare for." I smile and her eyes light up at that despite the one being blackened. The sight of her marred face makes me want to kill the bastards that did it. But their time will come. Right now, I have a child to look after.

I open the door and a spark of rage enters my veins again when I notice Elijah not that far along the corridor. He must have heard the majority of our conversation. I spy Lukas lingering also at the far-end, too far to hear anything.

"Lukas?" I call and Maer tightens her grip on my hand.

"No," she complains. I bend down to her level as Lukas approaches, wringing his hands guiltily but with a friendly smile on his face. She is frowning.

"Lukas was brave in telling me what had happened to you. And I hope that never changes. Do not blame him for doing the right thing. He cares about you and his actions only confirm it."

"I suppose so," she grumbles.

"Hello, Maer." He grins nervously when he approaches us, she doesn't say anything, "I'm making cookies for the festival, there's plenty of mix to go around?" her eyes glow at the thought of eating cookies no doubt.

"Will there be chocolate chips?" she asks in a small voice.

"More than what could fit in my stomach alone. I need another one to help me. Do you think yours is up for the task?" one of his sincere smiles has her grinning with a nod. She takes Lukas' hand. When Lukas realises I won't be coming, he gives me a puzzled look.

"You aren't coming?"

"I will follow in a few minutes." He looks behind me to where Elijah leans against the corridor's wall, arms across his chest. Lukas almost looks sad so I touch his harm with my hand. "Save me some chocolate chips, don't let her eat them all." I wink at Maer and she giggles.

"Sure." Lukas smiles before heading up to the kitchens with a much happier young girl at his side.

I do not exercise patience when I storm over to where Elijah stands, his face betraying nothing of his emotions. If it weren't for last night, I would sincerely believe that Elijah is made of stone. His brown hair hangs loosely at his shoulders today and the candlelight glints off of his high cheekbones and emerald eyes.

"Is there something I can help you with, Elijah?" I do not hide the irritation in my tone and it has his mouth tilting up slightly, almost in an arrogant way.

"Is she all right?" he points down the corridor to where Maer was just moments ago.

"She will be when I kill the bastards."

"You don't even know who they are." His deep voice echoes in the hallway.

"But when I find out, they will be as good as dead." I promise him, no doubt with wrath dancing in my grey eyes.

"Your arrogance will get you killed before you can do anything." His comment only makes the fire in me more uncontrollable.

"Arrogance is when you believe you can do something outside of your skill-set. I *know* that I can kill them swiftly and easily. Do not mistake the difference."

"I make no mistakes," he growls.

"Are you always so insufferable or is your pride just shaken because I saved your ass last night?"

"I could have handled it just fine on my own." His hands tense into fists at his sides.

"Oh, please. If I were not there, you would have walked deliriously into the kitchens and rubbed breadcrumbs into your wounds."

"You mistake me for a fool, Elyra." He leans off of the wall and glowers down at me, towering over my small frame. "I consider that very unwise."

"In case you have not noticed, I do not give a damn what you think is unwise," I spit at him. "Do not eavesdrop on Maer and me again." With that warning, I walk away from him only to find that he grabs my arm to pull me back to face him again. His face is the angriest I have ever seen it. It is nearly frightening.

"Who are you to give me orders? Do you not think that I care for the girl?" his fingers dig into my arm but I dare not let him know that it is hurting me.

"I doubt that you care for anyone." I sneer back at him and his eyes turn into emerald flame right before my own eyes.

"I care for a father who was slaughtered by his brother and for my own brother who was sent to Canaan for witnessing it." His words shock me into silence, "Do not think that you know me, Elyra, because that will be your downfall."

He releases my arm with such force that I stagger backwards. Elijah is already at the end of the corridor before I can comprehend what he has just revealed. My heartbeat rivals a horse's gallop and I cannot stop my uneven breathing.

Elijah's uncle had killed his own brother… while Elijah's brother was sent to Canaan… the male equivalent to Golnar. How long has he been there? Could this be where Elijah goes? It explains last night… I thought the arrows embedded in him were from Golnar… I never even suspected Canaan.

"His name is Benjamin," a voice says from close behind me.

"Sneaking up on me is never a wise decision, Breccan." His light laugh would have me smiling if not for the grave news I have received.

"Perhaps. I do not wish for that dagger to be thrust into my chest any time soon." I look at him and his sea-blue eyes are weary despite his happy air.

"I did not expect—"

"For Elijah to have a family? For him to carry dark secrets? Did I not warn you of this?" I think back to when Master Saltmist and I had first met and the realisation sinks in.

"You told me that he and I would be more similar than I would expect."

"Indeed. Everyone has a past, Elyra. I expect that you still carry secrets of your own upbringing. Are you not living a secret now?" I would roll my eyes if he were not so wise.

"I believe that you have surpassed your initial training. I also trust that you have just given Elijah the catalyst he needs to start fulfilling the next stage."

"What has standing on the spot for hours got to do with my training?" I huff. Obviously I have incredible calf muscles because of it but I just do not understand how this is supposed to help me.

"You forget that we are training you for magic, not war. This training was to teach you patience, to be aware of yourself as well as your surroundings. This will aid you in your use of magic as all skills reach a point of exhaustion. It is your duty to know when your magic reaches this point and to do so means to be aware of every bodily process that you have."

"Why can't you teach me? It would be so much easier to do this if it were with someone tolerable," I moan, not meaning to sound too petulant.

"Elijah has trained many a fine warrior in his time with me. He is the best warrior within the ranks of Drodal and I have no doubt that he will accomplish the task I have set him."

"We don't even know if I have any magic as of yet. All of this effort seems pretty futile." I sigh, wiping my forehead with the back of my hand.

"I see something in you, Elyra. Something that could be an amazing advantage in your quest against Myrna Verena. And I strongly believe that any advantage would be one worth your patience."

"I have been here almost a week and I have not seen much magic." I note and Breccan smiles, crinkling his eyes.

"We do not like to flaunt our talents. We prefer to use them at our leisure or in times of war but never for anything trivial."

"Pity. I would love to see why Master Saltmist is so highly revered." I smirk and he grins at me. A realisation hits me and I find myself saying, "The more time I spend here, the longer Jocelyn and Jasper feel that they are alone." Admitting this makes me feel a little vulnerable.

"That would only make your return more triumphant in their eyes. They may think you to be dead by now. News of your capture spread through Aneya like wildfire. Most do not believe that you still exist." I am silent for a moment as I ponder my thoughts.

"What if…" I trail off, too afraid to voice this fear but I know that I must, "What if they are both dead?"

"I know of only one person who would be able to answer that question and he lies within my dungeons." Breccan does not meet my eye with his subtle advice but I know who he is referring to.

"Don't blame me if my dagger accidentally slides across his throat," I mumble, bracing myself for the conversation ahead.

"I would expect nothing less of you." With that, Breccan Saltmist turns on his heels and stalks to the floors above me with hands laced behind his back.

I, on the other hand, have a traitor to interrogate.

Standing in front of the small curved wooden door that leads to the dungeons, my heart starts to race. I might as well be facing Myrna. Although I know that I would find that much easier. Myrna is power-hungry. She has a thirst to conquest and thus she is not on amicable terms with anyone in the borders of Aneya. She is evil for evil's sake. I can handle that.

But for someone to befriend me. To fight with me and for me. Someone that I trusted with my life and my duties… and then to shatter it all completely… I cannot fathom it.

But I must know what has become of Jasper and Jocelyn.

And so I stifle my fear and push open the small door with ease.

A dark spiralling staircase splays out before me, down into the depths of Drodal. It is cold. It is foreboding. I walk down the staircase, my footsteps echoing within the silent chasm that awaits me.

When I reach the bottom, only one brazier glows with a flickering flame. Numerous cells spread themselves before me, the iron bars on their front to subdue those who wield magic no less. It smells damp in here. The wet chill aches along my spine.

I make out Roran's golden hair before I can see the rest of him. Curled up in the corner of his cell, he hugs his knees and hangs his head into his lap. He is trembling with cold. The Eradanian navy and silver uniform still clings to his skin albeit ripped and dirty. I cannot help my sneer that he has the audacity to where Adrian's colours under Myrna's rule. He must have adorned this before entering Drodal. My breathing comes quickly as my blood boils.

Roran's head snaps up at my ragged breaths and his blue eyes twinkle with hope. He slams against the iron-bars before I even have

66

time to blink, hands gripping the bars as if he could tear right through them.

"You came…" his voice is dry from lack of water and the brazier sheds enough light for me to see that Roran looks ragged, barely alive. From the conditions or from his betrayal, I do not know.

"I am not past stealing your last breaths," I say calmly despite my raging blood. His eyes widen and then slacken in sadness. He releases the bars and even his posture turns defeated.

"You stole my breath when I first laid eyes upon you," he murmurs and I am struck by the comment. It reminds me of times with Roran that I would rather forget. Especially given his current affections.

"I am not here for the past, Roran. I am here for the present." He laughs darkly, handsome golden face contorting into that of an animal.

"Aren't they all related these days?" he leans against the wall and hangs his head, his dirty hair shielding his face from my piercing stare.

"Tell me what I want to know," I demand of him.

"Ask me and it shall be yours, Lenora." I stiffen at my true name, bristling like a dog would for battle.

"Do not call me that," I snarl. He pins me with a curious gaze, eyes almost alight with amusement.

"Renouncing your past, are you?"

"I am renouncing *you*. Nothing more." He comes forward and stands in front of me again. I do not yield to him.

"You know, I have wondered…" his voice is low while he cocks his head at me, "Why the great Lenora Belavier is hiding behind the name of the High Priestess of Delphor."

"You have no right to discuss such matters with me." The words barely come out through my clenched teeth.

How dare he mention her?

How dare he imply her name?

"Your reasons are your own, *Elyra*." He drawls her name and I ball my hands into fists. "But if she gets wind of this, I fear that you will come to harm."

He does not know.

He does not know that Elyra had been in Golnar with me.

How could he not know?

"As if you care about my safety," I spit at him, hand desperately wanting to grasp my dagger and slice it across his throat.

"That is all I have ever cared for," he bites back, gripping the bars with pleading in his eyes. It is my turn to laugh maniacally.

"Did you care about me when you lead Myrna over my threshold? Did you care for me as you watched her men beat and torture me in the confines of my own apartment? Did you care for me when you beseeched my good name across all of Eradan and ruined everything I have worked for since our King's death?" tears threaten to spill from my eyes but I hold them in. I will not give him the satisfaction.

"I did not mean for any of this to happen." His voice shakes tremendously but I do not care.

Without another word, I turn around. Ripping open my basque and pulling away my shirt, I pull my clothes down to expose my marred back to Roran who gasps in response.

"They whipped me. Branded me. Cut me. For three years." I hastily pull my shirt back on and clip my basque across my midriff and face him. He looks ready to break before my burning eyes.

"I once got hit so hard that I could not see for five days."

"Stop."

"Men used to seek me out. They used to pin me against the wall with bad intentions."

"Please stop." He covers his ears but I just raise my voice.

"I was once whipped for so long that many said that they could see the full length of my spine."

"I said stop!" he bellows and it rattles the entire prison. I simply regard him in disgust.

"Why should I afford you the mercy that Golnar never afforded me? These truths, these pains… they will not stop for me. And by the Aerix, I will make damn sure that they do not stop for you."

"Lenora…" he begs, voice twisting into that of sorrow. I point a shaking finger at him and try to control my rage.

"*You* did this to me. Not Myrna. Not her men. *You*."

"I didn't mean to—" he tries.

"Yes, you did!" I shout, losing control and he winces, grabbing his hair as tears slide down his cheeks. "You were supposed to be my friend! My soldier! My—" I cut off then, not willing to admit what we almost became to one another. That was a very long time ago. "And you betrayed me. The one person I could trust betrayed me. The irony kills me as much as your treachery."

"If I could take it all back, I would." He sobs. "I would destroy all of Aneya if it would allow me to win you back, Lenora."

"I am not a prize, Roran. Not to Myrna. Not to Golnar. And certainly not to you." With that, I turn my back to him and begin to walk away. Damn him. I will find what I seek elsewhere.

"They found out about Jasper!" he cries to me and I can hear his hands digging into the iron at the rate he is wringing them against it. I stop in my steps, shocked and stunned by his declaration. I turn and face him and he looks more defeated than ever. He slumps against the bars.

"Myrna found out about Jasper," he repeats in a small voice. Alas, Roran's past comes back to haunt me.

"That's not possible," I counter, disbelief extinguishing my anger for a moment.

"It's true."

"We are the only ones who knew—"

"Come on, Len!" he cries again exasperatedly, "Did you not find it just a little bit suspicious as to why Jasper was kept inside the castle? Why Jocelyn was sent to work and Jasper remained locked inside?"

"Myrna is barren… she needs an heir…"

"He was her bargaining chip. Her leverage. She knew what we were doing from the moment she took the throne. And he was her only way in stopping us. In dividing us."

"Well, I guess it worked, didn't it?" I snarl at him and he punches the wall beside him with a deafening cry of rage.

"It was him or you, Lenora! I preserved the kingdom because I knew that that is what you would have wanted. I chose him because he is the only one who can take the throne back from Myrna. I chose him to make all of the work you were doing worthwhile."

"It is not worthwhile if I am in prison, Roran." I have to physically stop myself from wringing his neck.

"I knew you wouldn't accept your fate. I knew you would escape. I tried to organise a rescue but by the time the plans were orchestrated, your name had faded across Zatria. And then it faded from Eradan. And now your name has faded into Aneya's history as legend. I thought you were…"

"They could not kill me," I growl, realising where this was going.

"You are only mortal, Len. I did not know what could have happened to you," he admits in a small voice. "It took me so long to come to terms with your death… so long. And then I saw your face riding away from Golnar. I thought I had died and gone to heaven."

"I can send you there if you'd like." I offer and he cries out again in agitation.

"By the Aerix, are you not listening to me? I am *begging* for your forgiveness. I have told you my reasons and still you are stubborn."

"The Aerix didn't save me from Golnar, Roran. I saved myself. I will forgive you if I ever deem you worthy to earn my trust again and not a moment before."

"Would you not have done the same thing?" he roars at me, his pleading face rattles my bones but I dare not let him know. "Would you not have saved Jasper's life?" I stare at him in silence and even though no one speaks, it is so loud that I can barely stand it.

"I would have tried to find another solution. I was working on another solution." Roran knew this; he was working on it with me. "When did I fail in my plans? When did I fail you?"

"You never failed me, Lenora. Never." A tear sheds from my eye and I wipe it away quickly.

"You put your faith in Myrna and not in me. That is where you have fallen. And so that is where you will be tested."

"Please—"

"I am tired of these games, Roran. Tell me what I came down here to know. Where are Jocelyn and Jasper *now*?" his answering silence stirs up unease within me.

"Jasper remains inside the palace. Guarded at all times."

"And Jocelyn?" he does not answer me immediately again. Instead, he looks at me in fear.

"What? What is it?"

"I tried to stop it. I tried to get her out of there—"

"Out of where?" I demand but he only stares at me, "Tell me!" I shout and he flinches.

"She was sent to work."

"Work where?" his face regards me sympathetically and I know his answer before he even has to speak it.

"She was sent to the brothel."

Everything stops.

I cannot think.

I cannot react.

What?

Jocelyn Maddox, my Jocelyn, King Adrian's daughter… is in a brothel?

I can't fathom it. Forced to work in… *that* industry and… by the Aerix.

"*Why?*" my tone immediately arouses his fear and for good reason.

"I had tracked her to the main brothel in Eradan and then nothing. She dropped off of the radar. I think that they gave her an alias, maybe even dyed her hair as a precaution. There is no mention of her anywhere in Eradan. I have been scouting the brothel every day and spoken to various men who use it and cannot find any woman matching her description."

"She's there, Roran. She's just good at hiding."

When we were children, Jocelyn could hide and lie her way out of anything. Her beauty charmed the men and her charm entranced the ladies. She was a sight to behold and an incredible woman. I should know, I trained her.

"Does Jasper know?" I ask. That poor family…

"Yes. He got beaten for his protests." Roran replies sadly and given his relationship with Jasper, I can only imagine what they are both going through.

"I should have never been sent away." I sneer. Everything was going perfectly. I was going to save Jasper, save Jocelyn and rally an army against Myrna to win back the kingdom. And Roran had ruined it.

"I know," he admits, "I will find her, Lenora. I promise—"

"No. *I* will find her as soon as I am released from Drodal. Until then, goodbye, Roran."

He does not say anything as I leave him to face his thoughts in the dungeon. As I slam the door and feel the overwhelming sense of solitude, the exchange begins to overcome my calm composure.

Jocelyn… my sweet Jocelyn… forced to endure a fate which I have been fighting against these past years. Jasper… held prisoner in his former home… my friends, suffering while I am compelled to complete a training which is useless to me.

And Roran… do I actually feel sorry for him? Do I forgive him for what he had done to me? Would I have done the same thing? Protected Jasper and condemned my friend to a torture I believed he could face?

I do not know.

And I will never know.

I don't know what to think. And before I can stop it, the emotion emits from me like a tidal wave but I frantically try to hold on to my tears.

Footsteps startle me and I whirl my head around to see Elijah walking along the dark corridor towards me. Despite the hate in my eyes, he sees the sadness shining on my cheeks and grows annoyingly concerned.

"Are you ever *not* around?" I murmur to myself exasperatedly and try to wipe the tears from my cheeks with my sleeve before he can see them.

"This is my home, Elyra. You are the visitor. And so I may roam where I please," he growls as he reaches me but I hide my face from him. Elijah only tries to angle himself in front of me.

"What saddens you so?" his deep voice asks and surprisingly, it rekindles the emotions that I had tried so hard to suppress before his arrival. Nonetheless, I know what I have to do. I just hope that I have the strength to say it. I wipe my face again and refuse to look at him.

"Um… I want you to…" a sniffle, "Release Roran from the dungeons and…" a pause as I force down more tears, "ensure that he is looked after."

"Elyra—" Elijah's face is so full of a concerned curiosity that I turn my face away and wipe the stray tear that had fallen against my will.

"But just don't let him near me." I sniffle involuntarily again and my voice shakes with restraint, "I'm not ready. I'm not ready for that yet."

"Elyra, please—" his hand reaches out to grab my elbow and he pulls me to face him, grabbing my face with both of his hands.

"I just… can't. Not yet." I feel almost delirious.

"What has he done to you?" his green eyes bore into my grey ones.

"Just promise me." I sigh. "Do not let him near me." His thumb wipes away the last remnants of the tears and I am surprised at how comforting it feels. Steeling myself, I place my hands over his and slide them off my face. As if a switch has gone off inside him, he straightens, face returning to his usual stony composure.

"It will be done." He nods. He gives me one last steely glance before he strides past me in a manner that makes me believe that he is eager to get away.

I do not really know what had just happened between Elijah and me. And I do not really have time to care. Nor do I even want to. I do not have the strength to visit Codax in his stable today for obvious reasons and so I head to the kitchens where hopefully I can find some cheerful bearings with Lukas and Maer.

And hopefully Roran and Elijah will stay well out of my way.

Chapter 7

The bonfire in the centre of the courtyard rages wildly in front of me and I marvel at the dancing flames. The rich tang of smoke fills the air and the crackling of embers tantalises my ears. This comfort is a far cry from my earlier distress but I would not wish it any differently.

Lukas had prepared a luxurious feast with impeccably seasoned meats and an array of flavourful accompaniments. It was a feast for kings. And even know his elegant desserts still line the long wooden table out in the courtyard bountiful with biscuits, pastries and cakes to rival the best pastry chef in Eradan.

Elijah had kept his word. Roran remains by his side at the other end of the festivities, bound by Elijah's aggression. At one point my heart rose into my throat as I saw Roran begin to approach me but Elijah's strong arm reached out to pull him back before he could even make one step. I nodded my thanks to Elijah and he merely blinked in response. Bastard.

Lukas is dancing with Maer around the campfire with many others and the grin on her face glows as if the flames of the bonfire live within her smile. Even though I am standing alone with my arms folded across my chest against one of the blossom trees on the edge of the courtyard, I do not really feel lonesome. The cheers and laughter is very infectious and with the full moon shining so brightly overhead, this is the probably the happiest that I have been in years.

The band silences upon their raised wooden platform under Breccan's hand. He is seated in an ornate carved chair, worthy of being a makeshift throne with its blue velvet accents and he is grinning wildly at the revelry.

"It is time for our guest to read the Prayer of the Aerix so that we may bask in their glory and hope for their return."

Ah, yes. The Aerix. They are our fabled gods. Some say that they once roamed this world as the undisputed rulers of Aneya. They are fantastic creatures… elegant and wise, brutal and ferocious. One could say they are but dragons but that term is too simplistic to describe them. They are larger than dragons, more ethereal than them too.

There were only ever five Aerix. Five lords to rule the lands. One for each element that this world is bound in. Embron was the Lord of Fire with scales such a deep red that they say it was hard to look at for fear that it contained the blood of his enemies; he lives and breathes the fire to which he was born to. Aera was the Lady of Air, her skin a pale white so as to match the clouds above us; her breath can steal that of others but she can also give breath at will. Teragon was the Lord of the Earth with scales of a green that could rival that of the rawest of emeralds; his sonorous cry can summon all those of this realm to his aid, plants and animals alike. Brinoir was the Lady of Water with skin such a deep blue that men have buried themselves in the ocean for search of such beauty; her breath can melt men to the bone with her searing steam but her wings can command any mass of her water she deems fit.

But the fifth beast is said to be the King of all Aerix, larger in size and more feral than the others, dangerous to all those that it comes across and even to the other Aerix. Others say that his purpose never strays from their friendship and that he is seen more so as an elder to the others. Onyxius is the harbourer of death, his black scales so black that some would fall into endless madness for staring at them too long, his breath unknown to all as he had never used it or all those that had the honour to see it did not survive the sight.

Some pray that the Aerix will return to us and lead us out of this darkness. But I am under the belief that we must save ourselves. Prayer will not help us defeat Myrna Verena and creatures that have not been seen in centuries will surely not come out of their shadows now for a meagre human war.

"I always hate this part of the festival," a gruff voice says from beside me and I grin at Brogan's mutual dislike for it.

"I am surprised that you have ventured outside of your forge. Trying to mingle with the rest of humanity, Brogan?" I can hear his smile before I look towards him and see it.

"I do not care much for names but considering I did not even get yours in our brief exchange, I believe that I am owed it." I struggle to hide my smirk but before I can answer, an unmistakeable figure emerges from behind the bonfire.

A Priestess of Delphor.

My heart thunders inside my chest. She has the same long and straight red hair as Elyra had... the same pale skin... but her eyes are blue and not the impressive brown of hers and this one seems to hold herself in a more pristine manner whereas Elyra was rather rugged. It is one of the reasons why we had gotten on so well.

Brogan stiffens beside me at the sight of this woman and I am surprised that I am not the only one who does so.

"Rayna Dior," he growls and his hatred for this woman is potent.

"You know her?" I whisper, my throat going dry at the sight. Gosh she is so like Elyra…

"She is my love's sister. The new High Priestess of Delphor as she had forced her to abdicate because of me," he manages to say through his clenched jaw and my stomach sinks. I feel as if I am going to be sick. Elyra was… and Brogan is… and he does not know… by the Aerix.

"Brogan—" I begin to say in the hope that I am wrong but a shout stuns me into silence.

"Come on, Elyra!" Maer cries in excitement as she stands with Lukas before Rayna along with many others readying for the prayer to be told. Rayna's head snaps up and her icy eyes widen at the sight of me and Brogan equally stares at me in shock.

Silence ensues from the crowd at the two responses and Maer shrinks into Lukas' side as she breathes in the tension. All eyes are on me. The dagger infused with Elyra grows heavy at my side.

"What is your name?" Rayna breathes though more out of incredulity than demand.

"None of your concern," I answer and I instantly regret it. Brogan grabs my arm and twists me to face him, his hand digging in so much that it hurts. His face is feral.

"What have you done with Elyra?" he growls and when I do not answer, he shakes me so violently that I can hear my bones rattling.

What do I say?

What can I say?

Memories of that night invade my mind and I am lost to them, the emotions I had felt now creeping in as if I had watched that vicious crime just now.

"I have not done anything to her!" I cry, hurt at the mere thought of having hurt my only friend in Golnar.

"What have you done to her? If you have harmed one hair on her head, I swear that I will cause you unimaginable pain." His desperation places an anchor in my chest and tears well in my eyes. When I do not answer him he shakes me again.

"Tell me you bitch!" he bellows into my face and it strikes me silent at the sheer violence. When I do not answer again, Brogan begins to draw his fist ready to hit me but suddenly, a wall of water separates Brogan from me and it hardens into ice right before my eyes.

I look over to Breccan and he looks positively furious, blue eyes like the raging ocean as he stands up from his throne, every muscle tense for battle.

"Raise your hand to her again and I will make you wish you had never been born, boy." Breccan's voice is animalistic, dangerous. I did not know he had that sort of rage within him. Why would he do this for me? The wall melts before us. It must have been a warning. I dread to think what he will do if Brogan disobeys.

"She has harmed my precious Elyra and I will not be denied answers!" he spits back. That statement arouses my anger once more.

"I would never hurt, Elyra!" I shout back to him.

"Then why do you wear her name?" Rayna cries from the crowd, running over to face me herself.

"Do you use it as a trophy?" Brogan sneers, "To remember what atrocities you have done to her?"

"I wear it to honour her," I snarl and Rayna and Brogan relax in either shock or sympathy, I do not know. The memory of Elyra threatens to leak from my eyes and a roll of thunder echoes overhead.

"Honour her, how?" Rayna asks, her voice contorting with impending grief. I sag in defeat and look between a furious Brogan and a distraught Rayna.

"Elyra Dior had served four months in Golnar," I announce to them and numerous gasps ensue. "And she had served it by my side."

"How did she even get captured?" Rayna cries, placing her hands over her mouth.

"She was caught by Myrna's men. They saw her as a prize that Golnar could make use of." I sneer in disgust as I recant her story.

"So you did know her?" Brogan demands with a quivering lip and I nod, placing my hand on the dagger as if it will give me strength.

"She was my friend in a time where betrayal had taught me that friendship no longer exists." I dare not look in Roran's direction.

"But you have escaped from Golnar," Brogan says, "Where is she?" I am silent to that question and Rayna screams at the implication that it holds. Brogan only nods, fists shaking.

"How?"

"I will not divulge to you the details that your heart cannot bear to hear. But please know that she was strong until the end." My voice quakes as I try to control myself and spots of rain begin to fall. Rayna starts crying then and one of her handmaidens rushes to comfort her.

"You were there when she..." Brogan gulps as he blinks back his tears, remaining a man until this is over.

"She had received what I had deserved and for that I am truly sorry. We had both been punished that day. And in our suffering, her body was not as strong as she made it out to be. But her soul never broke." My throat closes up and then the rain pours down on us in sheets, drenching us within seconds.

"Let us move into Drodal. We can finish the revelry inside," Breccan announces gravely and everyone follows suit until I am left alone in the rain with the extinguished bonfire leaking its remnants into the sky.

I do not know how long I have stayed here in the middle of the courtyard but it is only until the sadness stops. I dare not let myself cry in these moments. I refuse to let it in. But as the sadness eventually stops so does the onslaught of rain; it is as if the universe is tied to my grief. Only the Aerix know what suffering Brogan and Rayna are enduring.

"We should begin the next stage of your training," Elijah states solemnly from behind me. I tilt my head to the heavens in disbelief.

"No rest for the wicked it would seem." I almost laugh.

"You are not wicked," he replies in a small voice and I laugh coldly.

"You do not know what I have done."

"I know that you tried everything in your power to stop Elyra's fate." I whip around to face him then, eyes narrowing with oncoming rage. I notice that he is just as drenched as I am. Has he been here this entire time?

"Do you know no grief?" I cry out to him and he looks to the floor. "Why can't you just leave me be?"

"I know what you are, Elyra," he states loudly. "And we must allow you to see it tonight."

"Why?" I answer in a tortured way. "Why must I play your games? Have I not been through enough?"

"You must see who you truly are. And this is the only way. Accept your truths and it will be done."

"*No.*"

"I will give you one last chance to make this easier on yourself. Give in to your rage." I notice that he is taking a battle stance; legs apart and arms tensed. Why?

"*No,*" I repeat and he hangs his head almost sympathetically. He comes silently closer, every movement astoundingly graceful. Elijah stands in front of me and my glare never ceases.

"Just know that I tried."

Before I can let his words sink in, his fist lands a blow to the side of my face and my jaw cracks on impact. I lose balance from the hit but I do not fall.

"What are you doing?" I shout at him, rubbing my jaw and spitting blood from my mouth.

"I need you to get angry. The faster you do, the easier this will be." He lunges again with his fist and I dodge to the left.

"Are you insane?" I back-step as he tries to land a kick to my abdomen and I cannot believe that this is happening.

"Do it."

"Why?" I cry, hating that I do not understand these sick methods.

"Strong emotions release your magic," he says before he lands his fist into my chest, knocking the wind out of me and sending me to the cold stone floor.

"I don't have any magic!" I almost squeal and he hovers over me, figure looming in the darkness.

"That is because you have not accepted your truths."

"What are you talking about?"

"Raw emotions lead to raw power, Elyra. You must let the emotions in for your power to come out."

I wince at his words and find that I cannot do what he asks. If I let them in... if I allow myself to feel all those things that I have seen and done... I will not be better for it. The dagger at my side suddenly feels like it weighs more than it should. The weight of the true Elyra's soul boring into it.

"I will not," I snarl at him and he crouches down beside me, drawing his arm back ready to beat me unconscious. I tilt my head back into the concrete and close my eyes, at peace with this punishment.

But he does not hit me.

Elijah stands up and cups his knuckles.

"Maybe tonight was not the night after all," he murmurs to himself.

Taking that as choice to leave, I get up off of the floor hastily and touch a finger to my bleeding mouth and sore cheek.

"Coward," I call him before heading towards the doors of Drodal. But it seems that Elijah has not yet finished with me.

"It was your fault that Elyra died." His voice echoes through my blood like the reverberations of a struck bell. I stop dead in my tracks and turn to face him slowly.

"What did you say?" I ask incredulously and he laughs in mockery. Anger boils my blood.

"You could have saved her. Rayna would be happy, Brogan would still have his love and Delphor would have its rightful High Priestess. But you didn't. And so they all suffer now because of you." I ball my hands into fists and my jaw shakes with restraint. He only smirks at me. Elijah *smirks*.

I have never hated him more than in this moment.

"You know not what you speak, Warren," I warn him, hoping he takes head.

"So what was it? Did you just watch as she was slaughtered? Or did you simply fail in your attempts to help her?" he edges closer to me, taking a lazy step with each pierce to my heart.

"I'm warning you, Elijah." Thunder begins to roll overhead and it is deafening. The clouds start to darken around us and cast an eerie dullness to the courtyard.

"You let the pain be endured by someone else. I guess it was the easy option. It's what anyone would have done." He shrugs and my nails dig into my palms. I can feel the blood oozing from their minor wounds.

"It is not what *I* would do," I growl, knowing that I sound feral but I do not care. Let him come. Let him taste the animal in me.

"And what did you do? Offer your friend so that you may live?" he laughs after that and the thunder echoes loudly against my eardrums. Wind starts to howl around us, the trees lining the courtyard trembling in fear and almost being uprooted from their spots.

"*Back off, Elijah*," I threaten him and I know that he can sense the danger in continuing. It is his fault should he choose to ignore it.

"Was it easy to just let her die? Was it enjoyable to hear her screams?"

"Shut up." I can feel the anger surging through me like electricity in my veins. It is almost like a tidal wave beginning to crest.

"*You* are the coward."

And the tidal wave crashes.

I scream my rage into the sky and in answer, a lightning bolt, white-hot with anger, surges just an inch in front of Elijah and an explosion causes rubble and him to be flown backwards by the blast.

Smoke and the smell of burnt earth fill my nose. I release my fists as I take slow deep breaths to try and calm the crashing rage within me.

When the smoke clears, I see massive chunks of concrete scattered across the courtyard and in the centre is a gaping black hole. Across from that is Elijah. Lying on his side and staring at me, his emerald eyes wide. Parts of his clothes are burnt and his face is lined with soot, hair detangled from his usual half-up half-down style.

I feel nothing but hate.

I point a shaking finger at him and try to steady my trembling voice.

"I warned you. You did not listen. And now you have paid the price." I don't even give him a backwards glance as I head to the watchtower again in the hopes that no one will dare follow me.

I have had enough of people for one day.

***

I have stood here since the encounter. Watching Broxen still itself after my onslaught.

Breccan was right.

I have magic.

Destructive magic.

I could have killed Elijah.

Good riddance, a part of me says.

However my hatred for him has softened in the calming of my rage. He was following Breccan's orders no doubt. He was supposed to find my magic and I suppose that he has. He did not need to be so cruel about it. But maybe… he knows my trigger. And he used it today.

A chill creeps down my spine.

In a way, Elijah knows me better than anyone has in my life. He knew my shame. He knew my secrets. And he used them against me. I do not know if I should thank him or wring his neck.

What am I?

I have never had a whisper of magic in my entire life and now all of a sudden I'm... a monster. I almost killed a man today. I do not know who my parents are so cannot trace my lineage and my 'father' had definitely had no influence on me apart from my independence and intolerance of men. Apart from that... there was only King Adrian and he was no mage. Just a kind man.

Hours pass with me in torment and the first light of dawn threatens to ruin the darkness. A tear slides down my cheek in anguish of my persistent troubles.

I hear the door creak open and heavy footing appear on the watchtower. I know it's him. I feel as if I will always know when Elijah is in my proximity. I just don't know why. And it scares me.

He does not say anything. And I do not make him. We are simply silent. I lean over the balcony and stare at dawn's rising, letting it be my focal point.

"Elyra—" His deep voice is soft but I cut him off swiftly.

"She was a light," I say and my voice almost breaks at the mention of her. "She just... *emanated* light. In all that she was. It was effortless."

"Please, you don't have to—"

"She was not meant for Golnar. Her soul was bound for peace but Golnar would not let her have it." I spit out those words as if they are venom, "In my time there I had assumed the role of Golnar's Ghost and had saved many women from the clutches of impure desires. Elyra was no different. The guards sensed her purity. They sought to conquer it. I did not let them.

She had given me her silver hairpins as payment. As if I needed any to have saved her life. It was the last remnants of her home and she was willing to offer them to me. She was a generous woman. A woman I had grown to respect. And to love. And to consider a lost sister to which I have always wanted. But it seems as if Aneya prefers me to live in solitude. To roam this earth as nothing more than a soldier, fighting for others who would never fight for me. She would have fought for me. And so they took her."

I take a deep breath and Elijah does not interrupt. He does not say anything. Good.

"We had several months of peace. Of friendship. But the guards did not like this newfound glimmer of happiness. Not when Golnar was made to torture, to maim. They had sought to exact their revenge.

Seven guards cornered us into a closet. They had corralled us out of our lines at nightfall before we could reach our cells. They laughed. And they jeered. They had called us 'rare beauties.'" I sneer, "It seems that beauty is a curse these days. They tried me first. After all, I suppose I had been the subject of their arousal for a longer amount of time. They pinned me to the wall. It took five men. The other two started roving their hands along my legs."

"I don't want to hear this," he says gruffly and I ignore him.

"I fought back. I beat two of them unconscious. Their faces unrecognisable beneath the gore. The others discovered that I was the ferocious one. The stronger one. So they turned their eyes on Elyra instead."

My voice trembles with grief, with horror, and it is a struggle to carry on.

"Three men had to hold me down on the concrete floor. I could not move for the life of me." I look to the heavens as my eyes flood with tears, long overdue tears. "I can still hear her screams. I can still hear her begging me to help her. They were slow. They were methodical. I did not stop fighting. I struggled until my limbs shouted in agony…until her screams stopped. I even dislocated my shoulder trying to break free but I was too weak by then to do anything of use.

Elyra was nothing if not wise. She knew her fate. And so towards the end… she looked at me and smiled. She *smiled*. She told me not to worry. That she will never leave me. She said that I was a gift during her numbered days.

I watched them squeeze the life out of her in the most brutal way. And I could not do anything to stop it. I watched. And no matter how hard I fought, I was not strong enough. I was not good enough to save her.

They released me afterwards. Thinking that I was defeated. Thinking that they were safe. I killed every last one of them in that closet. The walls were stained red with their blood. The floor was decorated with various appendages and entrails. I slaughtered them. And then I carried Elyra's broken body to my cell. Where I cradled her in my arms so that she would know how much I loved her despite her final moments. They had to knock me out in the morning so that they could get rid of her. As if she was the shame in Golnar and not the guards that run it.

She was taken from me. Lost forever. But I still had those pins."

"The dagger." Elijah realises and as if on cue, I withdraw it from its sheath and marvel at its hilt.

"I wove the silver into its hilt and fashioned it in a way that would remind me of her. Elegant. Swift. Beautiful. I used it to escape from Golnar and it was as if she were escaping with me. Like how it should have been. And now she will always be with me in my travels so that I may never forget how I had failed her. So that I may take that failure and save others." I take a deep breath to steady myself.

"I think about her every day." I finish, sheathing the dagger once more.

Elijah does not say anything. He only walks forward to lean against the rail beside me, staring at the horizon too. He has cleaned himself up since my outburst. He adorns brown trousers and a white shirt that brings out the tan in his skin. His hair is neatly brushed back into its half-up half-down and I cannot help but marvel at the sight of him.

"I am not just the Warren of the Woods," he begins in a grave tone, "Some would know me more so as the heir to Axton Falls."

My breath catches at that.

Axton Falls is a wealthy yet small kingdom just West of Broxen. It is nestled upon a cliff that is said to be the beginning of an incredible waterfall. Some say that when the sun hits Axton Falls, it shines like a diamond, an array of colours appearing in shards in thin air. It must be such a beautiful place.

"My mother was poisoned by her own hand-maiden after she had given us Benjamin. The woman was a consort of my father's. She wanted the kingdom. She wanted my father. But he had loved my mother too much to leave and so the consort exacted her revenge.

My father was a kind man if not brutal. I was the heir and so I should follow in his footsteps. But my heart lies in Broxen. It always has. I am a hunter. A warrior. Something he could not understand. But my uncle could. When my father would beat me into submission, my uncle would tell him to stop. Tell him to let me hone my skills and that a warrior is still useful within Axton's ranks.

One morning, I returned from my usual nightly hunt and heard my father and uncle arguing loudly. I peered into the great hall to find my uncle stabbing my father in the chest repeatedly. I watched my father's blood seep into the foundations of the kingdom he had coveted. I watched the light fade from his eyes. I even saw a glimmer of love on his face before it slackened in death.

I drew my arrows but they were no use. Not against an air mage. My uncle stopped the arrows as soon as I had released them. So I ran at him with my blade. He choked the breath out of me. It was… unimaginable pain. To suffocate so deftly by another's hand. It was only when Benjamin came in that his attention turned elsewhere. I told Benjamin to run and he did not. So my uncle realised his leverage.

As I was catching my breath, he began to choke my brother before my eyes. He tried to call for me. Beg me to do something. I saw the whites of his eyes that day. My uncle would not stop until I promised to accept my exile, renounce my title and to flee these lands. I did so for Benjamin's sake. The look on Benjamin's face as he saw me leaving is one that I will never forget. Having to leave him with that power-hungry monster… I could barely do it. I could only do it knowing that he is better off alive in his hands than dead before he is twenty.

I came to Drodal where Breccan gladly accepted me for what I was and never told anyone of my past. He is a great man."

"Yes, he is," I murmur and his mouth lifts up a little in response.

"Last year I had received word that the heir of Axton was claimed by Myrna's men. That he was being sent to Canaan for being a mage even though he hadn't even received his powers yet. My uncle had sent him to Canaan for being the only other threat to his rule of Axton Falls.

"I charged the carriages. I slaughtered many men. Heard Benjamin's cries of hope. But there was one soldier who I could not defeat no matter how hard I tried. Twice the size of a normal man. Twice as strong too. He bore a mask made of iron… I never saw his face. He pinned me to a tree with his longsword and made me watch as he beat my brother. Benjamin was unconscious by the time he was through. I thought that I would be able to know my own blood no matter what I faced… but even as he lay before me, I could not make out Benjamin's features.

"By the time that I had pulled the longsword out of my chest, the carriage was already out of sight and my wound was so grave… I had to abandon my brother to seek a healer. So *selfish*." He bites on that last comment and I can understand why.

"I visit Canaan every day in the hopes that I will catch a glimpse of my brother. I hear the crack of the whips and the screams of pain coming from there and I cannot bear the thought of him enduring it.

A couple nights ago, I got too close. The guards saw my approach and began to fire arrows at me. Others followed me on horses. It took all night to let them be subject to Broxen's madness but by then, the arrows had wrecked my flesh for too long.

One day, I will get Benjamin out of there and take back Axton Falls in my father's name. But without allies, I am but one man against his former home who would sooner slaughter their real heir than risk my uncle's wrath. And I don't blame them. Who would want a coward as their King?"

So it is Canaan that Elijah visits. Not Golnar as I had once believed.

I do not say anything for a while. We just stand in silence. I am surprised at the mutual understanding that has just passed between us. A truth for a truth. That was the cause for the arrows embedded in Elijah the other night. How sad. It is a side to Elijah that I have not seen and may even like. He holds the same insecurities as I do about our pasts. And though he does not know who I am... it is nice to know.

I would not say that we're friends... but I would say that we are no longer enemies either.

"You are not a coward," I decide to tell him bluntly and although I can feel his shocked eyes upon me, my stare remains upon the horizon. He regards me for a moment more.

"And you are not a failure." I shake my head at his comment because it is something I know in my heart to be false.

"I could have saved her. I should have been stronger."

"You cannot wish for more strength when your body is already at its prime. You fought for her. And that is what matters." Another silence passes. I realise that this truth is similar to his own... he was not strong enough to save Benjamin from that carriage. And he has accepted it.

"Your father would be proud of you."

"He hated me," he sighs. I can only imagine how many beatings Elijah had to endure because of his father.

"I know that he was not the nicest of fathers but it seems that they are rare to come by these days. Believe me, I know." He looks at me in question then but that is a story for another hopeless night. "I do not condone what he did to you. But you are strong enough to still hold respect for a man who did not respect his children and still want to reclaim the Falls in his name. I would say that requires great courage. Something he would have admired despite his bitterness." He does not say anything for a while and it is quite comfortable.

"Will you ever tell me your true name?" he says into the cold air and I do not let my surprise show.

"Why does it matter?"

"It matters to me," he murmurs and the seriousness in his tone leads me to look into his intense eyes. I am not sure what is lurking there but it catches my breath in a way that I have not felt before. I clear my throat and look away from him and notice that he inches away from me a little.

"A name is but a word... and yet it has the power to inspire both fear and admiration. But it remains just a word."

"You would not have me know who you are?"

"I would have you know me as I am today. Not for the legend that I once was. I have not earned the right to keep that name and so I choose not to adorn it until I have deserved to do so."

"You are wise. For someone so infuriating," he comments and I can hear the smirk in his voice as he straightens off of the balcony.

"Careful, Elijah. Lightening is an unlimited resource. I have no qualms in summoning it again." The words come out without me realising it. How can I be so calm about this new magic?

"You would first need to gain a shred of self-control. Something I believe is not in your nature." His eyes twinkle with amusement.

"I'll control my foot when it lands in your throat if you continue." I warn him but instead of it being my usual threatening promises... I can feel the playfulness lining my words.

Elijah opens his mouth to reply but he does not get the chance.

A roar so loud echoes across all of Broxen, startling nestling birds from the cascade of trees and causing them to caw and take flight hastily. We have our weapons drawn before either of us can even comprehend the sound.

"What the hell was that?" Elijah exclaims but I think it is more so for himself than for my own ears. I place a wicked grin on my face, excited by this new development.

"I don't know. But I plan on finding out." And without waiting for him, I plunge myself to the bottom of the watchtower and am not surprised when I hear a louder thud land behind me.

"You are insufferable," he growls from next to me and all I can do is chuckle as we both run into Broxen before the rest of Drodal had even lit their lanterns.

Chapter 8

Running into the heart of Broxen may be deemed unwise before daylight. But that roar was not human. That roar was no creature I had ever heard.

Pushing through branches and hurtling over logs, Elijah and I run towards the source of the cry. We had agreed that it came from the centre, if not a little to the West. And yet still so close to Drodal… that is what scares us most.

Sunlight begins to trickle through the dense canopy of dark green leaves and Elijah pauses within a wide clearing lined with ancient oak trees and covered with ferns. I stop next to him and extend my hearing.

It is quiet.

Too quiet.

Something bad has happened here.

I look at Elijah and see the same thoughts appearing on his face. He looks at me gravely.

"Something unnatural has come to Broxen." I dare not tell him that that fact is pretty damn obvious; it is an effort not to roll my eyes.

Drawing my dagger as carefully as I can, I narrow my eyes across the expanse of the forest and as I turn West, a sinking dread defiles my stomach.

Without saying a word, I walk past Elijah towards the dread. I can almost smell the suffering in the air and that is when I realise that it is not my imagination as a rancid aroma waves through the nearby trees.

With Elijah close behind me and armed to the teeth, I push back the spindly twigs that guard this imminent tragedy and I am not prepared for what I see.

The once emerald jewel of the heart of the forest might more so be described as a ruby in this instance. Blood. So much blood. Smeared across the ancient skins of the trees, as if the guardians of Broxen are weeping the victim's blood after being forced to witness the slaughter. Dripping off of the ferns in a monotonous thud that sends chills down my spine. Soaking into the earth as if it has not already bore such bloodshed and gore.

I can make out eight victims. Or what is left of eight victims. Various loins lay scattered amongst the ground, their ripped and jagged ends suggesting that whatever had done this had torn them off violently and without mercy. Legs. Arms. Torsos. Fingers. It seems that whoever comes across this creature is promised a slow and brutal demise. I pray that I am not one of them.

"By the Aerix..." Elijah says from behind me. I sheath my weapon and start walking around the site, observing every detail.

"It is not safe, Elyra," he whispers to me and though he remains rooted to the spot, machetes drawn, I know that his eyes are surveying the clearing for any sort of incoming threat that may subdue us.

"The creature is long gone," I state knowingly as I crouch down to survey the slender arm of a woman.

"There are no tracks. There is no way to know that it has left the vicinity. The leaves remain undisturbed." He recants, the warrior in him observing the details of this scene as much as I am.

"This creature slaughtered out of anger. The sheer destruction of these limbs suggests that this thing was bred to kill. And maybe as this is his first appearance, he was also a little ravenous. My guess is that this is a warning."

"For what and to whom?" Elijah sheathes his machetes and folds his large arms across his broad chest.

"The creature did not exactly leave blueprints of his plans amidst all of this carnage, Elijah." I snap irritably and his answering scowl is vicious. "Where did these people come from?"

"There are quite a few neighbouring villages to Broxen. Most are not on the map as they are only small. I suspect that this creature knew this and sought them out. It must be intelligent."

"But if he sought them out specifically as easy targets, why lead them here? Why not slaughter them inside the village?" I think aloud and to this Elijah has no answer for a while.

"You believe this to be a warning, yes?" he asks and I nod, "Perhaps it is for us." I blink in shock at his words as I try to wrap my head around them.

"Why would a creature this destructive take the time to orchestrate such a slaughter in warning to Drodal?"

"What is Drodal, Elyra?" he questions and his sudden agitation leads me to believe that I am incompetent. Not a feeling that I like so I answer his question in my head. Drodal is home to the mages.

It dawns on me.

"Myrna," I snarl, fists automatically clenching with my hatred. Typical of her to get someone else to do her ruthless bidding.

She must not know that I am here. If she were to discover me it would bring the war to Drodal even faster. I know Myrna. I have studied her, watched her and observed her wicked ways. She is nothing if not methodical and this is her simply testing the waters of Drodal's security and its boundaries no less.

"We must warn Breccan," Elijah states, genuine fear for his Lord in his eyes.

"So warn him we shall."

"I want every armed solider monitoring the perimeter of this Keep. The watchtower shall be manned at all times with triple shift patterns to ensure maximum vigilance. I do not want one man out of place. I do not want to hear of one incident happening within my borders and if I do then may the Aerix help you all. Is that understood?" Breccan had called a meeting of arms as soon as Elijah and I had told him the events of this morning. He is no longer the wise and caring Lord of Drodal but a fierce General desperate to keep his people safe.

"Yes, sir," the guards say in unison. The grand hall is filled with every last soldier that Drodal has to offer and Breccan has been ruthless in his demands of them all. If it was the security of my kingdom at stake, I suppose that I would be too.

"The safety of my people must come first and I will not stand for any man deeming these precautions unnecessary. I advise for anyone who disagrees with me to stand forward now and proclaim his resignation from my ranks." When no one answers, Breccan's eyes unmistakeably glow with pride as he folds his arms behind his back. "See to it." He finalises and the guards disperse without a second to lose until it is just Elijah and I in Breccan's company.

Breccan sits down on the edge of the raised platform at the end of the hall and places his face in his hands. It is now when I can truly see his age reflecting off of his strong form. He almost looks weak, deflated.

"Is there no peace?" he says into his palms.

"My Lord, we will do everything in our power to stop this war before it begins," Elijah promises strongly and I admire his diligence even if it is slightly misplaced.

"I fear that if Myrna has managed to develop a creature born from hell itself... we may not stand a chance." Breccan's voice is weary and I can sense how tired he is of war.

"Elijah and I will scout the nearby villages to discover if there were any witnesses to the attack or to the beast that devised it. From there we will track the monster so that we may see what we are dealing with and thus formulate its weaknesses to our advantage."

"Since when are you and Master Warren allies?" it seems that Breccan cannot help his smirk and his blue eyes twinkle like the sea under sunlight.

"I have said that I'll work with him. It does not mean that I like him," I answer sternly.

"Easy, Elyra. Do not forget who will be protecting your arrogant ass in those woods," Elijah warns and it is as if the old him has resumed his role.

"Don't forget who will be protecting yours," I snap back and in spite of our bitter tones, I cannot help but see it as rivalry banter. Breccan looks between us both for a moment and then sighs resolutely.

"As much as your strategy enthrals me, Elyra, you must learn to control your magic before hunting this creature." I stand stiff at his words.

"How did you know?"

"It is not hard to miss the burnt black hole now decorating my courtyard."

"I am sorry about that," I say in a small voice, "It is all just... so difficult to even comprehend right now. Magic has been the last problem on my mind."

"Hence why your training is more vital than it has ever been. Go, now. Train with Elijah. Just do not burn him too much. I like my soldiers fresh, not fried." He winks and I gulp my nerves down.

How am I supposed to train with magic when there is a creature out there ripping innocents apart?

How can I possibly learn to control lightening with Jocelyn and Jasper needing my help?

How can I simply *rest* when Myrna Verena is plotting to attack a place that I have come to hold most dear?

Wait... this problem may actually be beneficial. If I can hone whatever magic that I have, it can be an extra weapon in my arsenal against her. An extra advantage. Blades will not be enough against a mighty mage such as her but what if I were to become her equal... her rival?

With newfound enthusiasm, I turn to Elijah with a grin on my face.

"Come on then, Warren. You have some lightening to catch."

Chapter 9

Three days it has been. Three days. And no sign of the magic I believed that I had. Maybe the other night was simply a fluke… a coincidence in the universe that happened to correspond to my emotions on that particular night.

Elijah has been hounding me. Sometimes beating me. To arouse that same anger that I felt that evening and nothing. We have even tried patience as control but all that does is get me irritable which then gives rise to a cranky Elijah. Those sessions never end well.

But as a beneficial note, I have been able to see more of what Elijah can do with his magic. He has performed demonstrations so that I may see the calmness with which he operates, the finesse and the care he holds for his element. I have seen him conjure plants from thin air and move limbs of trees from his path without lifting a finger. I have watched as he assists with the health and happiness of Broxen's trees and all who dwell within them. And I still believe that there is more to see. I think that his magic could do more beautiful things than simply be a brutal force in war. But like Elijah himself, I suppose his magic is not accustomed to such uses.

"Again," he demands of me in a harsh growl. Again, he watches me with a heightened temper as I continue to fail in conjuring magic. Neither a spark nor a flicker since that night.

"No," I growl back. "I have been playing your games for three damn days now. I'm through playing games." Elijah strides towards me angrily, his bow and machete bouncing against his body.

"You are through when I say that you are. And you will not be leaving this wretched courtyard until you show me something worthwhile." His emerald gaze sears my face with its wrath and I can feel my own rage boiling to the surface.

"Has it ever occurred to you that what I did before was a coincidence? That maybe nature decided to scorn you for being so insufferable?" he scowls hard as he towers over me but I do not back down.

"There are no coincidences in magic." His jaw sets into a hard line.

"Do you realise that another town could be suffering the way the other villagers had?" I bellow into his face but he only turns sterner. My stomach churns involuntarily at the thought of that beast tearing people limb from limb.

"I have not forgotten," he spits.

"Then *why* are you bothering to hound me with insults to divulge a magic that may not even exist when innocents are being targeted?" I plead with him.

"I am doing my job." He steps closer in defiance, so close that I can feel his breath on my face.

"Your *job* is to protect Broxen," I counter harshly, "So protect it." He takes deep, shaking breaths as his scowl burrows holes into my own eyes. The rage that I feel at Elijah's wasted time sparks through me like electricity. "We're done for the day."

With that, I turn on my heel to head back into Drodal.

"If you think—" Elijah makes a move to grab my arm forcibly but as soon as his fingers touch my skin, he convulses wildly and crouches low on the ground on his knee, panting and looking at me frantically. I am about as stunned as he is.

"I didn't do it," I offer quickly even though it will probably sound more like an admission of guilt. He grimaces for a moment and then the corner of his mouth turns up slightly and his eyes glimmer amusement.

"Did you just... *electrocute* me?"

"No," I answer. Well... at least not intentionally. Did I do that? He smiles lightly before rising from the floor. He eyes me suspiciously.

"What?" I sigh exasperatedly, folding my arms across my chest. "Static shock happens all the time."

"That was *not* static shock."

"Well..." I throw my arms up in frustration. "You should learn to be nicer to women."

"Nicer to women or nicer to you?" he challenges, inching towards me again, his green shirt ruffling in the slight breeze. I can barely make out the first planes of his toned chest but I quickly look away, shuffling on my feet.

"Both." I shrug, not meeting his intense gaze.

He nods at me for a moment, biting his lip in thought. For some reason an involuntary tingling sensation travels to my core. I desperately try to act indifferent. When he makes no move to speak,

I turn my eyes to his and catch his gaze upon my mouth but it is for so brief a time that I may have just imagined it. He nods again with a lick of his lips.

"Here." He hands me my dagger which he takes off me before every session despite carrying his own weapons. I hastily strap it to my side and relief floods through me knowing that it is back in my company. He begins to walk away, his back muscles working strongly to match his strides.

"Are we done here?" I ask him and he looks back at me and smirks.

"No. We're going hunting." He grins and I cannot help my own as I fall into step beside him.

**

"What is this place?" I ask Elijah after walking for hours through the heart of Broxen.

Ahead of us lies a small village. Wooden houses are dotted around a small market and a tiny town square gives space next to the only inn. The people of this town are clad in simple clothes but it is their fear that strikes me. All of them cast wary glances over their shoulder every few seconds. Even some of the vendors in the market look spooked.

"This is the village I had traced those bodies too. Braelin is its name. Quite the market town, but not large enough for trusted vendors." I smack him hard in the shoulder but he does not cry out.

"You have been investigating without me?" I scowl at him and he shrugs with a smirk.

"I like the quiet," he counters and my scowl deepens much to his amusement.

Standing up from our crouched positions in nearby brush, we head into Braelin. Many gawk at us both, no doubt as we look so startlingly different to that of their own people. Clad with weapons, walking tall and confident. Many cast fearful glances in Elijah's direction and when I look over at him it is not hard to see why. His face is set as if made of stone and his tense posture is enough for anyone to believe that he is there for a dark purpose.

Before I can correct him, he already grabs a passer-by by the arm. A man, not old, not young. His pale eyes grow wide as he beholds the warrior grappling onto him.

"I need some questions answered," Elijah says and I stare in horror at the way he is handling this.

"Please!" the man gasps, "I don't want any trouble!"

"Then tell me what I need to know."

"Please don't kill me! I must go home… my daughter… she is sick, and—"

"What happened here three moons ago?" Elijah's tone does nothing to ease the man's terror.

"Please, my daughter—" before Elijah can press him any longer, I step in front of him, breaking his hold on the man who frantically straightens his clothing. I offer him the warmest smile I can muster.

"My apologies, sir. My sentry is a brave warrior but his communication skills are lacking because of it."

"Why yes, I…" he cannot stop staring at Elijah with fear but I place a hand softly upon his forearm and the gentle touch turns his eyes back to me.

"Do not be frightened. We will find our answers elsewhere. Please, tend to your daughter. We will keep you no longer," he offers me a tentative smile and his cheeks redden to a blush.

"Thank you, miss," he offers and then disappears across the cobbled, uneven streets.

"What were you doing?" Elijah asks sternly.

"I am saving this investigation!" I snarl back at him in a whisper and his answering glare makes me roll my eyes. "Do you know nothing about people?" his silence tells me what I need to know. "This village has just been terrorised by an unknown beast. Nobody will want to relive it nor will they wish to tell strangers of their grief. You demanding answers and forcibly plucking people from the streets are not helping anyone!"

"I get things done," he growls at me.

"And by doing so you will ruin our chances of finding this monster." He stares at me a long while. "I know what I am doing." I tell him. I have liaised with many a people during my time in Eradan. Those skills will not be wasted now. He nods wordlessly and I take that as permission to lead. I say nothing else on the matter and start scanning the town square for a suitable target.

My eyes zero-in on the inn opposite me. It is dank, paint chipping off of the walls but the music is rife inside and so is the laughter. Perfect. I head towards the inn, not even bothering to look at its name.

"I am not sure if that is a good idea, Elyra."

"An inn means people. People mean gossip. Add ale to the equation and you get easy-talkers." I carry on walking but Elijah

95

steps in front of me and I halt; he holds his hands up as a placating gesture and I know that he does not mean to threaten me.

"I just figured…"

"What?" I snap, annoyed at having to wait. This beast is probably already on the prowl and I need answers now.

"You are fresh out of Golnar, Elyra. I am not sure if an inn full of drunken men is the ideal place for you right now," he says and I straighten at his words, caught off guard. Is he trying to help me? Or is he mocking me? I really cannot tell. And that just makes me more eager to prove him wrong.

I shove past him and waltz up the creaky steps and push open the rotting door. Laughter and booming voices fill my ears and the golden light from the hearth casts a warm glow on all the revelry. A single barmaid looks ready to pass out from serving so many customers. The room is full of various townsmen and women though the lack of women is astounding. I gulp down my fear as I notice male eyes watching me as I walk in. I will prove Elijah wrong.

Without a word, I take up a stool at the corner of the small room, the table before me sticky with the Aerix knows what. Elijah sits across from me without a word, constantly surveying the inn for danger no doubt. I can still feel eyes on me but I choose to ignore them while I use my own to find a target. I can barely think with all this noise…

There.

A young man, teenager, sitting by himself in front of the bar as the maid serves him an ale. He smiles at her hopefully but she dismisses him for the next person in need of a drink. And so the boy sits quietly gazing at his tankard sadly.

Perfect.

The barmaid is plain enough. Brown hair, brown eyes, nice slim figure. I think my own appearance could arouse this boy's curiosity and thus loosen his tongue. He is young enough that I do not expect anything vulgar. Yes, he'll talk.

I look down myself and the usual black basque amplifies my curves alongside the slim trousers. Smoothing my raven hair, I stand up from the table, leaving Elijah to his thoughts, and try to walk with us much seductive prowess as I can. Men halt their conversations as I stroll by but my gaze remains on the young boy at the bar.

He notices the silence and his face turns to mine. I smile amicably at him and his face pales before he turns back to his drink in shock. When I sit on the stool next to him, he casts me a wary glance but nothing more. His dull blonde hair and brown eyes are something to be admired but not adored. I chuckle to turn his attention back to me.

"Do I not interest you?" I ask, batting my long lashes. His eyes grow wide as he frantically tries to grapple for words.

"No, no… I, um… I'm not used to such…" his eyes rove over me for longer than need be, "company," he finishes with a smile.

"Nor am I," I return and he nods, his grin never ceasing. "Is it always this rowdy in here?"

"Unfortunately. One inn in a quiet town makes for loud and crowded conditions." I laugh seductively and his grin widens. "What brings a fine lady such as you to Braelin?"

"Who says that I am not a resident?" I raise an eyebrow and he blushes.

"If you were, I would have been given a hundred refusals to court you by now." I feel my cheeks redden with embarrassment at his compliment and I am conscious of how it is not entirely fake either.

"You flatter me, sir."

"You deserve to be flattered," he counters smoothly and I can sense his confidence growing. Right, time for pleasantries is over. I lean over to him innocently.

"Can I ask you a question?" he leans into me eagerly.

"Only if I can return the favour." I give him a contemplative stare and smile.

"Agreed."

"Very well, who is that man scowling at us in the corner?" that surprises me so I turn around and sure enough Elijah looks ready to kill as he regards the boy before me.

"Oh, him? That's my brother, my sentry. He does not play well with others," I tell him and he nods.

"And do you, ma'am, play well with others?" he does not meet my gaze but I give him a seductive smirk.

"Only with those who want to play with me," I offer and his blush reddens as his grin broadens.

"Are you sure he's your brother? He is wearing jealousy very threateningly," I turn to look at Elijah and his knuckles are white with the force of his grip on the table. I try not to figure out why.

"Oh, he's just protective. He doesn't like it when I… mingle." I look away innocently though I can tell that this boy is picking up on my devilish air.

"And your question?" he asks, leaning closer to me.

"Well… it is more of an observation. You see, everyone I have come across outside seems white with fear. Hardly anyone would talk to me." I pout sadly and he is quick to change my mood.

"Oh, please do not think it is you."

"But… they just looked at me like I was a monster."

"You are not the monster that they fear, trust me." His eyebrows rise as he gulps down a sip of ale.

"Then what is?" Finally, we are nearing the topic of interest.

"I'm…" he hesitates, "not really supposed to say." I cast my eyes down in humiliation.

"Please don't lie for my sake. I'm not welcome here, am I?" he places his hand on mine abruptly in an effort to console my sadness as my lip quivers.

"No! It is not you, I swear. Braelin was attacked not three nights ago. The people fear that the monster will return."

"What monster? I don't understand." I feign girlish confusion and he latches onto it like a dog in heat.

"It came in the night," he answers solemnly, "Stealing people from their beds. We heard the screaming before we noticed anything was wrong. Blood stained the town. Blood led us into Broxen. We found them there. Dismembered and dead."

"I am so sorry." I gasp, putting my hand over his and clasping it sympathetically.

"It is their families I feel sorry for."

"Of course." I breathe, "Did no-one suspect anything in the days before? Perhaps of being watched or followed?"

"The various villagers had said they were growing afraid of the shadows. As if it too, had eyes that observed them." The creature must be dark then… something made of darkness to have not been seen and linked to shadows. It had targeted these people. It had watched them before making its move.

"But why those people? Why not kill everyone? It seems rather suspicious."

"I know." He sighs. "Some say that those who were taken had dark dealings with Myrna Verena. But this monster… something that brutal does not think about who it kills. Its sole purpose is to kill. It need not think or show mercy." Another link to Myrna… dark dealings indeed. A rebellion? Or trade-bargains gone wrong?

"I can't imagine what you have all been through." I offer consolingly and I mean it.

"Enough about that." He shrugs as if ridding himself of those memories. "I wish to know more about you. How long are you in town for?"

"Unfortunately, I will be leaving this evening. We had only stopped to rest ourselves before the long road ahead."

"And I could not persuade you to stay the night?" he asks, placing his hand on my knee and travelling further up than I am comfortable. I try not to cringe away from the touch.

"Sadly not. I have important business that needs taking care of." I smile apologetically before getting up from my stool. I do not get far as the boy grabs my arm firmly and pulls me back to him.

"You're just going to leave? After all that? I thought you said you were playful?" alarm bells ring inside my ear but I force myself to smirk.

"I am sure you that will find out should we meet again, stranger." I wink and turn around but he pulls me back again, fingernails digging into my skin. My heartbeat races as panic rushes through me.

"I want to find out just how playful you are. Right now," he whispers into my ear and in my mind, it is not a boy whispering to me, it is a guard from Golnar. My heartbeat pounds inside my eardrums.

"I really have to go," I mutter and he chuckles darkly... is it him? Or is it Marcus underneath the stairwell? Is it the men that whipped me? The men who killed Elyra? Or is it *him*... no, it can't be.

"Maybe my friends could have a taste too," he murmurs against my neck and goosebumps trail along my skin.

I hear the scrape of wood against stone before I can contemplate what is going on.

Elijah has the boy pinned against the bar with his machete at his throat. He looks feral and outraged, a growl practically rippling from his snarling mouth. I place a hand over my thundering heart as I try to register what's going on.

"Do you think that just because a beautiful woman talks to you that you can somehow take ownership of her?" Elijah bellows into the youth's face.

"No, I—"

"She is not your possession. Women are not toys to satisfy your pathetic urges." His voice rattles the entire inn and all inside it have gone quiet at Elijah's outburst.

"I know, I just—" the boy tries to settle, his voice quivering. Elijah simply lifts him by his collar and slams his head into the worktop.

"If you want her, you will have to fight me to get her and I will *gladly* behead you right here if you dare question my claim."

"You're her brother!" the boy manages to screech and Elijah chuckles, an evil sound.

"You wish I was," he snarls finally before sheathing his blade, grabbing my hand and leading me out of the inn without another word.

When we reach cover under Broxen's leaves, I muster the consciousness to snap my arm away from his grip and face him.

"What was that?"

"You're asking *me* that question? What happened to *you*? You completely froze!" I am silent at his words; I need not explain myself to him. Everything turned so quickly… he was so sweet and then… it was just like Golnar.

"I don't know," I murmur evasively. He glares at me before pointing an accusing finger.

"I warned you not to go in there! I told you what could happen and you couldn't get past your pride to follow my advice," he spits.

"Go to hell." I sneer as I push past him.

"Is that it? You're just going to walk away?" I whirl around to face him yet again, my face taut with anger. I can hear thunder rolling around in my chest, or is it the sky?

"I thought I could handle it. I couldn't. It was not a matter of pride. It was a matter of false belief. And I lost." The rumbling grows louder and the skies grow dark.

"You cannot let Golnar control you, Elyra," he replies sternly and I laugh darkly.

"It wasn't just Golnar!" I shout back at him, tears stinging my eyes. Elijah stiffens. "You think that wretched prison is the first time I have had to deal with men and women corrupted by lust? I have had this damn curse upon me since I was born! It seems that being ugly gets you nowhere and being pretty gets you screwed in more ways than one."

"Elyra—" he begins softly but my tether is already at its end.

"Just leave me alone!" I scream at him and a blinding white bolt of lightning sears through Broxen's canopy right before Elijah. He is once again blasted backwards and the smell of burnt wood fills my nose.

The skies clear instantly when I realise what I have done. The clearing lays black and burnt in front of me, leaves charred and many branches struck bare from the bolt. Elijah's clothes and face are smeared with black and he places a shaky hand to his head and blood stains his fingertips.

I cup a hand to my mouth. I had just done that. I had hurt Elijah. I... I don't know what's wrong with me. Why can't I control it? He has made me so angry these past few days and nothing. But one encounter with a stranger has me setting Broxen alight.

I sink to my knees and cover my eyes as silent tears fall down my cheeks. It was not just an encounter. It was a series of flashbacks. Vibrant and painful like the scars coating my back. All the way from that moment in Braelin to when I was a child with *him*. I dare not say his name now. To say it would damn me as much as the deed I did back then. The tears do not stop.

I hear the sound of crunching leaves coming towards me. Elijah crouches down in front of my kneeling form and his steady breath calms me slightly.

"Elyra?" he murmurs and the sound warms every bone in my body. But I refuse to look at him. Not after what I had just done. "Elyra, please," he repeats but how can I? I had just made him bleed.

With gentle hands, he pulls my own away from my face and holds them for a while, his emerald eyes regarding me with an emotion that I cannot quite pinpoint. He reaches out and strokes my cheek with his thumb. A stillness takes over my heart and it is as if everything fades while I look at his face. The full pink mouth, the tan golden skin, the sharp angles of his face, the shoulder-length dark hair, the intense green smouldering eyes... he could be glowing. I open my mouth to exhale but nothing comes out.

"Can I show you something?" his deep voice caresses my muscles with warmth I have never known.

"Yes," I whisper to him and that soft mouth smirks slightly. I did not realise how much I love that smile until now.

From his side, he picks up a burnt leaf, as black as midnight, delicately in his palm and holds it out to me. It strikes me that a man of the forest has just watched it get killed by my hand.

"I'm sorry..." I tell him truthfully, "I didn't mean to—" he shakes his head with a warm smile and lifts his palm to his mouth and blows a tender breath on the leaf.

I watch with wide eyes as the charred dust melts away to reveal the glimmering emerald leaf as it once was. As it should have been. It cannot be possible. Watching my shock, his smile widens to a glittering grin. He takes my hand and pulls us both upwards, keeping the leaf steady in his palm. He brings the leaf to his lips again but instead of blowing at the face of the leaf, he blows across his palm and the leaf magically floats around us. Up and up until it reaches one of the bare branches and attaches itself onto one as if it were never harmed.

I look at Elijah in complete surprise and his smile is miraculous. He raises his eyebrows.

"You haven't seen anything yet," he taunts.

He faces his palms upwards and a gust of wind rattles from behind me. The cascade of burnt leaves float in whirls around us, ridding themselves of their charred skins and floating as if in a dance to praise their master until they too attach themselves to the bare branches. Elijah moves his arm out slightly and the crater I had created on Broxen's floor slowly turns back to the earthen base it was before, enriched with all its beauty. I look around and the trees are not harmed, there is not a damaged leaf in sight, the crater is gone…

Broxen is glistening again like new.

I can still feel the chill of that phantom wind on my skin and I touch my fingertips to my lips in pure awe at the beauty in what Elijah had just shown me. I knew he was powerful… but *this*… he is incredible. As I turn my eyes to him now, the Warren of the Woods is positively beaming at his work. Broxen is his home. Broxen is where he belongs. Broxen is Elijah's happiness.

His eyes are glowing as he beholds the trees around him. My heart swells. I have never seen him so in his element. So in love with what he does. His eyes fall onto me and that softness in him remains.

"I am not all that you say I am." Again, his voice tantalises my skin with its warmth. I have to stop myself from gasping at the sensation.

"Nor am I," I reply breathlessly and he nods, accepting that we have both done wrong here. He regards me curiously before he outstretches his hand slowly to push a strand of hair behind my ear and though his deed is done; his fingertips linger on my skin.

"Elyra—"

A shattering roar pierces my eardrums. A black shadow swipes at Elijah and the strength of the blow sends him flying into the trunk of a tree and I scream when his body falls limp to the floor. I turn around, dagger drawn, and am not prepared for the sight before me.

A creature, like none I had ever seen, growls as he stares into my eyes. His skin is the deepest of all blacks, stretching over his bones as if it barely covers them. It looks shiny… as if the skin is coated in some sort of liquid. His pale blue eyes are wide, black slits for pupils pulsating with its intent to kill. He stands on four clawed legs with large talons sticking out of every one of them; the large arch of his back suggests that he could stand on two legs if he deemed it necessary. He has no hair but his face gapes down to a large mouth, gums rotting black and teeth a stark yellow; the sharp edges of them tell me that he could rip me to shreds in less than a second.

The creature prowls around me in a circle and I follow, never turning my back to it. A foul smell reeks from him as if he permanently smells like dead flesh. I try not to think of Elijah unconscious in the corner or the head wound that is probably worse now than what I had inflicted. Why has he not attacked me yet when he was so quick to get Elijah out of the picture? I remain calm and focused as I draw all of my attention to him.

"You have been on quite the rampage," I state loudly, unsure if this creature can even communicate. He stops in his tracks, a low guttural growl emanating from his gaping jaws.

"You have been quite the hunt, *Lenora*." His voice is raspy and cold, the way death would sound. This creature knows my name. Three guesses as to why.

"Did Myrna tell you my name when she told you to kill me?"

"Such an intelligent creature you are," he rasps, saliva coating his canines with every word.

"I wish I could say the same for you," I counter and it chuckles, a harsh grating sound.

"How so?"

"Your little massacre led me straight to you. Get bored, did we?" his angry growl lets me know that I have him rattled.

"I did it to draw you out, you parasite!" he bellows, "I knew that as soon as blood was spilt, the great Lenora Belavier would come running. And so you have."

"It's a pity that you have failed then, isn't it?" I jeer, gripping my dagger tightly.

"Why?"

"I am no longer Lenora Belavier," I say before I strike forwards with my dagger.

The beast is too quick. He swipes it away with his claw in one swift movement and growls his rage at my attempt. He swipes his talons at my stomach and I dodge to where the dagger landed. But before I can reach it, he is before me once again. This time when he swipes, he lands a blow to my face and I feel the long cut etching down my cheek. He swipes his long arm out again and catches me in the abdomen, sending me flying backwards near Elijah.

Elijah.

Lying next to him is his machete. Great. I pick it up and face this beast who laughs in pity at my attempts of defence. I don't care. Let him laugh. He swipes again and I dodge to the left, swinging the machete across his leg and he howls in pain as putrid black blood spurts across my clothes. He flicks his talons out to catch my throat but I parry the blow with the face of the blade and slice at his abdomen. Another howl spurs the birds in Broxen's trees to take flight. The creature is getting angrier.

Let him.

I try to land the machete in his chest but he slams his body into me as a block and the force sends me to the ground. Before I can grab the machete again, jaws clamp themselves around my shoulder and my blood oozes along my skin while I scream. My vision blurs at the pain. I reach back to try and hit him off me but when my hand meets his slimy skin, the creature convulses and instead of ripping away the flesh, he simply lets go.

I try to stand but falter. The flesh of my shoulder is barely holding itself together and when I move, it only tears more. I have to get through this. I slowly stand up, screaming my pain as if it would somehow relieve it. The creature is cowering in the corner, the side of his head pink and blotchy from where I had touched him. Raw. I look at my hands. It must be that electricity… it is then when I feel that familiar sensation of electricity in my blood. My magic. It has been with me this whole time; I have just been dismissing it. A sadistic grin spreads across my face as I regard the cowering monster.

"Don't tell me you forfeit." I goad, "I was having so much fun."

The creature lunges towards me with an earth-shattering bellow and I dodge the first blow and I side-step the second. My dagger lies just ahead of me in the soil and if I could just get to it, then I can finally do some damage. Slipping to the floor almost costs me as the monster's claw lands an inch from my head but I quickly roll and take my stance.

I lunge for the beast without pausing for breath. The blade cuts across his stomach deeply and his purple guts gush onto the floor, I swing the dagger again and it slices across his throat, black blood spurting into my face. The creature sags from his wounds and I use all the strength I have to run forwards, taking the beast with me, and

104

pin him to a tree-trunk with my dagger in his throat. Blood oozes everywhere.

"You cannot win," he gargles, struggling to talk for fear of choking on his blood.

"Watch me," I say through gritted teeth, my shoulder barking in agony.

"You think that I am the only one? You're wrong," he says, trying to derail me.

"Then I will just kill you all," I answer politely before using the electricity in me to send a bolt of lightning down from the sky and into the beast. He convulses wildly against the tree and before I know it, his carcass is all that remains. Black, charred and completely dead.

With a snarl, I rip my dagger out sideways and the beast's head rolls along the floor. I don't take the time to inspect it before running over to Elijah. I slide under him and place his head in my lap only to find that blood begins to seep through my trousers from his wound. Panic pounds through my veins. Is he dead? Is he dying? I need to get him out of here.

Taking Elijah's shirt off him, I try not to marvel at his bare chest. I wrap the beast's head in the shirt and then lift Elijah up from the ground and hoist him against me. My shoulder cries out against the weight of Elijah on the bite wound but I cannot worry about pain when Elijah could be dying. That beast was here for me. And he could die because of it.

Trudging through Broxen took hours what with my injuries and Elijah's limp figure. He still hasn't regained consciousness and fear strikes me harder than ever. I do not let it stop me. On and on I go. It is nightfall by the time I enter the gates of Drodal at which point guards hastily call to wake Breccan. My muscles ache and tremble from the pain, sweat gleaming on every inch of me, fusing with the putrid blood of the monster as well as the scarlet of my own. But before I can break, the guards take Elijah off my hands. I grab one of them by the shoulder and turn him to face me, a face I have never seen before.

"If Elijah dies, I will unleash a hell so destructive that you will cease to exist," I threaten though my voice is little more than a hoarse whisper. The guard nods sternly and follows the others to the infirmary. I dare not even look at my shoulder.

Breccan emerges from the doors and in four strong strides, he is clasping my face in both his hands, sapphire eyes alight with worry.

"Elyra, what have you done? What has happened to you?" his voice breaks and I am surprised at how much he cares.

"I got busy," I mumble.

"By the Aerix, your shoulder." He gasps. "Take Elyra to the infirmary now!" he barks angrily.

"Wait. Don't you want to see Myrna's grand plan?" I offer and his eyebrows furrow in confusion. I throw the green bundle across the floor and as it rolls, it becomes uncovered. Numerous gasps ensue at the sight of the beast's head. Breccan's face blanches but then he turns to me slowly.

"You managed to kill a Bolgran?" he asks in complete shock and that shock mimics my own. He knows this creature?

Before I can ask him how, my shoulder sends me into a fit of dizziness and Breccan calls for the guards to take me to the infirmary again. Two strong men take either side of me and lead me into the bowels of Drodal, my flesh ripping away from bone at this point.

But before I completely black out, I hear Breccan's voice one more time as he mutters under his breath.

"If anything should happen to my daughter, you cannot even imagine the consequences."

Chapter 10

I do not remember much.

Only the severe pain wrenching my shoulder in half.

It is as if the beast had venom coating its canines and it is searing my flesh as it soaks through the wound.

I should have never let it get that close.

With my body aching severely, I slowly regain consciousness and find the familiar glow of the candles in the infirmary. This place is beginning to be my home.

Home.

Breccan.

That sentence still echoes in my mind: *if anything should happen to my daughter, you cannot even imagine the consequences.*

I cannot even process the anger right now. It cannot be true… not after everything I have been through… not with who he sent me to live with. It is not true. I am an orphan. I have no parents nor do I wish for any. It would just be more people to abuse my affections.

When my vision stops blurring, my anger spikes at the sight of Roran perched on a stool before me, head in his hands.

"You better be here because you're injured, Maar. If not, I will make sure that your presence here is deserving," I growl hoarsely. Gosh I need a drink desperately. It is as if sand paper is scratching against the walls of my throat.

"Lenora…" he exhales with relief but the daggers in my eyes soon have him amending his words, "Elyra, you're alive."

"Who healed me?" I ask bluntly as in all the times I have been here, I only know Ayla to be a healer and I cannot imagine her having that graceful touch for the life of me.

"The healers like to leave when they are no longer needed," he answers for me.

"Lukas? Maer?"

"We spared them the news until they had awoken." I nod; that was the right thing to do. They need not worry for my safety this way.

"Why are you here, Roran? Were my instructions not explicit?"

"I came because I was worried about you… you were so close to death." His eyes swim with the ghosts of the tragedy he had believed to be imminent.

"Spare me the flattery," I bite back but the harsh tone is even harsher upon my throat and so it makes me cough violently. Roran silently hands me a cup of water and I take it without thanks. The water coats my throat with a sublime caress and the rawness melts away. It reminds me of when Elijah stroked my cheek and-

Elijah.

With panic surging through my heart, I yank myself upwards, not caring for the pain that ensues. I feel something tear in my shoulder and scarlet begins to coat the bandages that have been placed there. I stand on wobbly legs and Roran is quick to support me but I shove him aside; the lack of strength only has him teetering slightly and it irritates me that I could not do more damage.

"Where is he?" I demand, edging near the door.

"There is no point—"

"Where is he?" I yell and Roran looks at me with a hurt that I have never seen so strong before in his eyes. He stares at me, posture slack with defeat.

"There was once a time when you would have broken down walls for me," he murmurs sadly and despite myself, my heart twangs at the words.

"Yes," I mumble back, "I would have." And with that admission I surge through the door and out into the stone hallway.

Breccan and Ayla stand in front of the door opposite me. Elijah must be in there. Without even looking at the two, I try to barge my way through them but Breccan's arms stop me. I try not to jerk away at his touch.

"Elyra, you have been awake for all but five minutes, now is not the time to be a warrior!" he barks at me and I cannot help my dark chuckle while I shrug his hands off me. I step towards him and his confusion is potent but he does not cower beneath my intense glare.

"I will deal with you soon enough," I snarl and even I am surprised at the ferocity I am aiming at him. Can he blame me?

"Elyra, please… your shoulder is already tearing from its stitching. You need to rest," he answers evasively but his sapphire eyes gleam with a fear and an agreement for our future conversation.

"I *need* to see him," I demand and Breccan nods his acquiescence much to Ayla's distress.

"Elijah needs rest, not a fight!" she cries but I push past her anyway and into the other infirmary room, slamming the door in their faces when they try to follow me.

"She's in no mood to obey right now." I hear Roran say but my attention flickers to Elijah lying on the bed against the wall.

The rooms are identical. The table, the various utensils and remedies, the candles... except in this room, Elijah lays unconscious. A bloodied bandage wraps around his head and another around his torso. A couple of his ribs must have broken from the impact. How did I not notice?

His dormant form is quite handsome. Mouth slackened with his easy breaths. No harsh scowl, no bitter words. He is peaceful here. But it does nothing to stop the continuation of panic in my veins. Why has he not awakened yet? Will he be the same when he does wake? *Will* he wake? I cannot shake the guilt for his injuries... I attacked him and then that monster almost killed him because it was after me. How can I ever look Elijah in the eye again?

I did not realise a tear has fallen until it splatters upon my leg. I frantically try to wipe the trail of saline from my cheek.

"Tears for me?" a gruff voice says and I look up in complete shock as Elijah's body shifts slightly on the bed. His eyes flutter open and my heart swells at the emeralds glistening back at me. His eyebrows furrow when he takes me in.

"Elyra... your shoulder." His voice is thick with warning but I do not take head. I am just happy that I did not kill him.

"Don't worry about me," I reply and I cannot take my eyes off the bandages. He notices my stare but I can't bring myself to look away.

"It was not your fault." I sigh inwardly at his words, how could he know what I was thinking?

"The fault *is* mine. If you were not with me, death would not be clinging to you." I stifle the tears now. I will not cry in front of him.

"It has nothing to do with—"

"It was there to kill me, Elijah," I say exasperatedly before gripping the bridge of my nose with my thumb and forefinger. "You were just in the way."

"I..." he begins but he falters. "I don't understand." With a deep sigh, I interlock my fingers as if to steady myself.

"I have a past of which everyone has heard of and yet all have forgotten. But it appears that one person has forgotten nothing. And so I still remain her target." I summarise carefully but it seems to only increase his confusion.

"Target for what?" He gulps.

"I have made enemies. Enemies in high places. How they seek to punish me, I dare not imagine."

"But what could you have possibly done to warrant that?" his head shakes in his confusion and I can see the irritation blossoming on his face.

"That's just it. I have not done anything bad at all. At least through my eyes. That is the irony of it all. Who is good and who is evil is purely subjective."

"Won't you just tell me the truth, Elyra?" he snaps at me and his harshness makes me wince. "I have no use for your lies. I *need* to know who you are." How can I make him understand that I do this to save him?

"The truth would forfeit your life. Something I cannot bear," I admit to him in a whisper but his eyes still narrow. No doubt he is thinking that nothing could harm him but... everyone has a weakness. And he might just be my own.

"Do you want to know what I cannot bear?" he asks softly and the question catches me off guard; when I do not answer, he continues, "Calling you by a name that is not your own."

"A name is but a word," I counter, like I have done so many times. He smirks darkly at that, a shadow passing over his face.

"To know your name would be a release. A release from a torture that I cannot evade." My heartbeat quickens though he does not meet my gaze. What is he saying?

"Why does a name matter so much to you?" I ask exasperatedly.

"Because how am I to know you otherwise?" he barks back. "I wish to *know* you, Elyra. And not just the things that are trivial. I want to know why you find that beauty is a curse. I want to know why you go to the forge whenever you feel upset. I want to know why Roran looks at you with adoration in his eyes despite the wrath you throw upon him. I want to know why I..." he trails off but I had stopped breathing the moment he began speaking.

"What?" I murmur and he does not meet my eyes again, he simply stares at the ceiling while he contemplates his answer. And before I know it, emeralds shine at me once more.

"I want to know why I cannot stand your presence here. But why I cannot bear to see you leave either." My breath catches and my heart thunders and I find myself avoiding his intense stare as I marvel at a brazier on the ceiling.

A hot sensation dribbles along my torso and I cannot help my nausea as I see that it is my blood. I dare a look at my shoulder and it is true what they said. My shoulder is now stained red and the stitching that once encompassed the bite has now torn away from my flesh.

I look to Elijah as the pain grapples with my consciousness; I can tell that he was not paying attention to it either. His face is full of panic and it is that panic that is the last thing I see as the world turns black.

My breath catches as I awake suddenly although this time, I am in my chambers. The four-poster bed is plush beneath me and the red sheets are draped from the top to conceal me from view. Sitting up, a wave of dizziness passes through me and I realise that it is now nightfall once more outside. I have been unconscious for a long while. Moving my shoulder, I find that the stitching is secure and the pain is now but a dull sting. I fear that this bite will be another scar upon my skin.

Moving towards the edge of the bed, I push aside the drapes to find a man standing in front of the large curved window that faces out into the courtyards and the gardens. The moon shines bright upon him and stars twinkle like I know his eyes will return as he stares at them.

Breccan.

I do not have any more emotion left in me right now to muster anger or sadness at his presence considering the information that I now know. The only thing I feel is the sweet sting of disappointment at how it is not Elijah standing watch in my chambers.

"You're awake," Breccan's deep voice announces. He slowly turns to me and his eyes betray the guilt that his voice refuses to show. I keep my voice steady.

"Explain yourself," I demand coolly. I am past surprise at this revelation. It is not the first time that fate has twisted for me.

"I do not know what you want me to say," he says hands linked behind his back.

"I want you to stop being the Lord of Drodal for one minute so that you might tell me why in hell you are my father!" I cry at him and he shuts his eyes as if the proclamation pains him.

"I…" he begins and his voice quivers on that one syllable, "I never wanted this to happen." I stand up then, passing aside the dizziness so that I may face him like an adult.

"Why did you lie to me?"

"I never lied. I did not know that you existed."

"So why now?" I exclaim and he stills, head bowing slightly.

"You had come to Drodal and I felt… I felt as if I had known you for years. The more time I spent with you, the more my soul knew that you were mine."

"But there is no way to know." I clutch my forehead, willing my thoughts to stop. "You did not know that I was born so how can you know that I am yours?"

"We have the same shade of hair colour," he says and I suppose it is true. Raven dark hair. But so do many people. "We share the same threatening techniques. You hold your dagger the same way I hold my sword. You are stubborn yet kind and strong yet vulnerable. You remind me so much of me the more I watch you grow."

"That means nothing to me. Physical resemblance and similar traits do not make me your daughter!"

"But you have her eyes," he answers quietly and I am stunned by the remark. "Her eyes are the first thing I noticed about you. I have only seen those beautiful grey eyes on one other woman in my lifetime."

"My mother," I whisper and he nods. "Who is she?"

"She is not the woman you wish her to be, Lenora." My throat bobs as I hear him say my true name.

"Who is she?" he looks at me but does not answer, he begins to wring his hands slightly. Obvious discomfort. "Tell me her name."

"She's gone," he snaps in a quick decision and I fight back the tears. No mother and an absent father.

"When?" is all I can ask without my throat burning with the intent to cry.

"The woman I loved died a long time ago," he replies dismissively, turning his head to the side to observe a tapestry instead of meeting my gaze.

"Did you ever suspect?" I ask him emotionlessly.

"No." He breathes adamantly. "I would have never left your side had I have known." I nod, desperate to reign in my tears but they flow down my cheeks anyway.

"Do you have any idea what I went through?" my hands are balled into fists at my side and I cannot stop their shaking.

"I am so sorry." I dismiss his guilt-ridden tone as anger sparks my veins.

"Do you realise what kind of man I was sent to?" I cry out, hurt tearing my heart in two.

Memories start flooding into my mind of lonely days and fearful nights with the man who raised me. I am about as vulnerable as I was back then… for all the woman I am today, I might as well still be that little girl crying into her pillow in the hopes that he would be too drunk to remember me each night.

"I chose to take to the streets at six years old rather than spend another night under his roof!" I shout at him and he rushes forward, taking my face in his hands. When I try to shove them away, he only grips me tighter as my sobs get worse.

"Lenora, I do not know what you have suffered but I would give my life to correct the wrongs that you have been dealt. I was not there for you then but I am here for you now and nothing could take you away from me. Not now. Not now that I know."

"You didn't save me, Breccan," I whimper and I am just reminded of being that six-year-old girl curled up in the corner of her bedroom.

"I could not save someone who I did not know existed," he admits sadly, stroking my hair out of my face, damp with tears, "You have my word that the man will pay for what he did—"

"He already has." I sniffle, wiping my sleeve across my nose.

"What?"

"He's long gone. I made sure of it," I answer stonily and his face still crumples in sympathy.

"I did not know," he murmurs. "What… what happened between you and him?" I shake my head adamantly at him.

"No-one knows. And no one ever will. Not unless I ordain it."

As I stare at Breccan's face, I cannot help but wonder how differently my life would have been if I had been by his side all my life. I would have been softer, less broken, less damaged. And yet… I would have been a different person. I would have been his born princess. I would have been courted by suitors he deemed worthy, forced into etiquette lessons and made to watch as he went to war as I maintained his court. That is not who I want to be.

I am a warrior. I have fought for Aneya and for myself. I fight for a man who took me in in my darkest hour and I will restore his children to their rightful place on Eradan's throne. I have been in countless battles and have shed much blood in these years. A court would not dare have me now.

And with this realisation, I realise that without my past, I would not be who I am today. Without *him,* without losing Adrian, without Roran's betrayal or Golnar… I would merely be another bystander as everyone watches the world perish by Myrna's hand. I will not be a bystander. I will fight her.

And I will do it with my father.

"I'm sorry, Lenora." Breccan breathes, a tear falling from his sapphire eye.

"I'm sorry too," I say and his mouth tilts upwards slightly.

"By the Aerix, I have a daughter," he says breathlessly as he crushes me into his arms with a hug that could break bone. He pulls away after a while and wipes his face free from tears with his sleeves.

"We must announce you to the public soon."

"What?" I exclaim.

"You are my heir, Lenora. Drodal must know that my blood lives on within you." He grins but I must stop him.

"No, Breccan. I do not wish for that," I admit to him and his weathered face furrows in confusion.

"You are ashamed of me?"

"No!" I cry, taking his hand. "I was an orphan. And then a child to a single father. And then an orphan. And then an addition to the Maddox family. And then I am an orphan once more… forgive me, but it seems that whenever I gain a family, they are soon marked for death," I tell him. "I want to enjoy my moments with you as a father and his daughter. Not as a King and his heir."

"Very well." He smiles. "Will you accompany me to the grand hall for supper?" he extends his arm but I decline with a sad smile.

"There is much that needs to be discussed, Breccan. And there is much that I must understand. May I meet you tomorrow morning instead?"

"Your wish is my own." He takes my hand and kisses it lightly and though I feel happy at this revelation, I cannot help the swarm of worry troubling my heart. "I shall leave you to your thoughts." Breccan leaves for the door but before he goes, he turns back to me with an unreadable expression.

"Had I have known… I would have come for you," he says and I can barely see him in the shadows.

"I know." I find myself saying and I believe that he would have. Breccan does not strike me as a man to neglect his duties.

I sit on the bed once more and ponder my various duties. I must see Brogan and Rayna… I have not consulted them since the party. I must check in on Lukas and Maer and find out if Maer has had any other dangerous encounters. I must consult Breccan about the Bolgran and how it has been made… come to think of it, I need to consult him on everything. I must try to find a way to tell Drodal that I am not a permanent fixture here as Jocelyn and Jasper need me. And then there is Elijah…

I do not know what is to become of us. The things he said to me in the infirmary… I do not know if this is some joke of his or if it is real but if it is real… I do not know how I would feel about it. I don't know how I feel about anything anymore. As just experienced, everything can change with one simple detail.

I just hope things do not change too quickly.

Chapter 11

After hours of trying to sleep, I find that it is useless. What is the use in tossing and turning when something more fulfilling could occupy my time? My body is restless and my mind chooses to do the same.

Sitting up on the edge of the bed, I cup my face in my hands.

So much to do.

So little time.

I am not sure when or even how I will be able to accomplish all of my duties but nonetheless those duties must be satisfied. The Bolgran, Elijah, Breccan, Brogan and Rayna, the Maddox family and Myrna… even the dangers posed to Maer.

But there is something I should do above all of that.

And if there ever is a time to get started, it is now.

I head out of my room and the candlelight flickers against the stone walls as usual. Sounds of merriment echo throughout the expanse of Drodal and despite myself I smile. It is nice that laughter still exists in a time of such darkness.

By the time I reach the grand hall, the merriment has already stopped and there are now hushed voices emanating from the small crack between the large double-doors. I peak through and find that the long tables and their benches have been stripped from the hall and only Breccan's throne and a single chair stands in there now. Breccan sits in his throne as Lukas sits in the other chair, surrounded by every remaining inhabitant of Drodal, sitting around him in a circle cross-legged.

"But are we ready for the most infamous legend of all?" he says excitedly and I raise my eyebrows. Maer sits eagerly at the front of Lukas' feet as does everyone else.

"She has awakened." I hear Elijah say from beside me and find him leaning against the wall with his arms across his chest with a smirk. He is hiding his pain very well.

"She never slept," I reply with a roll of my eyes. "What's going on in there?"

"They are telling tales of the past. Legends. Myths. To inspire hope and happiness among our people."

"Anything interesting?"

"Perhaps." There is a certain glint in his emerald eyes that sparks something in my blood. It unnerves me and so I silently walk through the doors and lean against one of the ornate pillars standing guard amongst the hall. Elijah follows suit but leans against one opposite me.

I catch Breccan's eye from across the hall and he smiles and gestures for me to come closer. I shake my head and though it saddens him, he nods. I cannot be so quick to show everyone at Drodal how our relationship has changed.

"It all began when the peace of Aneya was strong." Lukas begins, "When our King Adrian Maddox had ruled these lands with integrity and kindness. On his casual morning stroll, he came across a young girl in the streets of Eradan. A girl being held at spear-point by three Eradanian guards with a loaf of bread in her hand, stolen to fill an orphan's stomach. But was this young girl cowering in fear? No. She bared her teeth at the guards and was preparing to fight them despite the odds against her victory."

My breath catches in my throat at this story. It cannot be. The coincidence is inconceivable. I try to let my expression remain impassive but the shock has my posture completely slacking.

"She had tried to fight her way through those guards and her skills were so admirable for someone so young… that Adrian took a liking to her. He was further astounded more when he had called off the guards and the girl had bounded off to an even younger boy. The boy she had stolen food for. King Adrian knew then that this girl was special. And he was not wrong.

"Lenora Belavier had grown up inside the palace walls of Eradan, training alongside its General and soon becoming the envy of every soldier within the Eradanian ranks. She had become a warrior more fearsome yet more kind than any Aneya had ever seen. And through her pillaging of evil and her forging of alliances she had become Aneya's Warrior.

"And when Aneya's peace was threatened by Myrna Verena, Lenora Belavier sought to conquer it. She fought for our rights and protected our virtues with both sword and word. She ventured across the seas and rallied each realm of Aneya to fight against the darkness Myrna had created, had stirred the patriotic loyalty to our late King to a point where our own swords would join hers in battle." Lukas' voice ascends into something one would use in a speech before war;

he even raises his hand in the air to show his enthusiasm with a grin and the tears already brim my eyes.

"But she did not succeed." My voice barely chokes out. Lukas notices me then and raises his eyebrows slightly. I can feel many eyes turning to me and their focus burns into my skin but I dare not let it show how much it rattles me. All that matters is this story.

"True. She did not succeed in her endeavours to conquer Myrna Verena and restore Adrian's kin upon their rightful throne. Instead she vanished. Doomed to the fate she sought to conceal from others, consumed by the darkness she fought so hard to prevent. No, she did not fulfil her task. And yet, she remains a beacon of hope to a land condemned by greed and treachery.

"In dark times, she reminds us that we must all be strong as she once was, to use our blades as she had to slay our enemies with bonds of friendship and loyalty. She reminds us that though our fates may be dark in this tragic time, that we all have the capabilities of being Lenora Belavier. Aneya's Warrior." Lukas finishes with a soft whisper but the audience are silent with their awe at his story.

With *my* story.

I dare not look to anyone for fear that the tears in my eyes may shed. With haste, I leave the hall and thrust my way out into the courtyard. I gasp for air from the night sky as if I have been suffocating in that room the entire time. I can barely breathe.

My story is legend. I have been forgotten. Hope has been forgotten. And yet… my tales are not so worthy to be told to the night. I have not earned that right. I have not accomplished my goals. I am not worthy of their reverence. I never have been. I am but an orphan plucked from the streets by the right man. Without Adrian, who would I have been? A life-long beggar? A traveller? Or worse?

"I did not think a woman such as you would be startled so much by mere legends." Elijah sounds from behind me. I clench my eyes shut, dreading his presence. Not now.

"I am starting to think that my shadow is no longer my own," I murmur to him, clutching my head in an effort to calm myself. I choose not to face him.

"It is not my fault that the shadows of your past choose to haunt you. I am simply guilty for noticing it." He comes to stand beside me now and we both face the flowing fountain.

"You notice too much." Our breath is fog before us as we stare at the glowing crescent moon.

"You knew her," he states clearly into our silence and I cannot stop myself from wincing.

"Somewhat."

"Another life that the Ghost had saved?"

"Not even I could have saved Lenora from her fate," I whisper and Elijah looks at me then, tilting his head in question.

"I find it hard to believe that."

"How so?" I say, still refusing to look him in the eye.

"Golnar's Ghost alongside Lenora Belavier would be a formidable force against all those seeking to imprison them."

"Golnar's Ghost," I spit through my teeth, "Could not save everyone from the forge or else they would all be free women." He laughs to himself for a moment whilst clutching his jaw causing me to shoot daggers at him with my eyes.

"I wish I could carry on this charade of yours but I will do it no longer."

"Excuse me?" I demand, clenching my fists.

"What hurts the most is that you still choose to lie to me."

"I never lied."

"Oh?" he says before grabbing the back of his neck in frustration. "Do you want to know what I think?"

"No." I walk past him defiantly, desperate to go anywhere else, be with anyone else.

"I think that Lenora Belavier vanished because she was sent to Golnar, as all female enemies of Myrna are sent to when they have been captured."

"She was never there," I say though gritted teeth but he carries on anyway.

"I think that Aneya's Warrior could not bear the shame of her failure and so she sought a new reputation, a new purpose. If she cannot protect Aneya then she will protect its inmates from the only threat she could, the guards."

"You know nothing of what those girls endured," I spit at him but he is relentless as he approaches me slowly with every word he utters.

"And then one day, she found that despite her newly acquired title, she could not forget her old one. She had remembered her duties to Aneya and to the man who raised her and sought to see them through. Thus led to Golnar's Ghost escaping her confines. But though she has safe refuge within the walls of Drodal, she constantly struggles with her presence here as she wants nothing more than to finish what she had started all those years ago."

119

"Lenora does not exist! She is fiction! A myth!" I shout at him, unable to control myself. How dare he just assume that he can say all of this to me. He has no right.

"I think that Myrna Verena finally subdued Aneya's Warrior," he says as he stands face-to-face with me, unflinching from my rage. "I think that Lenora finally gave in."

"*I* did not give up. *I* was betrayed," I bellow into his face but he does not react. Elijah simply looks at me.

And then his eyes soften.

His posture slackens.

And he reaches his arm outwards to cup a hand to my cheek. His touch does not stop my heavy breathing or my rage, if anything it simply adds more heat to the flush of rage upon my skin.

"You know…" he whispers, his breath caressing my face, "I had always wanted to meet the great Lenora Belavier, famed for being the most skilled of all warriors. I always wished that she would come to Drodal in her quest for Aneyan allegiance against Myrna." He laughs to himself and it thaws my heart slightly, "I wanted to see what made this woman so great. And she has been standing in front of me this entire time."

"She deserted her people," I murmur, relishing in the touch of his hand upon my face.

"She did not desert us. She just… went away for a while. And now she's back." He smiles at me, stroking a thumb across my cheekbone.

"If it were not for Roran, I never would have left." I roll my eyes at that but I find my tension towards him easing.

However Elijah seems to take that tension inside him instead. He stiffens and retracts his arm from me and I am saddened to see it go. His emerald eyes are wide and I cannot fathom why.

"*That* is what he did to you, isn't it?"

"What?" I ask, completely confused for his choice of words.

"You said he betrayed you but I didn't think… well, how could I have known that he…" he rambles to himself, clutching his head in thought. It is strange to see Elijah so worried.

"Lenora!" someone calls from in front of us and I see Roran Maar emerging from Drodal's doors with a frantic look in his eyes. Gosh, he has timing. He must have seen me leave the hall after my tale had been told.

Elijah turns to face Roran and judging by the fear in Roran's eyes, it must have been one hell of a look. He turns back to me and I have never seen such rage on his face.

"He is the one that sent you there, isn't he? Roran sent you to Golnar." He says with absolute hate in his heart. Roran attempts to back away into Drodal but one flex of Elijah's wrist has him locked into place with roots ensnaring his calves.

"Elijah…" I warn but before I know it, he has already clasped Roran's throat with his fist and I can hear the life being choked out of him.

"You betrayed your friend! You captured Aneya's only hope in this damn war!" he shouts at him but Roran cannot answer; only gurgles of struggled breath come out from his mouth.

Surprisingly, I find the noises of Roran's torture unbearable. It grates against my ears and I decide to bear the pain no longer. I surge forwards and force apart Elijah's fist from his throat and it works momentarily. Until Elijah lunges again. Roran shrieks but my bellow soon causes them both to turn silent.

"Stop this, Elijah!"

"Don't you realise what he has done?" Elijah shouts back at me.

"No-one realises more than I, Warren. As you can imagine," I scold him and he does not meet my gaze.

"Please, I know that I have done you wrong in the past—" Roran tries to speak but Elijah cuts him off bitterly.

"You are a traitor! You give a bad name to Aneya's loyal soldiers."

"He is only in this position because he was doing his job *as* a loyal solider." I find myself defending him easily and am surprised that I am even doing so. "True, Roran was not loyal to me. But he remained loyal to those he swore to protect. He remained loyal to the Royal family."

"And in doing so subjected you to three years of torture and ruin!" Elijah cries and it breaks my heart. "What if it had killed you?" his voice cracks on that and I hold in my tears.

"Golnar could not kill Aneya's Warrior," Roran says, clutching his throat whilst panting.

"You did not know that it wouldn't," Elijah spits back at him and I place my hand on his forearm to grab his attention. I can feel the tension in his muscles. I can feel him bracing himself to kill Maar.

"He did what was right for the kingdom, Elijah. He wagered that I could beat the torments of the forge and his faith in me was upheld. The kingdom has lived longer than it would have through his actions. On this, you must trust me," he looks at me with pleading in his eyes and I know that he is accepting the truth.

121

Nonetheless, he looks back towards a defeated Roran and points a shaking finger at him.

"Your days are numbered, General," he threatens him.

"I am already counting them," he replies under his breath but Elijah simply storms back into Drodal, leaving Roran alone with me in the courtyard.

"And I will be counting them with you, my friend." He looks up at the term of endearment and I feel no regret in using it. There is no point in grieving for my past anymore.

"Lenora—" he begins, his voice breaking but I hold up my hand to quiet him.

"I need you to know that I no longer blame you for what you did to me. For Jasper's life, I would have done the same thing. And so on that, you must accept. But you must also know that I do not trust you. And as for that, you must earn as you once did before."

"I will." He promises with tears in his eyes. I nod at him, unsure of how I feel when I look at the man before me.

Once, my heart shone with pride and adoration for him. And now... it is as if our past has left the trenches of my memory. As if a stranger stands before me now with only shadows to guide me in his stance upon my life. Is he my Captain? Is he my friend? There was a time where he could have been more than that. But there are some things that you cannot simply forget.

"I must leave you now. But I must talk with you in the morning. Now is the time to begin again what we had once started." He simply nods at me and I turn my back on him, ready to make my next visit.

The familiar ring of bluebells surrounds the fiery forge in front of me. And as suspected, Brogan is hammering away at the steel in his hand, sweat upon his brow. No doubt, the chill of the night is a dull comfort to the sweltering forge beside him. He does not realise my presence for a while. My heart is thundering inside my chest and I know that I originally came out here to practise putting that thunder outside of my body. But it has been a long time since Brogan had found out about Elyra. It is my duty to respond.

After a few moments more, he looks up at me. I wring my hands together in nervousness though he is simply still. He lowers his utensils and wipes his hands against his khaki trousers. He eyes me suspiciously before wiping the sweat away from the back of his neck with a deep sigh.

"I am sorry I have not seen you sooner, Brogan," I tell him in a small voice and it is true.

"The fault is mine," his deep voice replies gruffly and I take a few steps forward until I am in front of his work-desk facing him.

"You are under no obligation to even talk to me right now but—" he holds a hand up to silence me and I purse my lips together, wringing my hands further.

"I should not have threatened you the way I had, El—" he tries to say my given name but pauses and it is heartwrenching. I suppose Brogan will have to be another to know my true identity; I don't mind this time.

"I understand your aggression. If it were my love, I would have reacted the same way for answers." He shakes his head and the baldness of it gleams in the light of the forge.

"You would have given me the answers without the need for such violence." He says more to himself than to me, and it saddens me. "As a warrior of Ceylon, I am trained to understand people I have known for two seconds as if I had known them a lifetime. I know that you are not a bad person. I was just… consumed by grief." His eyebrows furrow as he fumbles with his hands. It is only now that I realise that he has no one to show him sympathy or offer any comfort.

"You must know… that Elyra was my most trusted friend in Golnar. Or rather, the only woman I trusted enough to become one," I murmur and he closes his eyes tightly at her name.

"She was a strong woman."

"Where is Rayna?"

"The High Priestess of Delphor has returned to her people to release the news of Elyra's demise and assume her rightful duties." The snarl on his face tells me that he disapproves of this decision. A moment of silence passes between us and I know that I must tell him.

"I think that if we are to ever return to friendship that you must first know why your love was treated the way she was because of her affiliation with me."

"Go on." He agrees.

"My true name is Lenora Belavier." His ensuing gasp leads me to believe that this was not what he was expecting. "When I was placed inside Golnar, I immediately received harsher treatment than that of everyone else. I recall being brutally beaten by five guards upon my first night and their brutality did not cease there. Elyra received similar treatment although her purity attracted brutality of a different kind."

"You protected her?" he replies gruffly.

"I tried my best. For a long time, it had worked. Until the guards amassed their numbers."

"I bet she thought very highly of you." He gulps and wipes the back of his hand across his beard, no doubt to hide his quivering lip.

"I thought very highly of her, Brogan. She was an incredible woman."

"She was."

"I want you to know that she spoke often of a love. Obviously, I did not know it was you she was referring to. But she spoke of you so passionately and with such love that I frequently wished to find what she had found with you. She loved you very much." He does not answer me but I can see the tears in his eyes.

In a snap decision, I walk to his side of the forge and embrace him. He is stiff at first but then he soon clasps his arms around me tightly. I can feel the arch of his back shaking with sobs but I dare not comment on something that he expects to be silent. Instead I just comfort him, offering my condolences until the shaking stops. He releases himself from me after a while and he regards me in thought for a moment, any remnants of tears replaced with the expression of a fierce warrior.

"You are truly Aneya's Warrior?"

"Yes," I answer in a small voice, the truth alleviating a burden from my shoulders.

"And will you be assuming this role once your magic has been tamed?"

"Yes," I answer again and he nods.

"Then I will fight with you until the end, Lenora, as you had fought for my Elyra."

"Brogan, no—" his promise startles me.

"I pledge my axes to you in service of my loyalty and skill. I will defend your life with my own and aid you in your quest to free Aneya from Myrna's chains of servitude."

"The last thing I need is someone else dying in my name," I admit to him, begging him to reconsider this offer. If something were to happen to him because of this damn oath… it would be my fault.

"If I die, so be it. But I am in service to you, Lenora Belavier, whether you deem it wise or not. I owe it to you. And I owe it to my precious Elyra. If there were ever a moment for me to pick up my axes once more, it would be by your side; as she would have wanted it." I nod reluctantly at his proposal and the corner of his mouth turns upwards slightly, his red beard gleaming.

"I must ask that you bear to call me Elyra until it is safe to do otherwise. I understand that it may be difficult—"

"If anyone should wear her name with honour, it would be you. You have my word that your identity shall never be revealed from my lips."

"I thank you for that, Brogan." He smiles again and a mutual understanding passes between us.

Nonetheless, I must get back to why I had come out here in the first place. I owe it to myself and to Drodal to master the gifts that have been bestowed upon me. I need to know what I can do, what I am capable of. The courtyard has already served as a physical training ground; it might as well be one for magical training too.

I take a deep breath as I gaze upon the full moon shining brightly overhead. I centre myself, focusing on the slight breeze caressing my skin and my calm heartbeat. I take deep breaths, mind sending out tentative tendrils in an attempt to grip my magic.

And then something clicks into place inside me, like a jigsaw finally being completed and my senses explode with sensation. I can feel the gentle hum of the atmosphere upon my fingertips, vibrating in the air unbeknownst to others. I can taste the moisture in the air more clearly than before, sensing each droplet.

Inside me, I can feel a crackling energy, spindling outwards from my heart like a tree inside my chest, each branch spiralling to include every inch of my being, glowing white hot though it is painless to me. The power ebbs inside my veins, merging with my blood as if my existence somehow gives it energy, as if one cannot exist without the other.

I smile to myself, closing my eyes and absorbing myself in the feel of this great power that I did not even know I had. I feel stronger. I feel... happier. As if I never really knew who I was until I have felt this thrum inside me.

My energy crackles within my core and it is a strange sensation but one that I will gladly get used to. I can feel the lightening. I can feel the storm brewing in my chest. And as it does, a real storm emerges before me.

Black clouds pulsate amidst the heavens, threatening their gates with relentless mischief. Thunder echoes across Drodal, a battlecry for all those listening to know its presence. I sense the moisture in the atmosphere increasing and by my will, rain pours down upon me in mirthless sheets, drenching me in their power. I can feel heat blazing at my fingertips, the branches inside me eager to be released. And with a mental push, I liberate the storm welling inside me and lightening forks the sky, electric perfection stabbing the skies without mercy.

I raise my hands to the storm that I have created, relishing in the rain falling upon my palms. I open my eyes and the sight is quite beautiful. The colours may be dark and the nature of it fearsome but there is always beauty within a storm. Something that most do not see. But I see the strength and the wonder, the power and the grace to which it aspires to.

The noise is deafening and a flick of my wrist ceases the lightening and the ensuing thunder. I wipe my hand across the sky and the black clouds erase themselves from the night sky, the rain slowly coming to halt, leaving only a drenched courtyard in its wake.

I realise that I am exhausted. My muscles ache with fatigue and I am panting from exertion. The magic has taken a lot out of me it seems. I must not have noticed during my awe of what I had created. What *I* had created. I am the creator of storms. I have magic. I actually have magic. And it works.

An excitement fills my heart that I have never felt before. Despite my exhaustion, I know that I must practice some more. I want to see what I can really do. With a grin on my face, I set to work.

I am out here until the skies turn indigo with the soon-to-be breaking of dawn. But I cannot help but feel genuinely excited and proud at what I have accomplished. I have made so many discoveries in this time that it astounds me that it is even possible.

I strongly believe that should I be attacked, I will not falter in my magic though I wish to train more in a combative sense. I am eager to learn more. Even now, I can feel the electricity sparking through me and I know that it will always be there for as long as I live.

A sudden rustling has me on edge. I whip out my dagger and enter a defensive stance, poising my blade to strike at the oncoming threat. My heart beats fast and my eyes scan over Broxen in an effort to find the danger.

And then a pair of eyes illuminate in the shadows. Pale blue with black slits for pupils. I would know those eyes anywhere. A Bolgran. The eyes narrow at me and I brace myself for an attack. A low guttural growl emanates in the darkness. A warning. A threat.

"Try it." I dare it.

But soon enough, more eyes appear from all sides of me. Their blue glow piercing amidst the darkness of the early morning. They surround me from the edges of Broxen to the sides of the courtyard, encasing me with their malice. I count ten Bolgren. How are those numbers even possible?

The growls increases in volume, letting me know that they are out for blood. I dare not provoke them further with defiant words so I choose a silent approach instead, staring each of them down and in turn letting them know that I will not go down easily. That they have a fight on their hands.

Without warning, the growling ceases. And they retreat back into the shadows from whence they came. These Bolgren may not have attacked but they are planning something. Something that they saw fit to warn me of. Or maybe not. But there is one thing that I am certain of.

I want to know where these beasts came from.

And how I can kill them all.

Chapter 12

Without bothering for niceties, I kick down the door to Breccan's study and storm my way in there. Breccan stands behind his desk facing someone that I choose not to notice at this time.

"I want to know about the Bolgren and I want to know about them now," I demand of him, tense with the fear of their obvious threat. His sapphire eyes flick towards his guest in apology but I do not follow his eyes.

"Can't this wait, Elyra?" he answers with a false smile, desperate to keep up appearances with the other person in the room.

"No, it cannot. I demand answers now," I tell him mercilessly, crossing my arms.

"There are more important matters at hand here," He says through gritted teeth, still trying to smile calmly at the guest.

"Oh right, well I thought the fact that ten Bolgren appearing over your threshold would classify as a matter of importance." I snarl at him. Father or not, diplomacy can wait.

He stiffens at the mention of this news and then turns to his guest regretfully.

"Would it please you to explore the grounds while I consult with my Captain? I assure you that we will continue to discuss your proposal in due course."

"My Lord's wish is my own." My ears peak at the husky sound of a woman's voice and so I turn my head to face her.

It is a Zatrian woman, no doubt a warrior of her own people. Her burnt red hair stands in erratic bouncy curls and her brown skin glows with many days lying in the Sun's wake. Her long and slim figure is strong and athletic, the orange fabric she is wearing barely covering her femininities. Light brown war-paint coats her body in various symbols and patterns though only a smear of black trails across her cheeks and the bridge of her nose. She carries no weapon but her intense brown eyes tell me that she is lethal without one.

"And you are?" I ask in a civil manner and her full lips reveal an array of white teeth. I keep my face impassive at the sight of her.

"My name is Alanaat of the Eastern Tribes." I scrutinise her appearance and hold in my humour. The black symbols across her cheeks should have already given her away.

"I have had experiences with your people. They are a proud race," I state calmly, wondering why she would dare lie to the Lord of Drodal.

"Yes. Their pride can often cloud their judgement." Her lips remain a hard line and I smirk at her with feline prowess. She tenses her athletic form.

"I think we both know that you are no longer a member of the Eastern Tribes, Alanaat." Breccan's head flicks back and forth between us with incredulity.

"Of course she is!"

"She *was*. Before the black paint marked her as an outcast." I smirk inwardly at that; outcasts happen to be the favourite type of people.

"Elyra, you are being unreasonable!" he cries and I shake my head at his blindness. I am the one who has spent time with these people. I know their customs whilst he knows nothing.

"She is right, my Lord," Alanaat announces her voice unflinching. "But let's no longer pretend that this arrogant excuse of a woman is named Elyra." I smile at that, eyes turning amicable at the woman before me.

"It has been too long, my friend." I grin, outstretching my hand and she grasps it firmly with her own, her smile as wide as mine.

"You know this woman?" Breccan asks me in an outcry of confusion.

"Lady Lenora had… *gifted* us with her presence a long time ago." Al smirks with the memories of long ago. "She has remained a friend to my cadre and my people ever since."

"Cadre? What? I… I am afraid I am not following?" he looks between us with desperation and I laugh.

"Could you please give us a moment, Al? I will deal with you once I am finished here," I tell her with a mischievous glint in my eyes, one that she returns with a nod of her head before exiting the study.

"Am I the only one that is confused here?" Breccan says more to himself than to me. I chuckle lightly at the Lord frowning behind his desk.

"Calm down, Breccan. Alanaat and I know each other from my Belavier days when I had visited the Eastern shores of Zatria."

"And you're... you are friends?" he asks me with a puzzled expression.

"I suppose so. I never thought I would see her again after they exiled her." I remember that tragic day as if it were yesterday. Al was stoned by her people, beaten into exile. I lost all respect for her tribe that day.

"You did not follow her after they treated her so harshly?" my reminiscent smile fades with his questioning tone of my behaviour.

"I was called back to Eradan shortly after. It was then that I was... obtained." I dare not say betrayed or captured, obtained makes it sound more objective. "But I had ensured that Al and her cadre were safe. I had ordered her closest friends to take her to a shack I used to hide in from desert storms. I am assuming they have protected her ever since."

"I see," he says but I do not meet his eyes for fear of sympathy. Al and I had become close but she was ripped away from me before we really had a chance to blossom our friendship. And then there was Elyra... it seems that my friendships do not last long.

"Why is she here, Breccan?" I ask, suddenly acutely aware that her presence here must be more than for her to have simply got wind of my presence here.

"She came to discuss an allegiance."

"An allegiance against what?"

"We all know that a war is coming, Lenora," he tells me sympathetically. "If anything, it has become even more imminent since your return."

"There are few who know of my return," I answer, irritated by his remark.

"Indeed. But those few can taste war on the wind."

"I am not the bringer of war!" I cry in distaste.

"No. You are the bringer of revolution. A revolution which we are all eager to fight for." I clutch my head which has begun to ache.

"There is no escaping my reputation, is there?" he smiles apologetically and comes towards me to place his hands on my shoulders.

"You started this revolt, Lenora. It is you who must end it. You have more reason to do so than anyone else in Aneya. It is not your reputation that you cannot escape from, but your destiny... which, from my own experience, no-one can outrun." His ocean-blue eyes swim with adoration as he kisses my forehead, a fatherly gesture that I am not used to. I take a deep breath and return to the matter at hand.

"The Bolgren." His eyes widen at the mention before sighing deeply and sinking into his ornate chair.

"It is as I have feared."

"Go on?" I lead, placing my palms on his ebony desk and leaning towards him with a storm brewing in my eyes.

"A Bolgran is a dark creature. One that is not born, but created."

"Created how?" I demand. Why is Myrna creating such beasts and how is she doing it?

"There was a scripture that I had read long ago about creating a Bolgran and it disturbed me so much so that I have never mentioned it again. Until now."

"Get it over with, Breccan," I growl, I don't need his ghostly introduction. He sighs again, though this time it is shaky.

"A Bolgran is neither of this world nor any other. It needs a tether to tie them to this realm and they find this tether within our blood. But a Bolgran cannot be pure enough to remain human and so it is the merging of human blood and darkness that creates this putrid creature."

"And the merging is done how?" I resist the urge to scrape my fingernails into his desk. Breccan wipes the back of his hand across his forehead.

"One must bathe within the forbidden Obsidian Pool, contained within the deepest depths of Vangar. The black waters are said to burn the very core of your bones until there is nothing left but ash, until the sludge infuses your blood, turning the soul as black as the pool you bathed in. It is dark magic. And so it makes the bather the bearer of it."

"How is this related to the Bolgren?" I ask, nauseated with this process. Who would sell their soul for something so vile? I guess that I already have my answer to that.

"Because a Bolgran is created from the dark blood that now flows through the veins of the bather. A droplet of their black blood falls into the dark waters of the Obsidian Pool and evil forces unite to form a creature just as evil."

"The Bolgren must serve the bather then. A bond between the creator and the created." I furrow my brows, thinking about the magnitude of this situation. "Which means that she now has an army of Bolgren at her disposal."

"I never thought she would do such an atrocity." Breccan's eyes are filled with pain, a ghost of a time forgotten.

"If anyone were to bathe in the revolting waters of death, it would be Myrna," I mutter under my breath but he remains silent, contemplative. As if he is lost in memory. It is almost as if he is frightened.

"Breccan, ten Bolgren just appeared upon your grounds either as a threat to you or as a warning for me. Drodal needs its Lord. Because if there is to be a war, these Bolgren are sure to be at the front of it." He looks at me wistfully before nodding and straightening up from his chair.

"Bolgren are not invincible. They are vicious but can be killed as any human would. We should implement training for all of my soldiers immediately. They should amplify their skills in swiftness and agility should they need to evade a Bolgran's teeth and talons."

"Indeed." I recall how those talons feel as they scrape across your skin, how their teeth feel as they cut into your flesh. I instinctively touch my tender shoulder and feel the scars lingering there. "They should be prepared. I will leave you to your duties." I gently incline my posture forwards in a light bow before leaving his office.

I cannot wrap my head around what I just heard.

Myrna Verena subjected herself to the Obsidian Pool… she has converted her soul to darkness and for what? A revolting army of terrible beasts? She sickens me. How can one woman crave power so much? What happened to her to make her want to be so warped?

As I contemplate this, someone grabs my arm and hoists me into a nearby room. A supply room it would seem. Without thinking, I punch the person straight in the nose and a sickening crack and cry of pain makes me look towards them.

"Lukas?" I exclaim, watching Lukas frantically cupping his nose while it is pouring a fountain of blood into his hands.

"Why did you hit me?" he cries, using his sleeve to mop up the blood.

"Why did you drag me into a closet?" I return just as incredulously. But he smiles in that sweet way of his.

"I wanted to talk to you." I lean back, stunned, blinking a couple of times as if it will help my brain to understand.

"And you couldn't just walk up to me in the hallway to do so?"

"What I have to say isn't for any others who might happen to hear." He mops up the rest of the blood from his nose on his other sleeve until the bleeding stops and his white shirt is covered in scarlet. Nonetheless, his secret interests me.

"What is it?"

"I think that…" His eyes look around suspiciously, "Maer likes me." When I stare at him blankly, he sighs. "As in… *likes* me." He emphasises the word as if it is his doom and I stifle a laugh.

"So?" I answer simply, folding my arms across his chest. His innocent brown eyes turn wide as he wipes the back of his neck with his hand in confusion.

"I just… I love being her guardian when you're not around and she is such a great girl but—"

"Lukas. She's eleven." I point out, beginning to tap my foot in frustration.

"I know, Elyra. I just… I don't know what to do about it." He does not meet my gaze.

"Maer has spent a lot of time with you. I am not surprised if romantic feelings have arisen out of that. But so long as you do not reciprocate them, I won't have to figure out how to make slitting your throat appear as an accident." I raise an eyebrow to prompt him to speak but he just looks at me, sagging his shoulders, eyes aglow.

"You won't have to worry about that, Elyra. It is not Maer that I hold close to my heart." He regards me expectantly and I blink slowly, trying to process what he has just said. And once it has processed, I feel a sudden urge to run and hide.

"I should go," I say breathlessly, hand reaching for the door-handle. He steps closer, palms up as if trying to calm me.

"I did not mean to frighten you. I just… wanted you to know."

"And now I do." I open the door and the fresh air cools my burning cheeks.

"Won't you tell me what you're thinking at least?" he exhales like a scared child. He runs his fingers through his blonde hair. I cannot comprehend anything other than my thundering heart.

"Just… give me time." I gulp and he lets me leave. I do not wait to see his expression before leaping out into the hallway, the air caressing my reddening flush. My heartbeat quietens so that I can hear my thoughts.

Lukas likes *me*?

I mean… we have barely spent any time together apart from a few evenings but I have been so busy… I have not seen him in so long. How can I… how could he…By the Aerix. I clutch my head.

"I like the colour of your cheeks today," Elijah says jovially from beside me. I never even realised that he was walking towards me. I turn my face away from him to hide the flush from his prying gaze.

"Warriors are not supposed to blush, Elijah," I reply, annoyed that he has caught me in a vulnerable moment.

"Maybe so." I steal a glance at him and find him watching me in a peculiar way. "But women are." His green eyes are positively glistening today; it is hard to remain focused in the face of such beauty.

"Not me." I sigh. How can my life get any more complicated?

"Lukas finally told you, didn't he?" I look at him aghast but his face is surprisingly stern, not the amused expression I thought it would be.

"You knew?"

"I... noticed." He amends, holding his hands behind his back as he walks with me.

"I just... don't understand where this has come from." I sigh, brushing my hair behind an ear.

"How so?"

"There are thousands of girls living under this roof, thousands of them willing to be swept off of their feet by Lukas. And he chooses someone he barely knows." I look at him then and suddenly I feel embarrassed to be talking to Elijah about this.

Elijah gently grips my elbow and it stops me from my walking. I look into his smouldering green eyes and the breath gets knocked out of me. His full mouth tilts upwards slightly in a faint smirk.

"Maybe Lukas doesn't want a girl. Maybe he desires a woman." He searches my face for something that I do not know while my heartbeat races at the intimacy. I don't understand why when we are standing a foot apart but... something about Elijah's proximity electrifies me.

"There are plenty of them here too." Suddenly I become distracted by his shoulder-length chestnut hair, the array of colours so beautiful that I find myself wanting to touch them.

"Not like you." He breathes back, breath catching my face in a sweet caress. I part my lips involuntarily but his eyes never leave mine. His own narrow in concentration as he reaches out his hand calmly to place it on the upper side of my face so that he can stroke his thumb underneath my eye. The touch ignites the branches of lightening within my chest.

"In all my years... I have never seen an eye colour quite so beautiful," he murmurs and I am surprised at how softly he speaks that compliment. He continues staring into my grey eyes. "It is like the morning after a perfect storm. When the world is still enchanted by its onslaught, bewitched in the hopes that it will one day feel its wrath upon her face again." His voice is so husky and so different to the violent tone that I am usually accustomed to that I am stunned into silence.

Without warning, he retracts his hand in one swift movement and returns them to behind his back, face now being covered by the stern warrior once more. I look away from him abruptly, acutely aware that I have been holding my breath since his words. I gulp in the crisp air and it relaxes the tension lining my bones. But when I look into his eyes, I see guilt there.

"What is it?" I ask him softly.

"Nothing of importance." He smiles lightly but I know he does not mean it. I place my hand on his arm.

"Something troubles you. I can see the ghosts haunting your eyes."

"Today is… a difficult day for me." I wrack my brain to try and work out what it could possibly be but I still cannot forget the intensity of his previous words. Could Elijah think that I am attractive? No. Absurd.

"Why?" I decide to keep to the conversation at hand instead of wondering off into the realm of 'might' and 'could be'.

"It was a year ago today when Benjamin was…"

"Sent to Canaan." I realise aghast. By the Aerix. Today is the year mark for Benjamin's fate. The forges like to take their victims once the torture has been too strong. Today is when it could all end.

"I don't even know if he is still alive. But…" he looks to me with pain in his eyes. "I would have known, wouldn't I? I would have felt something if he…" he gulps, trying to suppress his emotions and it breaks my heart. He shakes his head to get rid of his emotions and smiles with a sniffle. "Anyway, I must go. I need to order a patrol so… see you around, Elyra."

"Elijah, please don't—" but he does not hear me, he just shrugs past me and walks defiantly to where he needs to go. I cannot help but think that though Elijah's steps are strong, that there is unimaginable pain shadowing his every footfall.

It is then that I decided how to fulfil my day.

I need two people to help me and I bet that they are not going to like it.

Chapter 13

"Lenora, have you completely lost your mind?" Alanaat exclaims to me but I just continue to grin while Roran puts his head in his hands as he sits down. "Breaking into Canaan and stealing a prisoner is suicide!"

I had organised Al and Roran to meet me in an empty infirmary room to tell them about my plot to break Benjamin free from his prison. I think Elijah deserves some closure and Benjamin needs his freedom.

"I broke out of Golnar myself with an unexpected passenger. Breaking into Canaan with the help of Eradan's General should be a piece of cake."

"You will be in pieces should you decide to follow through this stupid plan!" Al continues to shout though Roran has not said a word. "If you only need him to get in that why must I risk my life?"

"Because you know the Zatrian desert more than anyone. You would be able to get us there efficiently and safely which is what we must do should we survive this."

"This is insane." She laughs hysterically. "If we get caught, it will be death for us all!"

"Is it not worth it to save the innocent life of the only family Elijah has left?" I implore to her and she purses her lips together.

"What of the others?" I look at Al questioningly and she sees right through it, "I know you, Lenora Belavier, and you will not find it easy to save one soul amidst hundreds."

"That is true. But it is for their sake that I must. A plan to save one prisoner will go without fail. I would rather return to Canaan and Golnar with a sure-fire plan to save every single prisoner than desperately try to do it now and condemn them all." To this she does not answer, she just looks at me for a long while.

"I know that I have no reason to ask this of you after everything you have been through with your tribe, Al. But this is a man I care about who could lose his only brother today. He has been through so much already that I cannot bear the thought of him receiving word of his death. You do not have to enter Canaan with us; all I am asking of you is to navigate us through the desert safely so that we may rescue him from a terrible fate." She looks at me and smiles.

"How could I refuse Aneya's Warrior?" she jokes and I clasp her hand in thanks.

"Thank you, Al."

"You saved my life. And I am in a life debt to you. If this is something that you must ask of me, then I have no choice but to see you through it. Even if it is crazy." I laugh at her words and remember why I loved Alanaat in the first place.

I look to Roran who regards me in a contemplative manner. I am surprised that he has yet to say anything. I look into his clear blue eyes, searching for the man I knew before his betrayal.

"What do you say, friend. Ready to ride through hell with me once more?" I ask him and a smile slowly creeps over his face. He stands up and clasps my hand also.

"Always." He grins.

"Then let's get to it."

Alanaat had demanded that her cadre stay here much to their dislike. I was glad to see that all of the friends she had all those years ago still remain true even now. It was good to see them again.

Roran had spent the time preparing the horses and after a long debate, he agreed to let me ride Codax. After all, he has been my friend much longer than Roran's. Al's steed is a black athletic mare; I believe Mara is her name. Roran is going to borrow one from Breccan's ranks after bribing the stable boy. There is no way that I am going to tell Breccan about my quest this evening.

I spent the day making sure that my plan will work. I keep telling myself that everything will be fine but... what if it is not? What if I do more harm than good? What if Benjamin is not as much of a fighter as Elijah is and passed away soon after being entered into Canaan? No. Elijah's happiness is worth the risk. Seeing him the way he was today was unbearable. And maybe... this is my chance to do something really special for him.

As night begins to fall, the final preparations are underway. I am in my bedroom, dressing in my usual black attire though this time with a black cape to mark me as an officer to Myrna's crown. She had changed the light blue of Adrian's rule to a black so dark that that there is no end. Roran shall be adorned in her colours too although he does not need to, everyone will know his face as her General.

Maer sits upon the bed, wringing her hands together.

"Do you have to go?" she asks me in a small voice. I turn around and face her, kissing her forehead to give her some reassurance.

"It is a task that I must fulfil but I promise to be back before first light." She pouts her lip at me and it quivers.

"I feel like we're growing apart." I sit on the bed beside her and put my arm across her shoulders. She rests her head on my chest.

"I have just been very busy, Maer. Unfortunately a warrior never sleeps."

"I know. I wake up most days and you're already gone." She sniffles and I clutch her tighter. Does she really feel this way?

"Do you not like being in Drodal?" I ask her worried that maybe she does not want to be here.

"Yes, I do! Breccan has been really nice. He even showed me his secret lagoon today."

"Secret lagoon? That sounds pretty special," I admit with a grin, wishing that maybe Breccan will show me one day. Trust him to have a body of water all too himself.

"It was really pretty." I continue to stroke her hair absent-mindedly.

"And you have Lukas?" I pry, hoping that she would open up to me about him. She leans off of me then, holding her hands in her lap and looking at the floor.

"Yes. He is really nice. We have been spending a lot of time together."

"Indeed. I notice how much happier you are when he is around." I prompt her further and she bites her lip awkwardly.

"I… kind of like him," she admits to me, an apologetic smile as if I would be mad. It just makes me hurt more about what Lukas had told me.

"I know, sweetheart."

"You do?" she looks at me like a doe in the face of an arrow's course.

"It is not that hard to see," I tell her truthfully and she places her face in her hands.

"I know that it's stupid. We can never be…" she trails off and I sympathise with her for experiencing a love that can never be.

"Lukas will always be your friend, Maer. That is something you can count on."

"I know," she answers sadly and I know that she wishes there could be more. But she is so young. So young and naïve that it would be impossible. At least right now.

"Having him there as a friend is better than not having him around at all, is it not?" I find myself believing my words and I can see in her smile that she believes it too.

"Yes." She grins with a shrug of the shoulders.

I give Maer a tight squeeze before announcing my leave. I left her reading on the enormous bed and she seemed happy enough. Clad in my black uniform, I meet with Roran and Alanaat in the stables. We immediately saddle our horses and sit astride them, eager for the task to be afoot. I stroke Codax's long blonde mane and I sigh in contentment at the feel of his breathing along my legs. He whinnies at my touch and I smile.

"Codax is mine, Lenora. Remember that," Roran warns heartily from beside me on a white steed. The white coat of his horse really emphasises his golden form.

"Remember that it was I who gave him to you," I warn back and he nods a twinkle in his blue eyes.

"The desert plains are quite treacherous at night. It is rare that someone dares to race them in such conditions," Al comments gruffly from my other side, Mara blinking her brown eyes as if she too is goading us.

"Is that a challenge?" I cock my head towards Al and her white teeth greet me menacingly.

"How about it, Lenora?" she then looks to Roran as if sizing him up, "The General can come too. *If* he can keep up." Roran is taken aback by her words.

"The faster we get there the better. Who says we can't make it interesting?" he suggests and I admire his gall to attempt to make a bet with Alanaat. This bet is between them now.

"What are you offering?"

"If you win, I will give you one thousand gold pieces." Even I gasp at Roran's wager. That amount of money would make a great deal of difference to Al's life. I look at her but she is unflinching.

"Agreed." She grasps the reigns of Mara who is eager to go.

"Wait, what are your terms?" he asks hastily as she readies her horse. She only smirks as she surveys him and I know that she has something devilish planned. So I ready Codax too.

"Win the race, General, and then you won't have to find out." She teases before speeding Mara off into the night sky. I gently thrust my heel into Codax's side and we leave Roran behind as Broxen engulfs us, with him desperately riding after us.

Without even thinking, I laugh into Broxen with a lightness that I have not felt in a long while.

"I did not agree to this." Roran groans as he hides behind a sand dune opposite Al and me. We cannot stop our giggling at the prospect of Roran's punishment. The horses are tied to a makeshift post and even they refuse to look at the imminent sight.

"This is what happens when you lose, General."

"I cannot go into Canaan like this."

"They will understand." I have to cover my mouth with my hand to stop my laughing.

"I will not forgive you for this," he curses colourfully before revealing himself from the dune and I cannot believe my eyes.

Roran stands completely naked and devoid of his black uniform. His tan skin covers a brutal set of muscles that coat his entire body. Even like this, I can tell that he is lethal. His punishment is to enter Canaan wearing nothing but the large green leaf tied with a string to cover the part of him that even I would rather go life without seeing.

"This is ridiculous. What if this foolish prank jeopardises the mission?" he exclaims, folding his arms uncomfortably around his toned midriff.

"Then it is your job to make sure that it doesn't," Alanaat warns with a cock of her head and I can see that her feline eyes are contemplative as she regards his somewhat naked form.

"I can always find you a smaller leaf to suit your size if that would make you more comfortable?" I offer and his glare turns to me.

"That is not necessary. I find the breeze rather calming," He retorts icily and yet as he takes in my amused expression, his glare melts to reveal his smile. With all joking aside, I pat my dagger beside my hip and focus on my task.

"I think it's time that we break into prison," I announce and our plan is still as smooth as it was this morning.

Alanaat will hide with the horses to await our return while Roran and I approach Canaan's entrance. We figured we could use Roran's punishment as an advantage here just to make sure the events unfold as naturally as possible. As we breach the final dune, Canaan stands before us.

A shiver crawls along every bone in my body.

It looks exactly the same as Golnar. The cylindrical shape, the small entrance, the sand covered roof... I wonder if it is the same in all aspects too. My mouth becomes dry at the thought of having to go back in there... where so much evil exists...

But I know I have to.

Benjamin could still be alive in this Aerix-forsaken prison and I am not wasting any more time watching Elijah's grief.

Here we go.

Roran and I approach the structure carefully, Roran assuming the role of an embarrassed General naturally. As he hides to the side, I knock upon the steel door of Canaan and a guard opens the doors instantly, a small knife poised to strike at potential trespassers. The middle-aged man sees my uniform and puts his weapon down, furrowing his eyebrows.

"We were not expecting Eradanian Officials."

"That is the point of an impromptu inspection of your facility," I counter, lacing my voice with authority. He scowls at me for a while so I decide to continue. "But it seems that we have an unlikely predicament tainting our visit here."

"*We*?" as the guard inquires, Roran sticks out his arm to let him know his presence here.

"That would be me," he announces himself in an exhausted manner. The guard cranes his neck outside to find Roran scantily clad with his leaf and his eyes widen in surprise. But then, he realises who he is.

"General Maar, sir!" he clears his throat gruffly before saluting to Roran.

"At ease, soldier," Roran rolls his eyes at him and I try to look as impassive as possible.

"What happened to you, sir?"

"Well... you know how the Sentillian are. We are brothers. This seems to come at the price of tormenting pranks." I catch Roran flick his eyes to me and I smirk at his detriment.

"Please come in!" the guard rushes his General into the compound and allows me to follow suit.

The inside is the same as Golnar was when I escaped; a large dreary front room with a small reception area to the far side. On the other side are the elevator doors. I can feel the burning sensation on my hands as if I had just climbed up the shaft mere seconds ago. I can see the steam seeping out from the cracks in the door... what are those men enduring right now?

A nudge from Roran makes me realise that I had been frowning at the elevator entrance for some time and I immediately return my attention to the reception guard that had let us in. He is still staring at Roran with incredulity. Three guesses why. The most feared and revered General of the Sentillian Army of Eradan stands naked before him.

"Do you wish to stare at the General's body all night or do you wish to fetch him some attire?" I scold him and he jumps at the sternness in my voice. He immediately rushes into the reception area to get more dreary clothes for Roran to adorn.

"I still cannot believe you have made me do this." Roran says through gritted teeth as he leans in beside me.

"You should not have goaded a woman who knows the Zatrian desert like the back of her hand," I scold him in a whisper to which he only rolls his blue eyes. With a smirk, I look down at his naked form as he cups his manhood away from sight.

"I bet that you are enjoying this, Lenora," he says gruffly.

"One can never have too much humility, General." He catches my eye and his own grin mimics my own. It has been a long time since we were amicable. It is strange to be back in this habit with him but I also feel as if I should not accept it so quickly.

The guard returns with the clothes hastily and Roran adorns them just as efficiently; just simple black attire not near enough to the quality of what he was wearing before but at least it takes him out of his misery. Alanaat would not be pleased.

"May I ask how you came to be in this… state, sir?" the guard asks sceptically and once Roran is dressed, he just scowls at the man before him.

"I lost a bet," he growls and I have to hold in my laughter; I did not think that he would admit to it so easily.

"I see." The guard still scrutinises him and it is setting me on edge. He does not suspect, does he?

"I have already endured this torture and I do not intend to relive it by relaying it to you. I have a job to do, sentry, and I expect you to let me do it." I am surprised at the authority in Roran's voice but it does what it is supposed to; the guard is stunned into action.

"Of course! I meant no disrespect by you or your position as General. Please go ahead," he speaks his words frantically before running back to his station.

As we walk to the elevator doors, I cast a sideways glance at Roran who is smirking like a jungle cat after capturing its prey. The doors open by command of the guard behind us.

"We expect open access," I call back to him and the man mumbles some form of agreement to me.

We step into the elevator and it starts to descend to the residential level of Canaan. I suppose it is here we can expect to find Benjamin; after all it is an ungodly hour. Standing within the sweltering cylinder of the elevator shaft, my heart begins to pound with our impending task.

What if he is dead?

What if the guards suspect our motives?

What if I cannot save him?

Before I know it, Roran touches his hand to mine and I am startled by his touch. I look to him and I only see sympathy in his eyes.

"You can do this," he murmurs to me and my mouth tilts upwards ever so slightly in a smile. He always knew the right things to say. I simply nod in acquiescence and then the elevator stops as the doors open to reveal darkness and damp.

Just like Golnar, an array of cells line the walls as far as the eye can see. I have no idea where to even begin down here. I do not even know what Benjamin looks like. All we have to do is be as official as possible which should not be too hard given our pasts.

I take a deep breath and begin the long walk along the cells. My heart breaks at the thin frail forms I see curled up in the too-small living space. I can even hear faint sobbing echoing throughout the damp walls. The smell of dirt is toxic to my lungs and my eyes sting from not being able to help the poor men flinching from our presence.

I wish I could save them all.

But I must remain focused.

Benjamin is the focus here.

I try to drown out the pleas and cries from my mind until we come across a guard stationed down on this level. Perfect. We are getting nowhere with searching on our own.

"You there," I call to him and he stands startled from leaning against one of the walls. Roran tenses beside me not having expected my ask for help.

"No women on this level." The man growls at me and I give him a feline smile worthy of a lioness.

"I can take care of myself but you have my gratitude for your concern." I tell him cockily and I catch him gulping in surprise.

"What is your business here?" he eyes Roran and me suspiciously, but it is nothing I can't handle.

"We need your help in finding an inmate." I cock my head to the side as I study him, looking at my fingernails in an effort to appear bored.

"Which inmate?"

"A Benjamin Warren?" I keep my voice as innocent as possible but the guard's eyes still widen at the mention of the name.

"Warren? Why on earth would you be interested in him?"

"We have our reasons," Roran interjects, lacing his voice with authority. He uses his renowned scowl against the guard and he looks like he could unleash an all manner of hell upon an uncooperative sentry.

"I am just enquiring due to procedure…" the guard stammers through his sentence and I roll my eyes at him.

"Like you have ever cared about procedure." I sneer at him. "Now either point us in the right direction or take us there because the Queen does not take those who waste her time lightly and nor do we."

The guard stares into my smouldering gaze and it seems to snap him back into reality. He regards us both apologetically before pointing his finger to the left side of this level and leading onwards. Roran and I follow on from behind him, not needing to say a word.

I would like nothing more than to slit the throat of this grungy bastard leading us onward. Only the Aerix know what pain he has inflicted upon these men, what he would do to the women if he was stationed at Golnar. I clench my fists and my jaw together to stop me from doing something that could compromise this task.

"Are you all right?" Roran whispers so that only I can hear.

"Fine." I have no doubt that he knows that I am not simply fine but Roran knows when I am in no mood to talk. This is one of those times. And so he simply remains silent as we trudge our way through the mud down the vast expanse of cells stretching out before us.

"Warren is an interesting one. Keeps to himself, but always remains a target."

"Target for what?" I ask, possibly a little too quickly. I know that it is foolish to even think that he has survived Canaan unscathed but the thought of Elijah's little brother being tortured… I would like to kill the men and women that even dared. Nonetheless the guard turns to look at me condescendingly.

"Miss… are you aware of what *happens* in these prisons?" he asks incredulously and it is an effort to keep my dagger sheathed. I grind my teeth together and look at him murderously.

"Only too well, *sentry*." He shrinks back from my glare and pushes forward. It is only silent for a few more seconds until we reach a stop.

In front of an empty cell.

I don't even comprehend my actions until they are already being carried out.

I grab the guard's throat with my nails and push him against the wall violently.

"Where the hell is he?" I demand of him but his eyes are simply aghast at my aggression. Roran stands fast beside me, recognising the danger that I pose to this operation.

"He has a habit of roaming," the guard says through his teeth, barely able to choke the words out. In reflex, I apply more pressure to his throat and his eyes roll to the back of his head.

"Elyra, that's enough," Roran says sternly into my ear.

"Don't tell me what to do," I growl back at him, eyes never leaving the fading life of the guard before me as I squeeze even tighter. This man led us on a wild goose chase. Does he not realise how important this is to me?

"You will do as your commanding officer tells you, Elyra." The bitter authoritative edge to his voice has me lowering my hand and the man splutters his life out in coughs before my feet.

The rage flooding through me knows no end. I glare at Roran with all my might. How dare he stop me? Who is he to stop me when I was *his* commanding officer all those years ago? Does he not realise that he is treading a dangerous line with his words after all that he has done to me?

"Stand down, Elyra. Or will Her Majesty have to hear of your indiscretions?" my eyes soften at his words then.

Shit.

I had almost ruined this mission with my anger. Roran is merely using his authority over me in this scenario. We are agents of the Crown in this instant. And if Myrna ever found out that I was here… I do not even want to imagine the consequences.

"Apologies, General. You know how important this man is to our endeavours," I tell him calmly, going along with his scenario.

"And you know that I could have you stripped of your title and banished from Eradan's borders so you better keep in line before you do something we will both regret." His burning blue gaze makes me lose my breath. It is amazing how much power Roran truly holds. I simply nod in affirmation and he turns to the guard clutching at his throat upon the floor.

"Where could Benjamin Warren possibly be?" his piercing blue stare strikes fear into the mundane eyes of the guard as he rises to his feet, careful not to look at me directly.

"I don't know, sir. All inmates are to remain in their cells." His confidence astounds me but I roll my eyes nonetheless.

"Yeah, right," I mutter under my breath, turning around to face the empty cell. I will myself not to look at any of the other inmates who are either sleeping or staring at our encounter.

The guilt would be too much.

Benjamin is a target. Where do all targets go? Or rather…

Where do they get taken?

My eyes narrow at the sight of the quaint wooden door just North of us, sitting in the inner ring of Canaan's structure. The store cupboard. Where unknown tortures await. My heartbeat quickens at the mere thought of the room but Benjamin could be in there.

"Let's go," I say through gritted teeth and though Roran has no idea what just occurred inside my head, he knows not to question me.

"May I—" the guard begins but I cut him off swiftly.

"No. Return to your duties or lack thereof." I sneer and he shrinks back into the shadows to resume his post without another word.

In silence, Roran and I edge nearer to the door, all the while my heart thumping loudly inside my head. My breathing is laboured and I can tell that he notices but I simply focus on the door in front of me.

I can hear grunts and smacks faintly from the other side.

Without thinking of a strategy, I barge through the door with Roran at my heels and my stomach turns at what I see before me. Behind the familiar stacks of utilities are two hulking men and one woman towering over a slim figure curled up on the floor.

Benjamin.

It must be.

He does not even dare to see who has come in, he just remains curled up in the foetal position. My stomach turns when I see the bruises and the blood coating him. I dare not even imagine what bones could be broken.

The men and woman look upwards at the intrusion and stare wide-eyed at me.

"A woman," One says, cocking his head to the side. I ignore his roving eyes and simply stare daggers at them all, hand poised for the real one strapped to my side. I particularly aim my aggression to the woman. Plain and unassuming. Her impassive face stares back at me, fists raw from stifled punches. I have never come across a female guard in my times in Golnar. I had assumed that the atrocities would be too much for them to bear. But to participate in them all the same? Despicable.

"That's funny, I thought I saw three," I counter, baring my teeth as a show of aggression. They all sneer at that and I could not care less.

"Beat it, lady. We have unfinished business," the other man jerks his head in the direction of Benjamin who whimpers in response.

"Let me finish it for you." I snarl, "This beating is *over*." The guards look at each other in amusement.

"Please just do as she says," Roran says from behind me in a tired tone. I can tell that he wishes for blood not to be spilled this morning. It's too late for that, my friend.

"I don't take orders from whores." The man at the front spits at me and my vision flashes red.

"By the Aerix." I hear Roran touch his hand to his head in exasperation for the guards not taking head of his warning. I cannot help the murderous chuckle emanating from my smirking mouth. I unsheathe my dagger and play with it mindlessly, twirling it around my fingers.

"What's so funny?" the woman asks warily.

"Arrogance just signed your death warrant," I inform her.

"I don't think s—"

Before she can finish speaking, I throw my dagger so swiftly that when it lands in her throat, the others have no idea how it had even gotten there. Blood spouts from the wound in her neck violently and her friends simply stare wildly at it.

By the time the others try to move, I aggressively pull my dagger out of the woman's throat and slit the throat of the man next to me who falls instantly alongside his friend. The other one grabs me from behind with his bicep crushing against my jugular. My vision blurs very quickly but I shove the hilt of the dagger upwards into his groin and as he bends his knees, I shove the crook of my elbow hard into his jaw and he falls beside his fallen friends. Without a second thought, I kneel down and plunge the dagger into his back for good measure. No one can know that I was here.

"I hate this cupboard." I say to myself breathlessly.

I did not realise that I was staring at the bodies until Roran cleared his throat to bring me back to reality. My heart is thumping wildly inside my chest and splatters of scarlet coat my skin in patterns that I will always be familiar with. I stare into Roran's clear blue eyes and see the monster mirrored in their shine.

"I have seen you fight many times, Lenora. But I have never seen you quite like that," he murmurs, gazing at me either in shock or sympathy, I cannot tell. I hate the thought of both.

"Now is not the time, Roran," I warn him. "Help Benjamin."

While I wipe off the worst of the blood from myself, I can hear Roran helping Benjamin up alongside some mild conversation but I choose not to look at him yet. Not until I try to erase as much of the bloodshed as I can. All that remains are some mild stains on my black uniform but they are not noticeable.

"Who are you?" a surprisingly calm voice asks and I turn to look at Benjamin who raises his eyebrows at the sight of me.

Benjamin is tall with a lean figure attached to broad shoulders though not as bulky as Elijah's muscular form. His light brown hair is cropped short and his brown eyes glow a hint of amber. Stubble frames his jaw but I can tell that he would rather not have it there. It is obvious that starvation has weakened his bones and he has taken such a brutal beating... but even so, he looks regal, like the ruler Elijah's heart would not allow himself to be.

"I am a friend of Elijah's," I admit to him and he looks as if he has not heard that name in such a long time.

"He sent you?"

"I came by my wishes, not his own."

"He did not... wish to... rescue me himself?" his tone is laced with bitterness and my heart goes out to him because he really has no idea.

"He tried. Many times. Elijah has not left your side despite Canaan's steel walls." Tears well in his eyes but he swallows them down quickly.

"And what makes you so special to endure this feat?" I can see that he is trying to remain strong but the relief is flooding out of him.

"We figured," Roran smirks, "That if we were going to break into a prison, we could use the assistance of someone who has broken out of one." Benjamin's eyes widen at Roran's words before he turns back to me.

"Golnar's Ghost?" he whispers. Deciding that now is not the time for pleasantries, I wish to get out of this prison before the dreaded sirens ensue.

"If this place is at all similar to Golnar then the work rotation would mean that a guard is due in about ten minutes at which point we need to be halfway across Zatria."

"Are you well enough to walk?" Roran asks authoritatively to Benjamin.

"I'd run with two broken legs if it means getting out of this place." He flashes us a devilish grin and my heart swells at how similar it is to Elijah's.

"Let's go," I tell them both.

Heading towards the elevator is easy and as the door opens with us three grinning in triumph, a sinking feeling plummets through my stomach as I look at Roran. He notices my gaze instantly.

"What is it?"

"What do you suppose the guards will tell Myrna when she realises that she did not authorise this visit?" I ask him in a small voice. Benjamin's grin too falls from his face at the mention of this problem.

"It will be weeks before the word is even out, Lenora." He tries to console me.

"Lenora?" Ben looks between me and Roran in shock but Roran holds up his palm towards him to silence any response to my name. He does as he says and closes his mouth curtly.

"We need your reputation to be intact, Roran. I need you on the inside."

"We won't need that element when we return to Eradan. All of Aneya will know that we have come to claim it. There will be no need for disguises."

"And Jasper? Will he suffer for your insubordination?" he flinches as he realises the true consequences of his actions and I can tell that it is not one that he took into account upon taking this mission. He slacks in defeat and pinches the bridge of his nose with his thumb and forefinger.

"You're right." He sighs. "What do you suppose we do?"

I wrack my brains fiercely trying to think of a way that Roran can be safe from scorn. We are forever losing crucial time waiting to use the elevator and a plan must come swiftly if we should get out of here alive.

Come on, Lenora.

Think.

Think.

Yes.

"I have a plan that may work… but it might hurt a little." I smirk gleefully.

Chapter 14

Roran grunts as yet another punch lands against his jaw and spits blood from his mouth as he does. I have lost count of how many punches I have thrown against him at this point but if this plan is to work, then Roran will need to have had a completely incapacitating beating to make it believable to the guards.

I am unsure as to whether or not I am enjoying this. It seems to me that this plan allows for perfect cover as well as small vengeance for what Roran had done to me.

Benjamin can barely watch what is happening and tries his best to ignore it. I guess after being beaten so much, the last thing you would like to see is someone else undergoing the same fate.

"I think you are enjoying this a little too much," Roran says through gritted teeth. His right eye is purple and swollen and his left cheek has a large bruise appearing which does a lot to distract from his bleeding gums and split lip. He spits out blood from his mouth again and his teeth are coated in its sheen.

"It's been a long time coming, old friend." I return to him before swiftly landing one last final blow to the side of his face. He growls in anger from the force of it. "That should do it."

"You are lucky that I like you," he snarls, wiping the back of his hand against his bleeding and, now, broken nose. I fold my arms across my chest in defiance.

"It is you who is lucky that I like you, Roran. Or else I would not have gone so easy on you." He sighs knowingly before standing up from his kneeling position on the floor.

"I guess I deserved that," he mumbles and I smile. He looks to a frightened Benjamin who is trying his best to remain composed after seeing such violence.

"So, what do you think? An improvement?" Roran points to his face with a sly smirk and I truly admire him for accepting this plan without any reservations despite the obvious consequences for him.

"I would not go that far..." Benjamin replies uneasily and I gently grab his hand to turn his attention towards me.

"Roran and I have been in this field for a very long time. There is a reason why we are the best. And it is because we will do absolutely anything to ensure our missions are successful. I have taken beatings for him and he has done the same for me. This work relies on mutual trust so do not fear for him, he knows it is the best way of saving us all." Benjamin's eyes soften at my words and he looks to Roran who shrugs amicably with a smile. He nods, accepting what I have told him.

"Please do not take too long in chasing after me, Roran, or else I will fear the worst." My voice takes on a serious note, one that he picks up on instantly.

"Believe me, Lenora. After getting beaten like this, I waste no time in attaining vengeance." He winks.

"Just take your position." I roll my eyes and grip Benjamin's arm firmly to lead him into the elevator at last. Roran lies down on the floor as if he was just sneakily attacked but before he closes his eyes, he gazes at me with genuine concern.

"Be safe." My insides seem to uncoil from their tension at his words.

"Relax. This is not my first time breaking out of prison." And as the doors close, I can just make out Roran's cheeky grin as they shut completely and we begin our ascent.

"You care a lot for the General," Benjamin states in a quiet voice as if he is afraid to even make the comment. I waste no time in giving him my reply.

"I care a lot for your brother. So let's return you to him, okay?" he nods with the first real hint of happiness that I have seen from him yet. I am glad that he is excited about this prospect and not afraid of it.

I warn him to expect a little aggression from me on the counts of being a Palace Official and he agrees to it willingly. I believe that he is getting used to these ways.

The doors open.

I stride forward strongly, half-dragging Benjamin to keep up with me. I keep a stern expression on my face as I make sight of the lone guard at the reception desk and my dagger pulses against my hip, getting ready to be used should the need arise. The guard's puzzled expression is not new to me as he takes in Roran's disappearance and the prisoner beside me.

"Where is General Maar?" he calls to me as he steps out from behind the desk.

"Maar is conducting the rest of the inspection. He instructed me to prepare this prisoner for travel."

"And why exactly is there a prisoner in your possession?" I continue to walk briskly towards the exit without stopping to acknowledge him, Benjamin positively grunting beside me from the force of my pull.

"We were instructed to retrieve this man for interrogation."

"By whose orders?" it is clear that this man will not stop talking so I stop in my tracks and laugh bitterly at him.

"*I* am a Palace Official. *I* do not need to answer to prison dogs like you. This information is highly classified and you are verging on treason should you persist in your quest to interfere and trust me when I say that Eradanian prisons are not. Worth. Visiting." My tone gets increasingly more aggressive as I go on, the same as the guard shrinks back more and more as I begin to tower over him.

"A-a-as you wish, ma'am," he stammers, truly terrified.

"Good. Instruct the General to meet me outside when he appears," I ask gruffly and surge forwards again, Benjamin lurking with the sudden speed. My grip on his arm remains strong and I worry that he may have something to show for it on his skin later. But that is not my main concern.

We are so close to freedom and I do not want anything to affect it now when we are so close…

"Quit whining you useless pig!" I hear a woman snarl from far behind me. It stops me just as I have reached the exit doors.

"Please d-don't…" a man says shakily in response and my muscles tense at this situation. Without pausing for thought, I gently push Benjamin ahead of me and out the doors.

"Over the dune, a Zatrian woman is waiting for you. Go to her. And do it now," I whisper.

"No—"

"*Go.*" I urge him and he does as I say.

Taking a deep breath, I turn around to see the situation unfold before me. The guard that was here before has disappeared but another one is in his place, larger and seemingly more hostile despite being female. She is tugging a man whose wrists are bound in steel chains. The man seems Zatrian to me with his spiky black hair and golden brown skin. A new prisoner.

"It's time for your initiation." The guard chuckles darkly, completely ignoring the man's protests.

My insides freeze at the mere mention of the word. I do not need to be a guard to know what an initiation entails. It seems that women are not immune to such actions. I know that I am rapidly losing time before someone finds an incapacitated Roran but I will be damned should I condemn this man to that fate.

"What is going on here?" I ask in the most official tone I can muster despite my incurring rage.

The guard looks at me not as a threat but as a mere obstacle in the way of her fun. The prisoner however looks at me in fear as if I, too, am there to hurt him or would like him all to myself. The thought makes me sick. No matter how handsome he is; light blue eyes peak out from beneath thick black lashes which are a stark contrast to his otherwise dark features. I have not seen anything like it before.

"Who are you?" the guard asks me sceptically, shoulders straightening in preparation for the threat that I pose.

"I was sent here by the Palace to examine Canaan with an impromptu inspection." I fold my arms across my chest to show her that I will not let this continue if I can help it. The prisoner clenches his jaw and looks away. It seems that he is not happy that a someone not of Canaan has found him in this position.

"For what purpose?" her grip on the chains only grows stronger.

"For whatever purposes that I deem fit." She tilts her head back as she regards me and then she takes in the blood splattered over my black attire; surprisingly, she smiles.

"I have never seen a female Palace Official before. Let alone one who partakes in the violence of Canaan." Judging by her roving eyes, I was wrong to assume that this guard likes men alone. Even so, she does not know that the violence she refers to extends to the guards rather than the prisoners as she assumes. This is an opportunity not to shed more blood than need be.

"I am accustomed to compliance. Those who do not obey make it worse for themselves." The prisoner whimpers as if his only hope just vanished before his eyes. Little does he know.

"I see. What makes you think that I will give up my prize so easily?" good, she believes the ruse. I aim a sinister smirk at the cowering man.

"What makes you think that I won't let you have him afterwards?" I inspect my fingernails carelessly to entice her and I can see the wheels turning in her head.

"What if I don't want your sloppy seconds?" she raises a bushy eyebrow and I can see the man desperately trying to ignore our conversation.

"I will just be warming him up, I assure you." I look up at her seductively and I can tell that she is definitely considering this so I decide to give her a little more persuasion. "Maybe… you can even join us after a while?" I bite my lip and I know that I have her in the palm of my hand. How predictable.

"Use this room." She gestures to the steel door behind her, "Knock when you're through with this pig."

"Please, don't do this…" the man whimpers once again and I feel guilty for having tortured him mentally like this.

"Thank you." I say to the guard as I fiercely grab the chain from her and yank the man forwards.

But as the guard turns away, sniggering to herself, I swiftly force the pommel of my dagger against the back of her head and blood spurts against my face but she falls to the floor effortlessly nonetheless.

"What—" the man begins with a gasp but I just yank him with me towards the exit of Canaan. There is no telling when that alarm will begin to sound and sure enough its wails echo throughout the entire building, piercing my eardrums almost causing them to bleed.

They have found Roran.

It's working.

As soon as we touch foot on sand, I force the man to look at me by yanking on his chain and his turquoise eyes search mine frantically for answers, shock still clinging to his irises.

"You know how to navigate the desert, yes?" I ask him without sincerity.

"Y—yes, but—"

"You must go home. Do not tell anyone of this encounter or about me. But please, you must hurry should you escape their wrath." I plead with him and his eyes only glimmer with confusion.

"Why are you doing this for me? You don't know who I am. What I have done."

"Your past is irrelevant. No-one deserves that fate." He looks over the dunes to where he must suspect Benjamin has gone and understands my business here, how his life was saved also.

"H-How can I even… I-is there anything I can—"

"Just go!" I beg him, hearing the guards scuffling around Canaan at wind of the intruder. It is enough to scare him into action and he gives one last thankful glance at me.

"I will not forget this day," he murmurs before running across the dunes as if being chased by wildfire.

I trudge quickly over the dunes to where Benjamin and Alanaat wait for me and I know that I must act quickly if I am to outrun the arrows that will no doubt be flying in my direction when they realise that it was me who infiltrated them.

"You saved someone else. Are you crazy?" Alanaat hisses lowly. She must have heard my exchange.

"He needed saving." I help Benjamin mount Codax and I sit behind him, grabbing the reigns.

"You better hope it does not cost us," she answers as she releases us from the post and mounts her brilliant mare. "Where is the General?" she then asks, looking at his horse still tied to the post.

"Where is she?" I hear Roran bellow from Canaan. "Traitor! There is a traitor in our ranks!" he is putting on a good show at least. Still, it answers Al's question and she surges forward on Mara and Codax follows suit.

We race across the dunes unseen thanks to Alanaat's extensive navigation skills and by the time we almost reach Drodal, we are all positively aglow with hysteria at having succeeded in our quest. After dismounting the steeds and letting them drink their fill of water, we stand smiling at each other in triumph.

"I cannot thank you enough for what you have done for me," Benjamin says appreciatively.

"We didn't even know if it was going to work." Al replies, casting me an amused smirk. Benjamin's face contorts into angst at the thought of us not having a full-proof plan.

"Not to worry," I gently clip his shoulder with my hand, "You're alive, aren't you?" I look at him, knowing that my eyes are alight with glee and he grins at me.

"You best wash the gore off of your face. Your brother will not be most pleased should he see you like that." Al fetches a pale of water and a rag and Benjamin immediately begins to rid himself of the blood coating his body.

When the water has turned scarlet, Benjamin is much cleaner than he was before. His face still holds host to severe bruising but that is to be expected. His light brown hair is clean of dirt and Al even managed to find a simple brown outfit for him to wear that was lying around the stables; it wasn't much but it is far better than rags covered in his own blood.

"You look great," I tell him reassuringly but I cannot shake the angst pulsating off of him as he cups the back of his neck with his hand nervously. "Is everything all right?"

"What if… what if he doesn't like me anymore?" he asks in a small voice, eyes never meeting ours.

"Your brother will be nothing short of delighted to see you, Benjamin. You are his brother." Al tries to console and he nods as if it does not really have an impact on him.

"What is it?" I edge nearer to him, leaning down so that he has no choice but to look into my eyes. All I can see is guilt.

"If I was strong enough… none of this would have ever happened."

"This has got nothing to do with your perceptions of strength. You did not give up. You survived. Isn't that what matters most?" I try to keep this brief because as much as I would like to spend hours consoling him, he has a brother to reunite with.

Just as Benjamin begins to give me a warm smile, Roran comes charging in on his steed; face as bloody as when I last saw it. Nonetheless his beaming grin is enough to make me chuckle. He leaps off of his horse and hugs me very much to my surprise.

"We did it! The plan worked. They don't suspect a thing. They are currently trying to figure out who that woman was and what her motive would be to steal a prisoner which, of course, will lead them nowhere! By the Aerix, it's just like old times!" without warning, he picks me up by my waist and spins me around, his smile never ceasing. I cannot help but laugh at his enthusiasm.

"Easy there, big boy. We want Lenora to survive the night without being crushed." Alanaat rolls her eyes at Roran and he sets me down with a pout.

"You are just upset because you want to see me naked again." He winks at her and she gives him a scolding glare that he merely shrugs away in amusement.

"Excuse me, what?" Benjamin says in confusion.

"Don't worry. There wasn't much to see." I clue Benjamin in and he grins at the banter between us all.

"Hurry up and change, will you?" Al cries and Roran mockingly jumps at her abrasive tone. "We don't have time for your childish games."

Roran does as he is asked and adorns the same brown outfit as Benjamin and washes his face to clear the blood from his own injuries. Once everyone is sorted, we agreed that I would lead the charge and find out where Elijah is. It turns out; I did not have a difficult search as I see him standing in front of the great open doors of the fortress. However… he seems to be arguing with the sentry posted there.

Not letting this damper my excitement, we silently move along the edge of the courtyard, Benjamin desperately trying to crane to see Elijah but having stone columns and trees blocking his view. I tell them to wait around the corner and their grins are heart-warming. Roran has to hold the back of Benjamin's shirt to stop him from running to where Elijah's angry voice sounds.

"I do not care if you have already checked; I need to know where she is now!" Elijah growls and just as I turn the corner I see that Elijah has grasped the collar of the sentry's shirt and has threateningly pulled him within an inch of his face.

At my emergence, he lets the guard go immediately but he is not happy to see me as I had hoped. The guard shrinks back into the shadows of his post.

"Something the matter?" I ask him cheekily and his familiar scowl only makes me smirk.

"Where have you been?" his tone is angry and it sets me on edge.

"I have been preparing a surprise—"

"This needed to be discussed hours ago!" he cuts me off and I stare at his wild eyes, wondering if this is the best time. I can only imagine what the others are thinking. Still, I desperately try to cling to any semblance of anticipation as my heart is about to burst from the secret I am withholding from him.

"But if you would just listen—"

"No, it is *you* who must listen."

"Elijah, please, I have brought you something—" I continue excitedly but he cuts me off yet again. I dare not gesture behind me yet.

"This is a matter of urgency, Elyra, can you not understand that?" I have never seen him so worked up and he is scaring me. For a moment, I forget about those waiting for my signal.

"What could be so important?" I ask in confusion. I can see the muscles in his arms tense and relax continuously. His strong jaw flexes. What could be so hard for Elijah to say? Does he have no idea what surprise lurks behind me?

"It is a sensitive matter so I must ask you not to over-react." I stop dead in my tracks and eye him suspiciously though he remains impassive. I know that I should just force Benjamin upon him but his urgent manner is making me suspicious.

"No promises, Warren." I fold my arms across my chest defiantly. He sighs in resignation. I can only hope that the others are not getting restless but I can imagine that they are instead listening intently to this conversation.

"I am concerned for Maer's motives in being here." I blink in surprise and forget all else bar that statement.

"Excuse me?"

"She spends a lot of time by herself despite being so friendly. She often wonders about the gardens as if looking for someone of interest. But the only person I see her interested in is Breccan."

"That is because she likes him," I growl at him, offended that he would have such presumptions. Is a little girl not allowed to want to spend time with an honourable man?

"Or because she has been assigned a task."

"If you are trying to tell me that Maer is some secret assassin then you must be more delusional than I thought. She is a victim." I cannot believe what he is insinuating. She is *eleven*.

"Or she may just play it very well, Elyra."

"I never thought that you would be so insecure as to accuse a child." I sneer at him and this arouses his anger.

"You think that I am doing this lightly?" he bellows but it does not deter me.

"I think that you are threatened by the dangers posed in this war and so the first people you accuse are the ones that haven't been here long!"

"*I* fear for my Lord's safety," he spits at me, animosity securing every inch of his posture.

"You fear the likes of an eleven-year-old," I bite back and it only adds more fuel to the flames.

"Are you so incompetent that you cannot even see the signs?" he exclaims. "She has had dark dealings in the past. Who is to say that those dealings have ceased?"

"They have," I snarl with all my might, "I made sure of it."

"Ah, I see. So when Elyra commands, Maer obeys?" I am completely shocked at his behaviour. I cannot believe we are even having this conversation.

I grow so angry that my branches of lightning ignite inside my chest but I control myself enough to keep it there. I simply step forwards, hands fisted with the effort of trying to keep calm and maintain the storm in my eyes instead as I glare at the man I just risked everything for.

"Maer may not be my blood but she is as good a daughter as any. If you accuse her, you accuse me. And trust me when I say that it will not end well for you should you continue this foolish presumption."

"I just wanted you to be aware—" he tries but I just hold up my hand to stop him. I don't need to hear anymore.

"This conversation is over."

I do not look at him as I stride past him, desperately trying not to cry. But before I forget, I turn on my heels and face him to find a very sorrowful Elijah still in the doorway facing me. I cannot help but feel that this is a betrayal. Just of a sort that I am not used to. But as I see Benjamin's form slowly appear silently behind Elijah, I know that I must tell him.

"You want to know where I have been all night?" I call to him shakily and his pained eyes only blink in defeat. "Turn around."

With a puzzled expression, he does as I say. Without even waiting for his reaction, I continue to storm my way down the corridor in desperate hopes of finding somewhere, anywhere… that I can go to forget this feeling. But before I completely lose myself, I hear the heart-warming sound of brothers reuniting. And I should be happy for them…

But all I can feel is my heart breaking instead.

Chapter 15

Still trying to hold in my tears, I continue on my way through the Keep.

I don't know where I am going... I am not even sure if I care.

I just cannot believe that after all I have done for him... after all that I have just risked... he accused a vulnerable child of dark intentions.

I know I should not care as much as I do. It is only a suspicion, an inkling at best. But if there is someone targeting my father, he should be looking at people with motive, people with the capacity to even commit the crime. Not a child that I consider my own.

Before I realise my surroundings, a strong arm blocks me in my path and I do not need much detail to know that it is Brogan interrupting my storm.

"Hello, gorgeous. There is something that I would like to discuss with you." His gruff voice growls at me; not in an intimidating way, just merely displaying his angst.

"Not now, Brogan," I whisper desperately trying to move past him but warriors of Ceylon are not slight figures and so he remains in my way. So instead, I try not to look at him, shielding my face with my block of raven hair, so that my eyes will not betray the sadness that I don't want anyone to see.

"You do not have a choice." His eyes narrow at me as he raises an eyebrow, something which Brogan is known for. I start to wring my hands together, still avoiding his gaze and after a few moments, he sighs loudly. "You don't know what I'm talking about, do you?"

"No," I answer and he inches his face closer, red beard almost touching my skin. I have no choice but to look at him and when I do, sympathy masks his expression.

"What is it?" he asks in a surprisingly sweet tone. I hug myself with my arms.

"I don't want to talk about it." Still holding back tears, I blink them back as a lump appears in my throat. He scrutinises me again, eyebrow still raised, until his face softens.

"Do you know why I am here, Lenora?"

I instantly look around me in fear at the use of my name and find the multitude of corridors empty. I exhale in relief and Brogan flashes me a devil-may-care smile. I smile at him too as I realise that he has willingly changed the conversation for me. He does not wish to push me on the matter that upsets me. I admire him for that.

"Bored of being a hermit, I suppose?" I counter sharply and his grin only widens at my new-found amusement, glad for it to be there.

"I wish it were that simple but no. Do you not realise what a pledge is?" I immediately balk at his words, all hints of amusement gone. I know why he is here. And though I know that this will be an explosive conversation, I would rather take Brogan's wrath than admit my feelings any day; and he knows it too.

"Brogan, I could not risk any more lives than absolutely necessary—"

"And you were able to risk the Zatrian and the General on a whim?"

"Alanaat can navigate the deserts in her sleep which we needed to make an efficient escape and Roran is practically the face of the Crown and was needed to earn the trust of the guards. There was no room for a hot-headed warrior!"

"I could have helped you," he growls under his breath.

"You could have ruined the entire mission," I spit back and he sighs again.

"I made an oath, Lenora. In my culture, that oath cannot be broken nor avoided at any cost and I intend to keep it that way. But never, in my life, has the object of my pledge completely disregarded it to go *behind my back* on a dangerous mission."

"I never asked you to make that oath. You made it of your own accord and I am not obliged to tell you my whereabouts or have you follow me. My shadow is my own, Brogan. And I will not have you lurking there against my will for the sake of your honour."

"This is not about my honour!" he cries, fists clenching at his side.

"You will have to prove otherwise then!"

"I vowed to protect you out of a debt that Elyra herself is not here to repay. You were her only light in a time of great darkness and I intend to protect that light in her name. If I fail here... if I fail *her*, I would never forgive myself which is why my entire well-being is jeopardised when you decide that you can negate me from situations that may have you killed. I will *not* fail her. And I will *not* fail you. Am I understood?" my heart goes out to him. I bet the loss of Elyra still threatens to crush him every day and this oath may be the last tie he has to her. And I will not see it broken.

"Fine. I will inform you of any quests that I dare to undertake but I expect you to be cautious at all times because I will not have you dying for me. This will not be one-sided. This will be a partnership. I protect your life as you will protect mine, yes?" Brogan straightens from his position and retracts his arm from my way.

"Agreed," he answers gruffly before giving me a final smirk and heading on his way down the corridor. That is another thing that I like about him, he never lingers.

Except now that Brogan is gone, so is my distraction. The heartbreak continues to crush its way through me mercilessly. It is so palpable that I struggle to breathe.

Elijah…

I must have been a fool to ever think that he… that I could ever…

After a long time of mulling over my thoughts, I find myself in front of an unexpected place. The door to Breccan's office. I do not know what force has led me here nor even if I wanted it to but there is no escaping the pull of comfort lurking behind the polished door.

I open the door more abruptly than I planned to and I see Breccan immediately turn around in shock. He is standing at his large window overlooking the courtyard as usual and as he looks at me with sheer concern in his eyes, I let out the sob that I had been holding in for what seems like hours.

"Lenora?" his soothing voice is all I need and I run over to him, not caring what I knock over along the way and embrace him tightly.

He is taken by surprise at first but his arms soon encase me and I feel the comfort and warmth that I did not consciously know that I was searching for on my walk through Drodal. One of his hands start to stroke my hair and I cry into his shoulder for a while in silence.

"Sweetheart, what is it?" he asks and I gently pull away just enough to look into his sapphire eyes, his raven beard softly scraping along my cheek as I do.

"Father…" his eyes glow when I call him that, "Does love always hurt this much?"

"Oh, my dear child," he says before tucking my head against him again and letting me shed my tears upon his shoulder. He continues to stroke my hair and I do not know how long I am standing there with him this time. Just that the comfort is calming me.

Breccan pulls away this time and cups my tear-stained face in his hands, the moonlight streaming in through his window making his concern shine more than ever.

"If I could make it go away, I would," he tells me softly and I give him a soft smile.

"I know," I murmur.

"He must mean a great deal to you."

"I do not think he knows how much."

"Trust me, Lenora; any man who finds himself to be lucky enough to have earned your heart would definitely seize it with both hands." Breccan leans forward to gently press a kiss to my forehead and it fills a hole inside the orphan in me that I did not know was still there.

"I see how it is." An angry voice says from behind us and I am shocked to see Elijah standing in the doorway, aglow with the amber light from the braziers outside.

He is holding a wooden slate with a bell jar perched atop it and inside is a miniature tree with various spindly branches. As I watch, black dust at the bottom transform into tiny leaves and float back atop their branches again to form a tree of blinding emerald. He had recreated our moment in Broxen just after the events that had occurred in Braelin town. It takes my breath away.

He came to apologise.

But now I realise that Elijah is positively enthralled in anger that I have not seen him in before. His clenched hands bearing the jar threaten to break the glass into a million pieces and I can see that it is trembling ever so slightly from his shaking grip. The strain in his strong arms is thick with tension and his face is so beyond stoic that it is in the realm of what I call a dangerous calm. But his eyes… his eyes can never lie. Elijah is hurt.

I look slowly between Breccan and Elijah and I discover the source of his anger. Breccan retracts his arms from me and folds them behind his back awkwardly. Elijah must have just been standing there long enough to see the kiss and our proximity and assumed the worst. Of course, no one knows the truth of our relationship.

"Elijah, wait—" I begin but he simply sneers before slamming the door shut.

I run and open the door in one swift motion and sprint along the corridor to where Elijah is pounding through in all his wrath. I catch up to him and block his path, desperate for him to listen to me.

"Elijah, please, let me explain—"

"What is there to explain?" he bellows and it makes me shrink back from the hate in his voice. "I came here to apologise for how I had acted earlier and I catch you getting cosy with the Lord of Drodal!"

"It is not like that!"

"Then how is it? I am anxious to know." He thrusts his arms out and I fear the jar will drop from his careless movements. I look into his hurt eyes and it pains me that I cannot explain it all to him.

"I can't tell you." As those words escape my lips, he continues to surge down the corridor and I hold my hands up in front of him to make him stop yet again. "Please, Elijah, it is not what you think!"

"Not what I think?" he bellows as he throws the jar down into the stone floor and it smashes into a million pieces. I cannot help my shriek as I kneel amongst the shards of glass, desperately clutching the pieces as if it would somehow fix itself. "I saw you in his arms, Lenora! I saw him kiss you! I am such a fool for believing that you could possibly… that I could ever…" he never finishes that sentence.

I can barely register what he is saying as I stare at what might as well be the broken fragments of my heart. The glass pieces are too small to ever be able to fix… the wooden slate is cracked in half. The small tree lies across from me broken in three places and the once emerald leaves have returned to ash and stayed that way. I stare at the pieces that I hold in my palms and am surprised when a teardrop falls among them from my eye.

I close my eyes to stop anymore from falling.

A cascade of emotions well up inside me. As much as I would like to electrocute Elijah for this, the branches of my lightening are not igniting amidst the strong waves of sadness that are also there. There is no taming Elijah; there is no trust between us. He might as well have just thrown me against the wall and it would have had the same effect. His jealousy is a place that even I dare not go and I will not be undermined by a fool who is blinded by it.

I open my eyes.

"My word… will never be good enough for you, will it?" I whisper and he stops whatever rant he was in when I drowned it out.

He says nothing as I stand up to face him, anger replacing the heartbreak that was there moments ago. I slowly open my clenched fists to drop the remnants of glass that were tucked away in there. I quickly wipe away the streaks left by my tears and look at him impassively.

"Lenora, I—" I hold up my palm to stop him from talking. I feel stoic. Emotionally drained.

"I have been through hell and back more than once, Elijah. I know a lost cause when I see one."

"A lost cause?" he cries out at me but it does not affect me as much as it once would.

"There is no reasoning with you. You always assume the worst when it could not be farther from the truth and I am fed up of waiting for you to see the light."

"What are you saying?" he asks gruffly, trying to act careless.

"I am saying that I do not wish to compete with a man who is blind to all emotions bar from his own."

"I am not as heartless as you make me out to be, Lenora." He steps forward and growls at me.

"That may be so but it does not change the fact that that heart is corrupt by jealousy and anger which in turn blinds you to the truth. I will not be a part of that." I turn to walk away but he shouts at me again.

"I saw him with his hands upon you! I saw him kiss you!"

"What you saw and what you think you saw are two very different things."

"How can you be so detached? Do you have any idea what I have been wrestling with since the moment I first laid eyes on you?" he cries again but I whip around to face him.

"You have given me nothing but grief since I set foot upon this Keep and you have not given me any reason to believe that you may feel otherwise!" I shout back at him and this time, he steps closer to me.

"I have many times, Lenora. You just chose to ignore it."

"I cannot ignore what is never spoken," I growl at him.

"I am not the only one to blame for that and you know it!" his voice booms throughout the corridor.

"I just risked my life by breaking into the brother of the very institution that tortured me for three years just to give you some semblance of happiness! What further proof do you need, Elijah?" I scream at him and he relaxes then.

He slowly closes the gap between us and he is an inch away from me now, eyes once again betraying what he wants most and I am not prepared for what I see in them. Desire. My heartbeat quickens as his hands reach outwards to gently cup my face between his hands. Their warmth radiates through me and his sweet breath caresses my face as his emerald eyes burn with a passion that I did not think he was capable of.

"Thank you, Lenora." His voice his husky and it sends anticipation running through me to my core. His soft pink mouth parts as his gaze travels to my own mouth and I can barely breathe. His lips come forward... so close... so close that I can almost taste their sweet kiss... and yet...

"I can't." I breathe onto his lips and he stiffens. My heart breaks at having to do this but I know that I must.

I cannot deal with his constant mood swings... I never know what he wants and for all I know, this is just a part of a strong swell of emotions caused by me saving his brother. I will not have my heart broken when finding out that this was a mistake because I am not sure if I can take much more of being played with. So it is best to stop it now because only the Aerix know what should happen should I let Elijah continue. Even so, everything I love gets taken from me. And I want him. I want him so badly. But maybe that is why I can never have him.

"I thought that... I thought that you wanted..." Elijah manages to say and his pain only adds to my own.

"I have taken a lot of risks in my lifetime, Elijah. But I cannot risk you." If something should happen to Elijah because of Myrna... I cannot even fathom it. I need him to remain safe. Even if it is not with me.

He immediately retracts and puts his hands behind his back, Warrior Elijah, his usual defence-mechanism bursting through. I do not understand why he is being this way when I just want to protect him and myself... unless... he sees my statement in a different light.

"I see. You can risk Master Saltmist but not me." He shrugs but I know that he is hurting. Still, his version of what I said stuns me.

"After everything that has just happened between us, you still believe that Breccan and I are involved?" I exclaim, completely dumb-founded by his logic.

"I believe what I see. And what I saw was you and him in a compromising position but please, don't let me stand in your way." His sarcastic tone sends me over the edge. I had just practically told him how I felt and still he makes these accusations because he refuses to let go of his jealousy.

"This is so typical. Elijah gets a breath of humility and starts blaming everyone else." I snarl at him.

"Are you so accustomed to men falling in love with you that you become completely emotionless when you come across someone genuine?" he bellows.

"I did not ask for any of this!" I throw my arms up in frustration but simply sigh with resignation. "My heart is my own, Elijah, and if I choose to protect it then it is no concern of yours." And with that, I finally walk away from him, needing to be away from his abrasiveness before it cuts too deeply.

"Off to warm Breccan's bed, are you?" he calls to me in a final attempt to hurt me as I suppose I have hurt him. Although his voice shakes with oncoming tears, the branches of lightening ignite in my chest and it is a tremendous effort to keep it inside me.

"After all that I have been through... after all that I have done, you think that low of me? That I would subject myself to the very things that I have been fighting against?" I answer, trying not to sob.

"I don't know what to expect of you anymore." He slackens in defeat and I know my refusal hurt him but he refuses to see how much it hurts me too.

"There is nothing going on between me and Breccan!" I practically shout to the sky, desperate for him to believe me.

"I just can't believe you," he replies, folding his arms over his chest.

All right, Elijah.

You asked for it.

I storm towards him until I am an inch from his face, lightening cascading around my form in white forks, eager to scorch anything that touches me.

"Do you want to know how I know that Breccan and I could never be involved?" I demand of him.

"Yes!" he growls.

"You really want to know the truth?"

"Yes, damn it!"

"Breccan is my father!" I shout in his face and he is frozen in shock but I continue nonetheless. "What you saw in that office was a father anxiously trying to console his heartbroken daughter who realised that perhaps she had fallen in love with his most trusted friend!"

"Lenora... I—"

"Save it," I snarl. "I don't have time for people who don't trust me."

With anger in my heart, I leave Elijah in that corridor and don't bother turning back when he anxiously calls my name over and over again. He knows better than to follow me. I head straight to my quarters and as soon as I open the doors, Maer jumps off the bed in excitement.

"You're back! I waited for you!" she grins and as the tears threaten to brim once more, I remember what she was accused of. I kneel on the floor and outstretch my arms.

"Come here," I ask of her and concern contorts her face. She runs over to me and I wrap my arms around her waist and then use one hand to stroke the top of her head.

"What is it?" she asks but I just I clutch her tighter.

"I will protect you with my life, you know that, right?" I pull away so that I can stroke her cheek with my fingertip and she looks so worried for me.

"Of course," she says, brows creasing in angst.

"I will always protect you. No matter what."

"I know," she whispers. Maer then touches her forehead to mine as she watches a single tear run down my cheek. "Elyra?"

"Yes, sweetheart?"

"Take my strength." Her youthful voice commands and I grin at her. She strokes away my tears with her small fingers. "It will all be okay."

"I know," I say as I embrace her again.

Except this time... Maer was holding me tighter than she ever has before. I just can't figure out if it is because she is consoling me... or if she has troubles of her own.

Chapter 16

After waking up before dawn, I decided that I could not force myself to stay in bed any longer. With Maer sound asleep curled next to me, I gently plant a kiss on her forehead and she moans in her sleep. She's so small. Too small to be embroiled in a world ripe with hatred and treachery. Nonetheless I am glad that she has found some sort of peace here at Drodal.

As I wonder the vacant corridors of the fortress, they feel colder than ever. As if the very walls can sense my sadness, as if they too are lonely with only the flickering flames of candlelight to offer any amount of comfort. The absence of life in these early hours only makes my thoughts louder inside my head.

Should I have denied Elijah? Even now, my heart aches for his embrace but my mind remains a steel wall against such actions. Someday, not excluding the immediate future, I plan on voyaging back to where my journey began and challenging Myrna's reign in Adrian's good name. Elijah as a mere acquaintance puts him at risk of her wrath let alone if we became something more.

I could not do it.

I will not do it.

Who is to even say that what happened between us would have even lasted? My emotions may just be rife with sensitivity. Three years with only female contact and ruthless men can do that to a woman. Elijah is strong and stubborn, a brutal warrior at his heart. But I have seen the softer side to him... his vulnerability, his chivalry. It is enough to drive any woman insane with desire.

But he does not trust me.

And I doubt that he ever will.

"Oh... Hi..." a timid voice brings me back to reality and I see Lukas carrying a bushel of porridge oats on his way to the kitchens. He looks awkward and I realise that I have not really been in his company since his confession.

"Lukas…" I breathe, ashamed that I have been too busy to talk with him. He gently places his bushel on the ground and I stand closer to him.

"I understand that you have been avoiding me—"

"Lukas, it is not that at all, I—"

"But I realise now how easily feelings of admiration can be confused for adoration and I apologise if I had ever offended you—" he fumbles around nervously with his clothes but I cut him off, saddened at the sight before me.

"I apologise for my absence. It was not fair to you or to your show of honesty towards me in the days prior. But you must know that I have not been avoiding you. I was working on something rather important and I realise that this should not have allowed me to neglect my duties to you. Can you forgive me?" his young face slowly emits a small smile as he looks at me.

"On one condition."

"Anything." I agree, sagging with relief.

"Can we please just… start over?" his face almost scrunches up in anticipation for my refusal but my soft laugh relaxes him.

"I would like that very much." I put my arms around his neck and embrace him, his hands lightly on my waist. When he pulls away, only happiness is on his face as he picks up the bushel of oats.

"I must go. A fortress of hungry mages does not bode well for our safety." He grins and I laugh again.

"Go." He leaves with a final smile and I am glad that we are going to return to normal.

"Lukas is a wonderful man," a stern female voice says from behind me. Ayla. I have not seen her for the longest time. She stands propped against the wall, straight mousy hair framing her pale face.

"He is," I agree with her, not sure as to why she is talking to me. We have never been amicable and I bet that I have not seen her purely because she does not want me to.

"I would hate to see him hurt." Her faded blue eyes scrutinise me and I do not like what she suspects.

"I would never," I reply confidently, trying not to put too much venom in my words.

"Please, it is so obvious that you are hiding something." She removes herself from the wall and crosses her arms before me.

"My business remains my own. And I will not have you prying in places that you will regret," I warn her, not liking her cold gaze.

"I was not the only one who witnessed your debacle at the Festival. You are hiding behind the former High Priestess's name and no one has even bothered to question as to why that is or what your true name is. And all because of Breccan's orders."

"I am not obliged to tell any of you who I am. I am allowed my secrets."

"Not if those secrets are a threat to everything that I hold most dear," she spits back and as much as I dislike Ayla, I admire her perceptive abilities.

"I am withholding my name so that the threat against Drodal is diminished," I scold her. Why can't she see that I am the one preventing the threat?

"And yet the Bolgren have only started attacking this region since you came to be here. Odd, don't you think?" she tilts her head slightly, piercing eyes making the edges of her face sharper.

"I do not like what you are suggesting," I say through clenched teeth. With a cold smirk, she edges slightly closer to me.

"I would watch your back if I were you," she threatens before walking away to begin her duties without another word.

I did not even realise the sparks tingling blue at my fingertips. She is lucky that I did not touch her. I make an effort to calm myself but it is short-lived.

A piercing shriek of terror echoes throughout these empty corridors and it startles me into an instant run towards its source. It leads into the entrance courtyard of Drodal and an onslaught of shrieks ensues at what lies in the centre of it.

A tall sharp pike stands in front of the fountain, forced into the ground with brute strength. The sky is still indigo with early morning but the darkness does not hinder our understanding of what is driven onto its top.

A man has been impaled on this stake, the sharp point forced through his chest until it has run him through completely. His body is limp, dripping cascades of blood down the stake's edges, some even turning the fountain's waters scarlet. Dribbles of flesh mark the wood and some of the man's ribs can be seen protruding from his chest from being forced outwards.

This man had suffered a terrible death.

Early morning servants must have found him here and screamed to alert the authorities. I pray to the Aerix that they will somehow be able to forget this sight. I am just thankful that Maer is still asleep.

Breccan appears beside me and strikes action into those who are not needed here.

"I must ask that all civilians take refuge inside the Keep while we figure out who had performed this tragedy. For those of you who are severely affected by this sight, you have my permission to neglect your duties for today so that you may recover."

Soon enough, it is only Breccan, Alanaat, Roran, Benjamin, Brogan and Elijah here as we face the pike before us. I dare not meet Elijah's gaze though I can sense his timid glances towards me and Breccan. I know that Benjamin, Al and Roran were present during mine and Elijah's initial fight and my embarrassment keeps me from making contact with them. I put my sole focus into the scene before me, taking comfort in the impartial presence of Brogan and Breccan.

"Who would do something like this?" Al gulps. A quick glance at her tells me that she is nauseated by these events. I suppose her cadre would have given her comfort in this time but she had instructed them to take care of the civilians.

"Master Stone, have you ever seen something of this brutality in your experiences of war?" Breccan asks and Brogan's eyes do not leave the man's carcass.

"This technique is sadistic. Whoever did this wanted to cause their victim pain. You will not find many warriors who will go to such lengths as these to attain it. This person lacks emotion."

"Do you think that it could be revenge for your conquest last night?" Breccan aims towards me but it is Roran who answers.

"Eradan is a brutal capital, Breccan. But not sadistic."

"May I remind you who runs the capital, Maar?" Elijah says in a small voice. But I barely register his presence.

"Myrna may have ordered such an attack but she did not perform it," Roran counters.

"Even the cannibals in Skull's Bay would not display such... gore." Al breaks her gaze from the body and clutches her stomach.

"You can go, Al. Thank you for your input but you may tend to the civilians with the rest of your group," I tell her softly and she mimes a thank you before briskly heading into Drodal, far away from such horror.

"Could it be possible that Axton Falls are aware of your escape, Benjamin?" Breccan asks.

"No... Lenora was very thorough. Not even the guards suspected who she was and most guards did not bother to learn my name. This man does not appear to be anyone I know from Axton." He looks to Elijah who nods in confirmation, agreeing that it could not be a man from their province despite their uncle's brutal nature.

Nonetheless, I approach the carcass, curious to see the face of him. While the others continue to murmur their suspicions behind me, a sinking feeling appears in my stomach as I edge nearer, the blood dripping onto the stone floor pounding in my ears.

Upon closer inspection, I can see flecks of golden hair beneath the blood coating his head and I see youthful brown eyes wide-open in fear with a once sweet yet vulgar mouth gaping with terror.

I know this man.

I stagger backwards, dizzy with my discovery.

Roran lunges forwards to stabilise me and I clutch my head, positively sick with realisation.

"Lenora, what is it?" Breccan is at my side in an instant, putting a reassuring hand on my shoulder as Roran takes my weight.

Without a word, I take a few paces beyond them, hugging myself in an attempt to stop the shame from eating me alive. I am surprised that Elijah did not notice this man's identity but I suppose he was not concentrating on his face more than his threats in their last encounter.

"This boy is a resident of Braelin town," I whisper and only the wind whistles across the silence. I sneak a glance at Elijah and his eyes widen as he too realises what I have come to know.

"Braelin? I have never heard of such a town." Roran furrows his eyebrows in thought.

"It is not on most maps," I murmur back to him.

"We had investigated the Bolgren massacre not too long ago. This boy was our informant." Elijah fills them in emotionlessly and they all place their gazes on me. But I can barely breathe.

"They are watching me." My voice is barely audible.

"Lenora, please—" Breccan begins but I whirl around, anger flaring at their audacity to go after an innocent party.

"They know who I am and they know that I am here!" I clench my fists and the skies darken to reveal the terrible swirl of emotions that I am bearing.

"It is not possible. We are the only ones who know." Benjamin tries timidly but as my eyes narrow, a roll of thunder erupts through the sky and he shies away next to Elijah.

"We have a traitor in our midst," I growl, looking at them all in turn, the wind howling above and threatening to rip the blossom trees surrounding the courtyard at their roots.

"Do you honestly think that lowly of us?" Brogan demands, massive forearms rippling with tension, most likely aching for his axes that he has adorned across his back since our agreement had been made.

"It would not be the first time," I counter and all gazes turn to Roran who stands like a doe at the tip of a spear until he realises their train of thought.

"Oh, come on! I did what I had to do back then and I do not need to explain myself to you. Lenora understands and my past has been forgiven. I will die before I ever feel the shame of her mistrust again!" he snarls at them all.

"Let us be rational about this. We do not know for sure if anyone knows that you are here and the fact that..." Breccan stumbles over her name, "Myrna... is not here destroying my Keep is evident that she remains unaware of your existence."

"The Bolgren threatened *me* days prior. And now they have brutalised a man that *I* had contact with. These creatures are out for blood and they lack the patience to wait for it. They will be coming for us soon," I tell them and they seem unsure of my assumptions.

"You really think that there will be a massacre?" Benjamin's small voice deters me from my ensuing storm and the skies calm as I realise that I must be scaring the people I love most.

"No, Benjamin. What we have here is a war. And I will be damned should I let them conquer this city."

"What shall we do?" Elijah's voice is strong and I am surprised that he is looking to me for advice. Normally, he would have challenged my knowledge and authority and I bet that he is simply negating from his norms to get back into my good graces.

So I choose to ignore him.

That is, until everyone looks to me with pleading eyes for guidance. Even my father, the Lord of this Keep, expresses sadness and I can see that he fears the death of his city and his people. I turn my gaze away from them all, taking a deep breath to calm myself. When I look at them once more, the defenceless guilt-ridden girl is gone and has been replaced with a well-trained warrior who has been in these situations her entire life.

"Rally the men," I announce. "For today, we prepare for battle."

Chapter 17

"Remember to aim!"

"You must have balance when you lunge!"

"Remember to strike up and across!"

"Do not let the weight control you!"

"Block! You must remember to block!"

The series of shouted advice has been going on since dawn. All of us are taking rotations with the hundreds of warriors prepared to fight for their home. We are teaching them how to survive, something I did not think I would have to ingrain into these men in such a short amount of time. Between learning how to use combative magic for the mages and standard combat for all else, it is a wonder how no one has collapsed from exhaustion.

I decided it best to take lead on providing the training although my reasons are different to everyone else's. The group thought it best because of my extensive background as Aneya's Warrior, 'who better to teach them,' they said. I had to hold in my sneer. I am doing this purely in the hopes that whatever guidance I can provide may just save these soldiers from a swift end that they do not deserve.

After all… it may be my fault as to why Drodal will be attacked.

I began with separating the masses into smaller groups, firstly by weapon of choice. From there, I had asked that all mages separate themselves into groups of the same element and was surprised at how many mages did in fact lurk within Drodal's walls; nothing compared to the number of standard soldiers but the more mages we have, the better our outcome will be. The mages would be training in solitude within their groups, learning from each other on ways to use their magic offensively and defensively while the others learn with us from the source; the mages can then join us when their abilities have been practiced to full capacity.

I had arranged rotations between us as we all have different guidance to give. Alanaat is teaching the soldiers who favour hand-to-hand and spears; many of her group had no experience in any weapon but wanted to defend their village so she thought it best to teach them simple manoeuvres with basic weapons. Elijah favoured teaching what he could to those who favoured archery thrown in with a small amount of blade training as no archer should be left defenceless should something happen to their bow. Brogan is teaching many who favoured the axe or similarly heavy weapons although most were terrified when finding out who their teacher would be. Roran as the General of the Sentillian Army is teaching those who favour the sword and throughout his training, I can see how much he must miss his men. I, on the other hand, am providing any training that I can to any group who would listen; my background is not so singular.

Once each group has been taught everything they can about their favoured form of combat, we, as teachers, started to rotate to provide basic techniques and advice to every group. By this time, the mages had even joined us for some standard training and the barking of orders can be heard throughout all of Drodal.

The group now in front of me looks as exhausted as I feel, their posture slacked and faces drawn from having been practicing since dawn. It is now dusk. The sky is beginning to darken and the shouts of my fellow teachers have been dying off one by one as they could not have possibly taught them any more than they already have. And so all those who wish to learn as much as they can still flock to me for instruction and so long as someone will listen, I will be there to provide it. I will not deny them.

"A dagger is one of the most useful weapons that you could have within your arsenal. It is small and light and can be easily attached to your belt should you need it. You could be the best with your weapon in all of Aneya but as soon as you are disarmed, you fall prey to death instantly. Having an extra weapon at hand will prevent this from happening to you."

And so it continues on for another hour, advice that I can only hope is sinking in. That is until Roran appears close to me as I teach in the courtyard, the hundreds of soldiers stopping in their paired-training to bow their heads at the General. I roll my eyes at him as he approaches me.

"You are disrupting my class," I tell him, trying to avoid his approach by entering the swarm of soldiers before us. I correct the angle of a soldier's forearm along the way and stop to change a woman's grip on her dagger.

"Elyra, please..." he says, remembering to use that name in front of the men, "You have not eaten nor rested this entire day..." I walk away from him to further inspect the soldier's positions.

"We are not finished here." I bend down to widen the stance of a woman to strengthen her block.

"There is nothing more we can do," he implores.

"*I* will not give up on these soldiers."

"We are not asking you to. We are simply saying that enough is enough." I whirl around to face him.

"And suppose the Bolgren attack within the hour? Do you think that they are ready to fight? To die?" my words have him speechless and he sags in defeat as he gestures for someone at his side to come closer before walking off himself.

Lukas stands before me with a grin, holding out a bowl of rabbit stew and a plate of bread. The smell makes my stomach lurch as if it could somehow demolish it instantly without the patience to eat it.

"A leader needs her strength," He tells me softly but I look to the soldiers before me who are salivating at the food in Lukas' hands.

"Them first," I counter and with that, Lukas jerks his head behind him and I see Benjamin and Elijah pushing a gigantic pot of stew into the courtyard and preparing to serve the soldiers running towards them.

"They had the same idea that I did." Lukas shrugs and my heart swells with happiness at their compassion, even Elijah's. Though we still have not spoken.

I take the food from Lukas with a warm smile and walk towards the edge of the fountain where I sit and begin to eat. Some guards had cleaned away the brutal display before training had begun and I am grateful for that. I cannot help but wonder if the boy had any family. Lukas sits down next to me.

"I enjoyed your classes very much," he says and I almost choke on my spoonful of stew.

"You were not supposed to attend!" I reply sternly but unable to stop eating. He shrugs again.

"I want to defend my fortress should the need arise."

"The need will never arise so long as I am here to prevent it." My stomach growls loudly as I start to scrape away the remains of the stew with the bread. Lukas' eyes are aglow as he watches me.

"Nonetheless, I am glad that I could have witnessed you in all your glory... *Lenora*." I drop the last bit of bread in surprise as I gape at him in horror. He only chuckles.

"How?"

"I have told the stories of Aneya's Warrior many a night here. It is only fair that I should recognise her when I see her." I recall the time when Lukas had spouted my origins within the grand hall.

"For how long?" I ask, not able to look him in the eye.

"I suspected for a while. Aneya's Warrior was not only praised for her skill in war but also for her beauty." I blush at that, "But what made me realise it was seeing the way you commanded these people, teaching them aspects of war that only an expert would know. It was quite phenomenal."

"These soldiers will die if they are not prepared." I sigh.

"But their chances of survival have greatly increased because of you. Here at Drodal, our soldiers are not forced to go to war. We go to war as our choice to protect what is ours. For most of us, Drodal is the only happiness that we have ever known. We will not stand-by and watch it crumble."

"I admire that."

"I knew you would." I look into Lukas' warm brown eyes and I am glad that he is here with me.

"How is my Maer?" I ask him quietly, hoping that she is doing well amidst all of these preparations.

"She spent most of her time with me in the kitchens and actually helped me when she managed to tear her eyes away from you."

"She watched me?"

"She *scrutinised* you. Her eyes would not leave you. I think she was in as much awe of you as everyone else here."

"I do not want her here for this, Lukas," I admit to him and he sighs in agreement.

"She will be safe; I will make sure of it. Just make sure that you come home to us both." Only sincerity is on his face and I really hope that no harm comes to Lukas either.

"May I have a moment with you? Alone?" Breccan stands across from us suddenly with an expression that could kill eyes as terrifying as a stormy sea as he stares at me with arms folded across his chest.

"Of course, sir." Lukas leaves swiftly and I think I know why Breccan is here.

"Breccan—" I begin to explain as I rise from the fountain but he does not give me a chance to speak.

"I have been training with the mages and conducting battle strategies all day only to find that my daughter has been starving herself of food and rest!" he tries to keep a hushed tone but his anger makes it difficult. Everyone is too busy with their meals to hear us anyway.

"I just ate some stew, everything is fine." I try to reassure him but he runs his hand through his black hair in frustration.

"I have enough to worry about without fearing for your health and safety!"

"There is no need to worry about me. I am fine. I have done this many times before."

"Yes but without my prior knowledge!" he does not meet my gaze as he stares at the ground and I sympathise with him.

"Do you want to tell me what this is really about?" I ask him softly and when he looks at me, I can see tears coating his eyes.

"How can I possibly watch the most precious thing in my life go to war?" I say nothing in reply but simply embrace him as tightly as I can as he does the same.

"You and Drodal are precious to me, father," I whisper in his ear, "It is my duty and honour to protect you both. You need not fear for me. Fear for your people. They are the ones who need your encouragement."

"You are right." He nods, pulling away from me, running his hand through his hair again.

"Promise me that you will not do anything reckless should this war befall us?"

"I will try," I tell him as this is the best answer that I will allow myself to give. He accepts this and walks back into Drodal to continue his duties.

"Excuse me?" a woman asks me and I find the courtyard once again filled with the soldiers who were only eating moments ago.

"What is it?" I ask, stunned by the hundreds of pairs of eyes staring directly at me in this moment.

"We do not mean to sound ungrateful…" a man begins next to the woman who originally spoke. "But there is just one piece of advice left for us to take head."

"And what is that?" I place my hand on my hip, waiting for their answer. All of them look between each other awkwardly until the woman speaks again.

"What is it like to fight a Bolgran?"

My heart stops.

Of course. This is the first encounter with Bolgren that Drodal, and perhaps even Aneya, has ever had. And I am the only one who has fought one in the flesh and successfully killed it. I remember its pale blue eyes and sinister fangs dripping with venom, its long claws swiping swiftly and surely to disembowel me, its membranous arched body ripe with strength and brutality...

As I look among the hopeful faces of the soldiers before me, I dare not tell them these gruesome details for fear that their own terror will diminish their courage.

"Bolgren are fast. Ruthless. Unforgiving. It is your job to be quicker, fiercer and merciless. This entire day has taught you how to master your arsenal but what you must remember is that no measure of steel can compare to your wits. So keep them about you and you will survive," I tell them and they all nod in agreement before dispersing quickly into Drodal for some well-earned rest.

"Alone again, I see." Brogan approaches me with a cocky grin and I cannot help my smirk in his presence.

"Not for long enough, my friend. To what do I owe the pleasure?" I ask him, curious as to why he is approaching me at this late hour. He should be resting for the war ahead. There is no telling when they shall strike.

He cocks his head at me before reaching behind his back and swiftly pulling out a package that was hidden there. It is long and covered in a navy sash which immediately makes me think of Elyra. I gulp at the sight of it and he holds the package across his palms and out to me, ready for the taking.

"What is it?" I hug myself, Elyra's final moments flashing before my eyes in a whirl of pain. I cannot look at it.

"Your dagger has been lonely for far too long." In one rapid motion, he removes the sash and I am blinded by shining silver.

I have never seen such craftsmanship. A blade lies across his palms but unlike any blade I have ever seen before. It is double-ended, each side curving outwards ever so slightly to form a weak 'S' shape, both ends so sharp that it could pierce you with the slightest touch. It is made of polished silver, its centre so gilded and intricate that it makes me gasp. In the very heart of the blade is a shining blue sapphire, glinting purple in the night sky.

Brogan catches me admiring the blade and he smiles weakly.

"Sapphire was her favourite," he murmurs. I instantly look up to find his grief-ridden eyes.

"It was hers?" I ask in disbelief.

"It was to be a wedding present upon her return." I step away from him then, shaking my head.

"I will not take this." He steps closer to me, forcing the blade into my line of sight.

"I made this for her and she never got the chance to wield it. Use it in her name like you use your dagger. Let her be a part of this rebellion as much as we are. Let her protect you in your endeavours against the bitch who had her killed."

My heart warms at the thought of Elyra being more present with me than she already is and I desperately try to stop the tears forming in my eyes. I can see that Brogan is doing the same. I reach out and take the blade in my hand at its middle. It is light. Swift. It is as if it was always supposed to be in my hand.

"I would be honoured," I tell him and he grins.

He reaches back and pulls out a make-shift sheath that he must have made to cater for its unusual shape. It is made from black leather with gilded silver upon its end. I sheathe the blade with ease and strap it to the other side of my hip, opposite to where I keep my dagger.

"Use it well."

"I plan to." He nods at me with a grin and leaves in his usual brisk manner. Brogan is not the sensitive type.

As I stand in solitude in the courtyard once more, I realise that in all my time spent training others, I have neglected in training myself. I do not know the first thing about combative magic. Sure, I can create one hell of a storm but that takes time and patience, something war is not inclined to give. I need to learn how to use this magic in close combat and so instead of much needed rest, I decide to practice.

The sky is dark and a soft breeze caresses my skin as I take a deep breath. I know that my powers are often ignited by strong emotions but Elijah had taught me that patience is the key to control. I will need to control the storm inside me should I be able to use it combatively so the first thing that I do is centre myself.

Continuing to take deep breaths, I can feel the branches of the electric tree inside my chest sparking to life slowly, not enough to lose control, but enough to know that it is awake. Thunder rumbles overhead as I get in touch with the storm inside me but I am careful not to succumb to all its might.

I recall how I had electrocuted Elijah accidentally when I was angry with him and how I noticed sparks at my fingertips when confronting Ayla… if I could somehow summon those sparks, it may just be a brutal weapon in close combat.

I close my eyes and feel sub-consciously for my tree and I can feel its white power rife with electrical energy. It would make sense for that energy to transfer to my hands for use and so I will the branches of my tree to extend. I can feel them entwine through my veins as they progress from my chest to my shoulders and along my arms until they reach my hands. I feel warm and tingly from the unusual sensation.

I open my eyes and stare at my open palms as blue sparks of electricity emit from them. As I flex my fingers, they begin to dance across my hands almost as if in a frenzied excitement at the thought of being used. The blue hue softly glows upon the stone beneath my feet and it is almost bewitching.

I know that these sparks will be a strategic way to disarm my opponent but there is no way to test its strength until I am on the battlefield. But will it be enough? I know that sparks are effective but could I possibly be able to turn them into something more? Something powerful? Maybe even ranged?

I close my eyes and imagine the electricity strengthening as if the branches are stretching and becoming wider until my hands glow effervescently with charged energy, its crackle echoing in the darkness. My face contorts with the effort and I feel out of breath but I need to see what I can do. And so, gritting my teeth, I will the electricity to take shape, contorting and concentrating the energy to mimic the picture in my mind of a perfect sphere. Sure enough, a blue sphere of spitting lightening glows in both of my palms, branches of electricity biting at the air.

I try to laugh but it comes out in a huff of air as a weight in my chest, that I did not even realise was there, begins to impress more weight upon me. Sweating, I look at the balls of lightening and wonder if they can move. Deciding to aim them at the courtyard's stone floor so as not to cause damage, I thrust my palms outwards and the spheres propel towards the ground. On impact, the energy disperses across the stones, blue veins spiralling outwards until the energy is absorbed and disappears.

Interesting.

I look at my now empty palms and grin. And as another roll of thunder echoes in the cloudy sky, I wonder if I can create streaks of lightening and bring the storm from the skies to the ground.

Even now, I am sweating with the effort of maintaining this charge but I must discover my true potential. The weight in my chest grows heavier and my vision begins to blur. This magic could be what keeps me from death in the oncoming war and I *will* see this magic tamed even slightly.

I imagine the branches inside me now protruding from my skin and as soon as I think it, bolt of lightning zap outwards from my palms. I quickly aim my hands at the ground again and the bolts snake into the earth with tremendous force, cracking the stone that guards it.

As the energy disperses once more, I stagger backwards, losing my balance as my legs turn limp. When I reach the edge of the fountain, I sit upon it, breathing heavily. I take deep breaths until my heartbeat quietens and all that is left of my impromptu training session are the cracks embedded within the paved slabs. I wipe my forehead with the back of my hand.

At least I have made some progress.

"Elyra?" a small voice calls and I instantly stand up from the fountain at the sound of Maer.

I turn around to find her a few feet away from me. She looks nervous and I realise that she is pulling a small tray with wheels behind her. On top of the tray are two teacups and a pot of tea. It sparks my curiosity.

"You should be sleeping," I tell her and she walks forwards, tray in tow.

"But I brought you some tea." With one arm hugging herself, she sits down next to me, letting the tray roll in front of us. She begins pouring the tea into the cups and watching her precision, I do not have the heart to tell her that I do not drink tea.

"You should not worry about me."

"It seems all I do these days is worry about you." She sighs and my heart sinks at the knowledge. She sits up after pouring the tea but leaves them there to cool.

"That is not my intent."

"I know." She shrugs, looking so small compared to me, even in shadow. "But that is what happens when you love someone. You fear for them."

"Maer, I—" she quickly turns to me and I am startled by her abruptness.

"Must you go to war?"

"Excuse me?" I ask, taken aback by her sudden change.

"We could leave. Tonight. Just you and me. To a place where no-one could ever get to us again." She is frantic and excited. And it scares me. Not for my safety. But for her well-being.

"You know full well that I cannot just simply abandon these people."

"But we could do it. Together. They have soldiers, they can fight. They don't need you like I do." It is times like these when I am truly reminded that Maer is but a child.

"They need my strength, Maer. Just as you did that day in Golnar." I try to reassure her but she carries on anyway, lost in her whirlwind of dreams.

"We could run away in the night. No one need ever know. Of course, we would need supplies but Lukas can always help us with that. Maybe he could come too! Our own little family. We could—"

"Maer, *stop*." My tone is stern and authoritative and she stares at me wide-eyed because of it. I never wish to frighten her but she must understand. It is not in my nature to run away.

"I… I didn't mean to—" she stammers but I give her a soft smile to show that I am not mad at her. Instead I put my arm around her and clasp her to my chest in a light embrace.

"I know that this is hard for you." I stroke her hair while I talk, "But if you cannot find the reason as to why I must stay then let me ask you this: where would you be if I had abandoned you?" Maer looks up at me then, eyes glistening with tears before sobbing into me.

"I c—can't bear to watch you d—die…" her voice is muffled as she buries her face in my chest. I clutch her close to me as if it would somehow relieve her pain.

"Death cannot take me. It fears me too much." I try to joke but she only sobs harder.

"No! You don't understand! Nobody here does!" she cries but I grab her face between my hands and force her to lock eyes with me despite her floods of tears streaming along their sides.

"No, *you* don't understand. Not even Onyxius himself could drag me to the depths of hell without gaining my permission first. I refuse to leave you in life and in death. I do not ask you to stop worrying but I must ask you to have faith in me. Do that and I will never be touched. Do that and I will always come back for you." Her sobbing stops and she wipes her eyes with her sleeve. She seems to sag from defeat.

"You are too noble for your own good," she murmurs.

"On the contrary. I believe that my nobility is for the good of everyone." I offer and she smiles ever so slightly but I cannot shake the feeling that something troubles her.

"What is it?"

"It's nothing." She tries to smile and then reaches for the two teacups, holding them in her hands. I just look at her sceptically.

"I trust that you have ceased all dealings with those who had beaten you?" I find myself asking her and she is surprised by my question. So am I. I do not know why I even decided to ask her that.

"I would rather die than continue on the path that they set out for me," she answers me so quietly and I find myself questioning if she is telling me the whole truth.

"Maer—"

"I don't want to talk about that anymore. Please, drink." She hands me my teacup and I try to hide my grimace as she anxiously watches me take it.

"I wish you would start trusting me enough to tell me your troubles." I absent-mindedly take a sip of the tea and the taste is as bad as I thought it would be. A shiver runs down my spine and I hastily set the cup back down.

When I look back at Maer, I only see guilt.

"Hopefully by tomorrow, my troubles will all be over."

Before I can stop it, my vision fades into the realm of unconsciousness with Maer's apologetic face being the last thing I see before darkness makes it disappear.

Chapter 18

Silence.

Sunlight illuminates the back of my eyelids and yet... there is silence.

No birds singing their morning song, no leaves rife with the chill of the wind.

Dampness coats my side as I feel that I am one with the earth. I open my eyes and the crisp daylight makes me wince and I shield my eyes from the sun. I am in a deep trench; a floor of dirt beneath me and walls of dirt beside me with a ceiling of leaves above bar a small yet significant gap that allows me to see the sky.

And then I gag.

A putrid smell fills my nostrils and my stomach heaves because of it. Covering my nose, I look behind me to find a carcass of a small deer; its midriff has been torn wide open as if another animal had feasted upon it before it was left here.

What in Teragon's name...

A small tear of parchment catches my eye, embedded within the wall to the right of me. I take it hastily, unfolding its crumpled remains:

I did what I had to do.
Stay here. Stay safe.
For me.
Love, Maer

Oh, Maer... what have you done?

Despite my mouth being devoid of all moisture, faint remains of valerian root still coat my tongue.

I curse to the skies above me.

She drugged me.

Maer had actually drugged me. And she used the tea to do it. She must have hauled me here on that contraption she brought with her last night. Was she that desperate to have me not fight in the war that she would leave me here? Did she lack so little faith in me that she thought that this was the answer? How could she be so selfish?

But… why would she leave a carcass in here with me? Why is there a canopy of leaves obscuring this trench from plain sight?

And then I take in the silence.

No wind.

No birds.

Nothing.

Something is wrong.

The earth will only be still in the face of great evil and—

The Bolgren.

Drodal.

They're here.

Maer picked the wrong day to try and protect me.

I leap to my feet, fighting against the foul stench of the deer's carcass. Maer was a fool to think that a trench would stop me from my rightful duty. I am relieved when I touch my sides to find my weapons are still there. She was not wise enough to take those from me at least. Without pausing for thought, I plunge the blades into the dirt one at a time and use them for leverage to pull myself up and out of the trench.

With heavy breaths, I sheath both of them once more and try to take in my surroundings. Never have I felt frustration towards a forest before but does Broxen really have to look the same no matter where you go? I do not even know which way to turn.

Distraught and covered with dirt, I close my eyes to calm my galloping heart. Once it slows, I hear it. I hear them. The faintest of sounds echo throughout Broxen. Muffled sounds of war. I open my eyes instantly and begin sprinting in the direction that I had heard them, terrible thoughts also running through my mind.

The Bolgren. They are here. They are attacking Drodal. And I have spent the entire morning unconscious in a trench! I will be sure to punish Maer for what she has done despite her best intentions but I have bigger and more tragic circumstances in mind.

By the Aerix, I just hope she is okay.

Please, let her be all right.

Let them all be all right.

So many people in that Keep that I love… so many that could die…

And I was not there to save them.

My thighs ache as I pound Broxen's floor with my footsteps, running and longing to reach my goal faster than my feet will allow.

Please be safe.

Please.

I cannot lose them.

Not one of them.

Not now.

The sounds get louder and I can make out vicious roars and heartfelt battle cries. The clash of metal against talons reverberates against my eardrums and I try my best not to balk. No, I will not waver. Not at the sounds of terrified screams nor of blood being split. I will not allow myself to fear war for I will make war fear me.

Just please be safe.

As I start nearing parts of Broxen that I recognise, I find myself having to drown out the cries of terror and malicious onslaught.

I must get there.

I must save them.

And then I see the massacre unfolding before my eyes as the forest begins to give way to Drodal's entrance. Bolgren, vile and ferocious, are attacking Drodal from everywhere I can see. There are Bolgren on the watchtower, Bolgren along the balconies, Bolgren inside its very walls... but most of all, the Bolgren are flooding in through the entrance doors to Drodal despite the efforts of its men. So many... so many Bolgren, hundreds, gnawing and clawing to fight their way into the gates despite their brethren already being inside.

Many bodies lay waste in the courtyard that I have come to love. Blood splattered on pillars, on paved stone, splashed among the fountain and dripping from the blossom trees. I hold in my grief and turn it into anger as my feet go from soil to stone.

I scream. With all my might. I scream. Thunder and lightning echo overhead but I simply focus on unsheathing the marvellous blade that Brogan had forged for me and preparing to shed some black blood upon the mass amounts of scarlet coating this place.

Before the Bolgren can register my presence, I start defending a place that was previously conquered. With my double-ended blade, I start slashing every way I can, feeling nothing but rage when the metal slices through flesh. When I catch a glimpse of long talons, I duck. When I see a flash of venomous teeth, I evade.

Bolgren drop like flies under my wrath, their carcasses falling all around me in large piles. But as more die, more seem to surround me in a never-ending pool of putrid black blood and clash of talons against metal. Soon enough, the Bolgren surround me in a circular constant onslaught, their roars matching my own ferocious growls.

I hear the cries of the battle within Drodal and see flashes of light as mages use their abilities but right now, in this moment, I doubt that I will ever reach the inside. There are too many. Too many beasts in this courtyard with only one warrior defending it. Even as my arms ache and energy wanes, I will continue to defend it.

That is until a Bolgran from my left side slashes its talons against my side. Red blood spurts from my wound and I clutch it with a cry. But this lapse of judgement allows the beast to flick his long arm outwards and backhand me across the face, sending me flying further into the circle of beasts. The others do not attack me. Instead, they wait for the one who dealt the blow to finish me off.

My blade got knocked away from me and it is just beyond my reach. But the Bolgran puts a sharp foot onto my abdomen to hold me in place. It leans forward, dripping venom onto my torso. My dagger is trapped beneath me and I have no means of defence against the fangs poised for my jugular.

Let them be safe.

Let them *all* be safe.

Suddenly, an arrow travelling faster than light pierces the head of the Bolgran before me in a violent surge. It dies upon impact and falls upon the dozens of bodies that I had slain just moments ago. In shock, I look to the watchtower and find a bloodied and battered Elijah readying another arrow into his unusual bow, spitting blood as he does.

He fires arrow after arrow, slaying Bolgren from all directions, the arrows too quick to dodge after being shot from his impeccably tense bow. I am in awe.

How did he know that I was here?

Nonetheless, I know an opportunity when I see one. And I was not about to let this one go amiss. I hastily pick up my blade and join it with my dagger and begin slashing just as much as before, if not more ferociously with my new sense of strength at Elijah's silent rescue. Together, we slay Bolgran after Bolgran, arrows narrowly missing me but always hitting their target. Just as my blades never fail to make impact.

With our joint efforts, I find an almost euphoric sensation taking over me. It is almost rhythmic… our timing, our blows… it is like a dance. As if his arrows set the beat and I dance with my blade accordingly. It is quite beautiful.

And as I slice open the jugular of the final beast blocking the entrance to Drodal, I find myself drenched in black blood and exhausted. Hundreds of Bolgren carcasses lay waste to the courtyard that might as well be a burial ground. My knees buckle in exhaustion and I give way to the floor, squelching atop dismembered limbs.

But despite my lack of energy, I manage to look up to the watchtower and see Elijah smiling at me. It is a smile for all smiles to envy… for it is not an ordinary smile. No… it is full of happiness, of warmth, of admiration. I find myself standing up again, blades in hand at his expression, captivated and entranced by its sheer emotion.

And then I see the true emotion lurking there.

Hope.

Hope that maybe this war is not a lost cause after all. Hope that we may just be able to fight these monsters. Hope that we can conquer these beasts… together.

Without another thought, I plunge myself into the walls of Drodal and am saddened to realise that our efforts in the courtyard were futile. Hundreds of more Bolgren attack those who remain inside the fortress. Fireballs fly past me to ignite some of the beasts while some spontaneously combust without their help. Some choke to death as others are flung against walls with air magic and die from shattered bones. Shards of ice get plunged into the hearts of many beasts the same as I see some Bolgren suffocating as roots erupt from their mouths.

I see spears being lunged, axes being thrown, swords being swung and daggers being thrust. I see so much thirst. Thirst to defend their home from these vile creatures. I cannot help but notice that as some warriors realise my presence, a smile spreads across their faces before they continue to fight with newfound strength.

It makes my heart swell with pride at the lot of them.

And yet, I do not have time to admire them before I frantically search the halls for any one that I might know, anyone that could possibly tell me how my loved ones are faring. I kill any Bolgran that crosses my path swiftly and easily, not letting them affect my search. However my hope begins to dwindle as I travel further into Drodal. I see blood splattered on the walls, dozens of dead bodies lining the ground and I notice how few Bolgran carcasses there are to Drodal's men.

Please be all right.

They have to be.

They must be.

A strong hand swipes at me and I land against the stone wall of my current corridor, breath knocked out of me. Blood trickles along my brow as stars dance against my vision. I sink to the floor in a daze but as soon as I do, a hand grasps my throat sharply and picks me up so that I can look into the eyes of the person now holding my life in their hands.

I was careless. Too lost in my thoughts of my loved ones that I neglected my surroundings. I had expected the attack of a Bolgran. I did not expect the attack of a woman.

"This is your fault," Ayla growls at me, trying to squeeze the air out of me with both hands.

"What?" I choke out.

"You brought this hell upon us." Her eyes are filled with fury and her hair is laced with sweat and blood although mostly her own.

"I did nothing," I spit back before swiping my arm against hers with full strength; she releases me for a bare moment in surprise and it is enough for me to take my blade and aim it at her throat. Ayla holds her hands up to me in surrender but the anger remains in her eyes.

"Then where were you? Where were you as these beasts began their attack hours ago?"

"I was unknowingly put to safety by someone we both deeply care about," I snarl and her eyes widen at the mention of Maer; after all, Ayla spends a great deal of time with her when she is pried away from me or Lukas.

But there is something else in Ayla's expression that makes my anger turn to curiosity. She looks... confused.

"Maer... she is not with you?" that one statement freezes my heart instantaneously.

"Where is she?" I demand, pressing my blade further into her throat until a trickle of blood appears. I try to ignore the pounding in my head after being slammed into the wall but it seems to just get amplified by my worry. The wound in my side continues to ooze to my detriment but I dare not focus on anything else bar Maer's safety.

"I have not seen her," she replies angrily, no doubt due to the fact that the tables have now turned.

"Where is Lukas?" I ask instead. He said that he would keep her safe. He must be here with her somewhere. Please, let him be here somewhere.

"He was defending the kitchens when I last saw him with a handful of others." Just as she finishes speaking, I throw her to the ground with resolve.

I must get there.

On the ground, Ayla continues to stare at me with pure hatred. I only look at her with disgust, unable to find the reason behind her resorting to such lengths as to do me harm and all due to meagre suspicions. Why does she hate me so much? Is it because of our mutual care for Lukas? Or perhaps our love for Maer and Elijah? I have done my best to stay out of her way but she always manages to get in mine. Why? What is her fascination with me?

I am so focused on my thoughts that I do not even realise that a Bolgran has been charging straight toward us from behind me before it is too late. It swipes its talons against my thigh in one sure movement and I crumble to my knees, clasping the wound. The blood seeps through my trousers quickly until it joins the blood from the wound on my side. All the while, my head throbs.

Having seemingly incapacitated me, the Bolgran turns to Ayla who remains an easy target on the floor. I hear that the battle too has moved to this floor of the fortress and I can hear many fighting the beasts to prevent them going any further. Nonetheless, the beast grabs Ayla by her throat with its talons and pushes her against the wall. Blood seeps from her neck as its talons close in and she frantically tries to pull its arm away but she is too weak.

I hold my blade in my hand, weakly at first but then my grip strengthens with resolve to not let my wounds affect my morals. I hate the girl but as I watch her eyes roll into the back of her head from asphyxiation, a glimmer of a plea flashes at me before they completely glaze over.

May the Aerix help me.

But as I stand up and get ready to kill the beast, a sharp cry of a man makes me turn around. A cry of a man that I recognise. In the ensuing battle, I can see Roran on his back, grappling with his sword against the gnashing teeth of a Bolgran, the sword being the only thing stopping the beast from ripping out his throat. He roars in anger out of getting himself in this position.

Time stops.

I look at a struggling Roran, biceps bulging with the effort of keeping the beast at bay. And then I look to Ayla, pinned against the wall and moments away from suffocating. It is as if there is not a brutal war ensuing before my eyes, as if there are not hundreds of soldiers who probably need my aid right now. There is just Roran and Ayla. Both struggling. Both compromised. Both an inch from death.

I can feel my hands igniting with electricity before I see it. One moment I was looking between a friend and foe and the next, my fingers are sparking with blue energy. Ayla's eyes roll to the back of her head violently and Roran's arms are a second away from giving way...

With a cry of rage, I throw my blade at the Bolgran crushing the life out of Ayla with so much force that its head is cut clean off with the attack. Its head lolls on the ground and rolls a few feet away while its body instantly drops Ayla's to the floor before collapsing itself, twitching with its last remnants of life before turning completely still. I rush to her aid and she is struggling for breath. She opens her eyes and is shocked at my appearance. That semblance of life is all I need.

I quickly turn my head around and hurtle a surge of lightening at the Bolgran attacking Roran who has managed to hold on just as I knew he would. The Bolgran is propelled into the wall thirty feet away, blue veins biting it and making it convulse until they fade away. Roran gets to his feet without hesitation, brandishing his sword ready for the beast to attack again with a cry of rage. But just as the beast begins to charge him again, he looks at me quickly with a brisk nod of thanks and then advances upon the Bolgran to meet it head-on in battle.

What a man.

I turn back to Ayla who is coughing profusely on the ground and spitting out splatters of blood. I help her onto her side so that she does not choke and I brush the hair back from her face despite it already being covered in blood. Once her breathing steadies, I release her and get to my feet. A quick glance at Roran makes me smile as I see he has vanquished the beast and has moved on to help the civilians with their battles.

"Why?" Ayla's raspy voice makes me turn back to her, eyebrows furrowed in dislike yet again.

"Excuse me?" She sits herself upright against the wall, wiping blood away from her neck dismissively, still gasping for as much oxygen as she can get.

"The General is your ally, your friend. I have been your enemy since you came through these doors. Why was he not your first choice?" she keeps her tone impassive but her eyes betray her curiosity.

"I do not decipher friend from foe in war," I tell her as I pick my blade up from across the Bolgran's carcass and wipe the black blood against my trouser leg. "There are only lives to save. Roran is strong, I know his capabilities. You needed the help more than he did." I sheathe my blade and look at her, conscious of the war ensuing behind me as we hold this conversation.

"And if you were wrong? If Roran were to have died?"

"Then I would live with the consequences knowing that there was nothing I could do," I tell her softly, turning on my heels and leaving her on the floor in a state of shock.

Running to the kitchens, it is surprisingly quiet. Judging by the numerous corpses of Bolgren and men alike, a battle had already occurred here. Slipping on pools of blood as I go, I slide into the kitchen, hoping with desperation that Lukas would still be in here. And when I do not see him, panic sets in.

Until I round the kitchen counter and find Lukas next to a large dead Bolgran with slash marks on his stomach.

"Lenora?" he says in a rasp. I gasp as I kneel down next to him, brushing his bloodied hair from his face and plugging his wound with my hands. He looks dangerously pale.

"I told you not to fight," I tell him sternly and he smirks lightly.

"I had no choice. We were unprepared for their strike. I had to help."

"And in turn endangered your life." His brown eyes scrutinise me for a moment.

"Where were you?"

"Maer took me far away in the hopes that it would save me." He chuckles slightly but winces in pain as he does.

"But you are too stubborn to be saved."

"Where is she, Lukas?" I ask him and his expression turns from jovial to anxious.

"She never came back." He gulps. "Last night, she did not return."

What?

Why would she leave me and not go back to the fortress? If she feared for my safety, why did she not stay with me?

A sinking feeling appears in my stomach.

"Lukas, where is Breccan?" my voice takes on a sharp edge and it does so involuntarily to me. He stares wide-eyed at me. "Where is my father?" he is not surprised at my words or maybe he just has no strength left to react.

"He was taken to his secret place so that he may be protected. Elijah took him there." Secret place? What secret place? He never mentioned one…

"That can't be right. Elijah was on the watchtower when I had arrived…" confusion warps my thoughts.

Why has he left Breccan alone when charged with his protection?

Is Maer with them? Is she safe?

"That is all I know, Lenora. I swear it."

"Lenora?" a voice says in surprise and I groan at the sight of Ayla in the doorway. Great. I stand up and head towards the door.

"Make sure he is looked after. He has a wound on his stomach but it does not look fatal. Take care of him."

"Where are you going?" she asks, trying to be apathetic.

"I have some questions for Elijah. And I will have them answered," I growl in her face.

Chapter 19

I have been in the heart of battle for a while now. Slashing and stabbing every beast that comes my way. I came here in the hopes of finding Elijah but it seems that the Bolgren have increased in numbers. The soldiers of Drodal are dwindling but we still fight on. Elements are being thrown in every direction and weapons are being swung at every cost. I have killed so many beasts that I doubt that any friend would recognise me for being drenched in so much putrid blood.

As I slit the throat of the Bolgran in front of me, another comes at me from behind. I thrust my open palm into its chest and electrical energy volts through its body and its convulsions stop alongside its heart in seconds. My palm has been ignited for quite some time. It is useful when there are so many creatures in one small space.

Bolgran after Bolgran after Bolgran… it continues to go on until screams increase and exhaustion follows through… until only a handful of us remain. I do not know who I am fighting with nor do I care. We are surrounded, every side of us being hounded by beasts. Soon enough, we are compacted into a small group; bodies tightly compressed against those of complete strangers, strangers that could die in each other's embrace.

I see a woman fall in the distance. Her screams reverberate throughout the fortress as her stomach is gauged out. And so another of Drodal's lives is stolen by our enemies. I look away from the Bolgren's salivating jaws to the lifeless corpses of men and women alike scattered across this corridor.

So much life stolen for the interests of one dictator.

I still do not know where Elijah is, if Maer is still alive or if my father has… no. I must get to him and I will. I will not let these beasts take more than they already have. These monsters have truly overstayed their welcome. And it is about time someone told them so.

I outstretch my hands beside me as they crackle with lightening, reckless licks of electricity already biting at the walls around me, sending rubble flying in all directions. The Bolgren are wary of this power and seem to be too bewitched by its volatile nature to take notice of the danger it poses to them. I do not know what will happen to the soldiers around me should I do this but these animals need to be killed and this is the only way I know how considering their numbers.

The soldiers scream in my ear as they realise my intentions but I do not take note. I push my palms outwards towards the floor as the energy glows brightly with a thirst to kill. With rage in my eyes, I—

"Lenora!" I look to the source of my name and find Elijah at the other end of the corridor.

His chestnut hair is matted with blood and his forest clothing is an array of red and black. His machete is by his side, dripping with the remains of his last victim. His bow is strapped to his back with the last of his arrows in their quiver. He stands strong, unyielding. And yet his emerald eyes are filled with a desperate plea. A plea to not destroy innocent lives.

Oh, my sweet, Elijah.

Now, I do not have to commit the act that you fear so much.

Not now that you are here.

"Ground them!" I shout to him, relieved to see him despite my scolded heart. Confusion flashes across his face for a mere moment before he realises my intent.

He closes his eyes for a second and then nods sternly at me to tell me that it is done. I do not need to look at the feet of the soldiers for confirmation; his nod is enough.

Without waiting any longer, I force the electricity into the ground below me and watch as it travels in frantic veins across the expanse of stone with motive to destroy all who lay waste to it. The Bolgren get electrocuted one my one as the sheet of energy travels between each of them, convulsing uncontrollably and gargling with pain. Some even have their skin melt away from their bones from the sheer intensity of the heat. Once the energy has travelled the length of the corridor, it dissipates just as quickly as it had appeared until all Bolgren lay dead before us.

I realise that there are likely more Bolgren between the floors of Drodal but this floor was bombarded with the most as they sought to conquer. I trust that the remaining soldiers will finish the others off efficiently now that the endless supply of beasts has been tackled. Piles of them lay atop one another, eyes melted into a white froth, skin swarmed with bright red burns and some are still emitting smoke from their flesh having been fried from the inside out.

It is a sight to behold.

One that I am not sure if I should cry out a victory in Drodal's name or vomit in the space next to me. Nonetheless... the sudden quiet is eerie.

Elijah approaches us quickly, stunned to say the least. Without looking at the others, I order them to assist in tackling the rest of the Bolgren that may inhabit these walls; they do so willingly. Elijah looks between me and the thousands of bodies that had once filled this corridor without room to breathe. I do not have time for this and I roll my eyes to tell him so.

"Where is my father, Elijah?"

"Lenora, do you not realise what you have just—" before he can finish, I grab the collar of his blood-encrusted shirt until he is an inch away from my face.

"Where is he?" I growl with pure aggression, enough to make him realise that this war is not over.

"He is safe," he answers and I release him out of angst.

"He would be safe *if* he was guarded. Why are you not with him?" I can barely keep my voice controlled as I stare at the man before me that should be protecting my father from harm according to Lukas.

"Breccan forced me to aid in this war. He could not bear the screams of his people any longer." He does not meet my gaze as he says this and I feel a sense of pride at Breccan's empathy but also a need to kill him for his foolishness.

"Is there anyone else with him?" I start pacing frantically, tugging at my hair with a need to know that he is safe.

"You think that I would leave him alone?" he asks incredulously.

"Just answer the damn question, Elijah!" I bellow and he does as I ask.

"He has two guards with him. Maer is also there."

I stop.

"W—what?" I cannot help my stammer. "Maer... is with Breccan?"

"Of course, Breccan did not want to leave her behind." His eyebrows furrow in uncertainty as he watches my surprise.

"Lukas said that she did not return last night."

"We found her near the entrance to Breccan's hideout. Breccan would not go inside without her."

199

I clutch my head, trying desperately to make sense of all of this.

Why would Maer not return to the fortress last night and yet return during war? If she had feared for her safety, why not stay with me inside the trench? If she was not in the trench and not within Drodal, where did she go after she had ensnared me? And then the leaves... they were used to hide the trench from view... and the carcass... something that grotesque could only be—

No.

I stop with my pacing and stare into Elijah's eyes deadpan.

"Elijah, what is this secret place?" my heart stops as I wait for his answer.

I could be wrong. I have been wrong before and this could be one of those—

"He has a secret lagoon beneath the fortress." My legs give way from beneath me and I lean against the wall for support, my chest weighing a thousand pounds. Elijah continues amicably as if it would somehow help. "It is primarily used for leisure but it makes for a great space should his life be in danger."

"Unless the danger is already with him," I tell him emotionlessly.

"What?" he gasps and I can see the realisation dawning in his eyes.

"Take me there. Now," I demand and he wastes no time in leading me into the depths of Drodal.

Lower and lower we go until the spiralling corridors become draped with cobwebs and coated with dust. We both slay Bolgren and aid survivors as we go but we both know that finding Breccan is more important at this crucial time. Drodal is nothing without its leader and should Breccan be compromised... I do not even wish to imagine the consequences.

When we face the final corridor breathlessly, I sigh grotesquely at the sight of the many beasts blocking our way to the lagoon's entrance. I cannot count them, there is no time. And if there is no time to merely count them then there sure as hell is not enough time to subdue them. And yet, before I can start ripping my hair out to frantically think of a plan, Elijah already has one covered.

With a cry of exasperation, he thrusts his palms out in front of him. When he does, two thick tree roots emerge violently through the concrete floor, flying upwards with the utmost intensity before surging forwards through the centre of the corridor. While the beasts do not have time to register what is happening, the roots reach the end of the hall and then shoot outwards, trapping each beast against both sides; due to the force of the blow, many beast's bones crack and some die instantly while others remain merely incapacitated.

The way is clear.

I look to Elijah with wide-eyes and to my complete surprise, he winks at me arrogantly. Elijah *winks*. It catches me so off-guard that he has to drag me to the end of the hall to where a couple of bookcases line the stone walls. The books that fill them are all antique and dusty to a point where most people would not take them any head. I, however, find them exquisite.

"We did all of this for a bookcase?" I find myself saying, unsure as to why they are significant.

Elijah rolls his eyes at me and then points to a blue velvet covered book in the middle-shelf at the centre of the bookcase. I take a closer look at it and see, in gold letters embroidered on its spine, the title '*A Pirate's Renunciation*'. It sparks my curiosity but without taking further consideration, I pull the book outwards slightly and something clicks; the bookcase is released from its locking mechanism and pushes forward like a door to reveal a dark spiralling staircase.

I look at Elijah and he is regarding me sternly. It amazes me how he can go from one extreme to the other, replacing his earlier amusement with seriousness.

"What is it that you think you will find down here?"

"Truth," I answer him. "I must ask that you hang back. I must confront her alone." Without giving him a chance to speak, I lose myself in the dust-encrusted staircase.

It is cold and damp and the hairs along my forearms stand on edge but I cannot tell if it is due to the chill air or the dread-filled anticipation for what I am expecting to find.

As I travel further and further down the winding stairs, the silence only makes my imagination take a morbid turn. My heart beats so loudly that it is a wonder no one else can hear it. I gulp a breath as a soft blue light fades into the bottom of the stairs to reveal a moss-covered archway and the sound of rushing water fills my ears.

Still hidden in the shadows, I expertly peer around the archway's edges to find a marvellous display of beauty before me. A waterfall gently drops a river of sapphires into the pool below it in an array of shimmering glitter. The pool is bound by engraved stone benches along its side with snowdrops dotting the grassy plane that covers the expanse of the floor.

Breccan sits on one of his benches, twiddling his forefinger in the pool with wonder in his eyes. Maer sits beside him but remains placid at the sight. Two standard sentries stand guard in the shadows upon the opposite wall, unknowing of the threat that is posed here.

Withdrawing my dagger, I gently poise it for action, ready to strike if need be. Who knows who else might be lurking here besides me. I move forwards cautiously, foot treading on grass so softly that if it were not for my call, I would have remained unnoticed.

"Breccan... step away from the lagoon," I call ominously. Maer and Breccan jump at the sound of my voice. I fix my eyes upon Breccan, refusing to let them stray for risk of betraying my emotions.

"What are you doing here?" Maer exclaims with feigned happiness as she stands up quickly with Breccan.

"Breccan, do as I say," I tell him again and his grin fades to concern. Nonetheless, he makes his way towards me. Maer looks between us, twiddling her thumbs anxiously before putting on a smile.

"I am so happy that—" Maer also comes towards me but when I aim the dagger towards her, she stops, brown eyes wide and darting to anywhere but my own.

"What are you doing?" Breccan cries but I keep my eyes on Maer.

"Get behind me... *now*." I breathe a sigh of relief when Breccan's body is behind mine as now I know that he is locked between my protection and Elijah's.

"I hardly think this is necessary!" he says but I refuse to acknowledge him this time.

I look at the eleven-year-old girl standing in the middle of the room. A girl that had been hurtled into a world of crime whilst all the while remaining the victim. A girl I have given my life to protect. A girl I have bled for. She is so small... so vulnerable.

Or so I thought.

"You are quite the actress," I call to her emotionlessly. She shifts unevenly on her feet.

"I—I don't know what you mean," she stammers and the lie pierces my heart harder than the arrow did that day we escaped Golnar together.

"Were you even a prisoner? Or were you simply placed there so that I would find you?" She hugs herself in her usual defensive stance and I feel no sympathy as I once would have. Breccan's hand touches my shoulder softly.

"Lenora, what is the meaning of this?" he whispers but I do not answer. He will find out soon enough.

"So what was the plan? They must have known that the 'great Lenora Belavier' had a soft spot for victims," I snarl bitterly at her.

"*You* are Lenora—" she tries and I laugh coldly.

"Oh, please! You knew exactly who I was the moment they plucked you from the streets! They ordered you to gain my trust and betray me just like all of the other snakes that I have encountered. Did you enjoy watching me suffer on your behalf? Or was it just a perk of the task?"

"I never asked for this," she mutters as her bottom lip quivers uncontrollably.

"So you became a traitor by force?"

"I didn't want this to happen."

"Will someone please tell me what the hell is going on here?" Breccan bellows. With tear-filled eyes, I stare at Maer who is already crying.

"Tell him." My throat threatens to choke my words as heartbreak overwhelms me, "Tell him how you were hired to gain his trust and murder him in the name of Myrna Verena. Tell him how you were told to find me and sell me out to her when all of this was over." She gasps at my knowledge, not knowing that I figured out this plan. "She has been feeding information to Myrna's men all this time. And we had absolutely no idea. *I* had no idea." But Elijah had. And I am not sure that I can ever forgive him for that.

"Is this true?" Breccan steps forward in complete shock but Maer's eyes remain on mine as her tears soak her cheeks.

"I love you." She sobs.

"What do you know of love?" I spit back. "All you know is how to abuse it."

"I tried to spare you!" she cries, wiping her wet nose with her sleeve. "I tried to warn you so many times. I had to resort to hiding you in the woods so that you would not die!"

"Yes and I must say I rather admire your cunning. Drugging me with tea because you knew that I would not refuse you. Disguising the trench with leaves to hide me and planting the carcass to mask my scent from the Bolgren. Perhaps you would have lured the beasts there after this war and be done with me."

"Never!" she cries.

"And the note was just an extra stab in the back." I can see my feral expression within the mirrors of her eyes. She has a right to be terrified of me.

"You were supposed to stay there! You were supposed to be safe!" she becomes almost hysterical now.

"And if I had done, Breccan would be dead by now!" my voice reverberates against the lagoon's stone walls.

"I would never have killed him! This started out as a task but soon became a burden." She crosses her arms over her chest in hurt. "I tried to stop but they beat me until I agreed to continue. I was hoping that I was safe after I told you about this in the infirmary but they still found me. When I realised that they would still carry out this war, I knew I had to save you."

My heart softens against my wishes at the memory of her telling me about the men who had beaten her. How they had wanted her to do something for them and hurt her because she renounced that task. And yet… the effect it has on my anger is only miniscule.

"Save me? Or leave me for dead? You wormed your way into my heart so expertly that I did not even think to question whether it was true. I had to defend your honour against growing suspicion and you just spat it back in my face." I look at her sobbing face and just feel disgust.

Maer betrayed me.

"Please, Lenny. You are the only mother I've ever had…" she whimpers and my heart contracts.

Mother. Lenny. So she did know who I was all this time.

"And now the daughter that I saved from Golnar… is no better than the man who put me there," I mumble, heartbroken so much that I do not think that it can be fixed. There are only so many times that a heart can repair itself before it is doomed.

"And you forgave him," Maer unexpectedly says and my eyes widen in surprise. Not for her audacity. But for her truth.

"He did what I would have done," I snarl back at her, taking a step forward with my anger.

"And what would you have done here?"

"I would have *fought*! I would rather die than betray my family!" I can see that Maer is becoming braver despite my increasing intensity.

"One child is no match for the forces of evil!" she manages to shout back at me and as much as it is odd for me to hear her raise her voice, I can merely focus on the anger now dissipating from my body… slowly being replaced by disappointment.

"But it would have been a start," I mutter softly, the words echoing more than my bellows were. "You just did not try hard enough." With this, Maer deflates and I can barely look at her.

That is, until a cold giggle cracks the tension in the room and two figures appear out of the shadows, the guards that had once been stationed there falling to the floor with wounds to their chests. One towers over the other with impressive mass and as they come closer, I only feel disgust.

Myrna's sentries.

It is undeniable what with their devilish and sadistic air. It is a man and a woman. The woman, I do not recognise; her short blonde hair and pale skin are plain, she is nothing extraordinary save for her beady black eyes that betray her malevolence. The large man beside her has biceps as large as tree trunks, torso strapped with studded leather with a spiked club strapped to his belt; he wears an iron mask, the plate of metal covering his entire face.

I tighten the grip on my dagger so much so that it is a wonder my palm is not bleeding.

This is the man that fought Elijah.

This is the man that imprisoned Benjamin.

This is the man of whom I do not know… but who I already have a vendetta against.

"Maer, stand with me," I say through gritted teeth, not wanting these two anywhere near her despite her being in league with them. She runs over to me instinctively and Breccan secures her to him.

The woman makes disappointing clicking noises with her tongue in the air like a malicious snake in the face of a mouse. The man says nothing.

"Now, that's no way to treat your friends." Her voice is cold and devoid of life. It makes my skin crawl.

"Friends do not beat each other if they are not complicit." I keep my voice steady but the venom remains. Her beady eyes meet mine in an instant and her sharp mouth points into a grin.

"So it is true then. You escaped that Aerix-forsaken furnace."

"Myrna was a fool to think that I would not." My eyes dart between her and the still male who has yet to speak and she catches my gaze.

"Oh, don't mind him. He hardly speaks." She looks at her fingernails in a bored-like manner.

"It is not his mouth that I fear." I eye his spiked club and know that it could break three skulls in one strike.

"But you should. Who knows what secrets he might be able to tell." Her eyes are alight with sadistic amusement and despite her curious words, I choose to remain unfazed. Instead, I notice that she is not an important sentry of Myrna's for I do not know her.

"I had expected to see Cindra here given the importance of this mission." The man next to her growls in agitation and the woman's amusement fades to reveal wrath; Cindra is Myrna's right-hand, a highly sought-after position.

"*I* am worthy of this mission."

"To catch me?" I smirk cockily, "I am in no mood for jokes, sentry." Her eyes narrow with hatred and I know that I have struck a nerve.

I feel Maer huddle against me as she grips my wrist with both of her tiny hands, hiding her face against Breccan. I can hear her soft whimpers and I know that I will do what I can to protect her from these people… no matter that she led them right to us.

"Give us Master Saltmist and no-one shall be harmed," she says through a tight jaw.

"Never."

"This is not a negotiation."

"Nor is it up for debate. Breccan stays here with me." With my decline, she then appeals to Breccan.

"Come on, Saltmist. You know that this would be a lot easier if you were to come with us willingly." I hear Breccan gulp behind me.

"I do," he says gruffly before stepping forward. I outstretch my arm to block him.

"Have you lost your mind?" I exclaim in his face but he does not meet my eyes.

"I have been summoned. Only a fool with no regard for his people could refuse."

"Forget the people. What about me? I just found you." I hiss at him and his sad expression grows.

"People will die," he pleads.

"Not before I do," I tell him sternly.

"Look," the woman says with disinterest, "let's settle this the old-fashioned way, shall we? Either you both come with us or I kill your friends." She shrugs.

"Excuse me?"

"Who should we choose?" she turns to the man and starts overtly thinking, "Perhaps the scrawny cook in the infirmary? Or the rowdy desert-flower in the halls? Or quite possibly…" she snaps her fingers and I hear scuffling from the stairs followed by ensuing shouts.

Within a few seconds, a large body is hurtled towards the floor with their hands bound and as the two burly sentries hoist him up, my mouth dries at the sight of a beaten Elijah. His lip is split and his eye is purple and swollen, new injuries amidst the carnage of battles prior. He clutches his side from, no doubt, sustaining a couple of broken ribs. He is exhausted. His green eyes meet mine with an apology but I only feel dread.

Desert-flower... Alanaat.

Scrawny cook... Lukas.

And now Elijah.

"Tick-tock, Warrior. Who shall taste their impending death?"

Chapter 20

I become a statue.

Unyielding and resolute.

This woman will not see my fear. Because in spite of this ghastly ultimatum, I cannot help but know that Roran escaped the clutches of Myrna's men, meaning his cover is still intact. It means that we still have a chance in this war.

The silence is deafening until Elijah takes in the man in the mask before him. In a split second, he surges forward with a growl unknown to most animals but is soon halted by the henchmen who brought him down here.

"*I will kill you,*" Elijah snarls and I have never heard such ferocity coming from his lips.

And then I remember Benjamin. And how he was held captive and beaten by a hulking man in an iron mask, a man whom Elijah has fought to an inch of his life in order to save his brother. And that man stands before him today.

"You best calm down, heir of Axton. You are in no position to make threats against someone who almost took your life." The girl sneers at him. The man says nothing; he just remains a tower of stone.

"Why are you here?" I ask of them irritably, trying to turn the conversation from Elijah and back to the matter at hand.

"Our reasons are no concern of yours. Choose a friend, Warrior. That is… if you have any left." The glint in her eye is terrifying but my answer is simply a glare. She sighs. "Fine. I guess we will have to decide for you."

With a snap of her fingers, one of the men holding Elijah suddenly grabs Maer and forcibly tries to remove her from my clutches. I secure her to me again with brutal force amidst her terrified cries and poise my dagger to strike the man's throat should he dare touch her again.

"*She* was not an option," I hiss through gritted teeth, Maer crying into my side.

"You are a fool to think that you even *had* an option," she says and the man tries to take her again.

Maer screams and upon instinct, I slash the man's throat without fail and he falls to the floor, blood gushing from his open jugular and onto the grass beneath him. The other comes towards me but when the woman presents her palm, he stops.

"Touch her and you die," I warn to all who may be listening.

"Funnily enough," the woman cocks her head, "I don't like your odds."

More of Myrna's followers appear out of the shadows, tumbling from the stairwell with fervour. Not enough to be considered a massacre but enough to let me know that I am in trouble should I decide to fight. Bodies appear in every direction and my dagger promptly feels very small in the wake of such an attack.

There is only one way out now.

Except, I am not entirely sure how much strength or control I have left.

But it will sure be a surprise for them all.

Sheathing my weapon, the woman takes it as a surrender.

"That's what I thought, *Warrior*." She upturns her nose in arrogance and while she rambles on about her superiority, I look to Elijah who instantly knows my intent. He nods subtly just as he did in that corridor not so long ago.

I would signal Breccan but it would be too obvious to the sentries before us. Besides, he has a greater purpose. I gently push Maer behind me and she has been with me long enough to know when I am trying to protect her. Breccan secures her to him and understands the fragile plan that I have underway.

I close my eyes and ignite the lightening inside me. It does not crackle and surge like it once would have as I do not have enough energy to sustain it. But it is there. My fingertips tingle with oncoming power and as I concentrate on the skies above me, thunder begins to rumble.

The sentries grow unnerved by the sudden storm but the woman stands her ground and tells them to hold their position. But as an ominous wind blows through the lagoon and the sounds of lightening echo in the space, the unease quickly shifts to fear.

"There is one thing you should know about me, sentry." My voice is quiet but the woman halts in her orders. Her eyes shift to me wickedly.

"What?" she bares her teeth with dislike.

"I am not just a warrior," I tell her.

And as I narrow my eyes in menacing, forks of bright white lightening break through the concrete ceiling and strike the men around us with a rumbling death. The woman and man in the mask cringe at each strike but my stare never falters. One by one the sentries fall, burning volts entering their skulls with intent to kill violently, until all that is left are the two standing before me.

The wind continues to howl, ripping at our hair and clothes but I can barely feel it as the smell of burnt flesh reaches my nose. Thunder rolls louder than ever before and with that comes the increase in terror.

"Get up you cowards!" the woman screams at the corpses as the masked man skulks to the back wall in disbelief. "Get up! What, are you afraid of a little storm?" my cold laugh stops her in her tracks.

"You should be." I thrust out my right palm and a blue volt of electricity soars from my hand and into the heart of the woman before me and she crumples to the floor lifeless.

All is silent.

The storm ceases but when I turn to where the masked man was, he has disappeared. I hate myself for losing him but this one may be a fight for Elijah to win. Besides, if what the woman said was true, he cannot say much of what he discovered here anyway which I am sure will work in my favour in the near future.

The ceiling boasts large holes from where the lightening had struck and when I stand beneath one of them and look upwards, I can see that there are holes from each layer of Drodal until I can see the sky. The holes cast an eerie glow to the room as beams of daylight join the sapphire hue of the pool.

"Is everyone okay?" I ask and my voice seems so loud in the newfound silence.

"Well… I…" Breccan stumbles for the right words and it is a sight to see. When he rubs the back of his neck with his hand, an unsure yet amused expression crosses his face, "Define okay?"

When looking to Elijah, battered, bruised and bleeding, one of those silent communications occur between us. His eyes are soft but his face remains stern. He is glad that we are all safe. But I know that the page of history that showed up today will haunt him until he can seek to rectify it.

I jolt with a sudden thought.

"Maer!" I burst out unattractively as I realise that I cannot see her.

A small head of brown hair with big brown eyes appears from behind Breccan and her persona reeks of caution. Looking at her, I can only think of one thing.

"Come here." I gasp with relief and she wastes no time in running towards me and clasping her arms around my waist in a tight hug and rests her head against my abdomen.

I enjoy the hug. I stroke her hair and feel her small frame clutching me with such love, such devotion. I turn her around and face her on my knees, placing both hands on either side of her flushed face. Tears run down her cheeks.

"Are you safe?" I ask frantically, eyes searching for any kind of injury along her body.

"I'm fine." She sniffles. "Do you still hate me?" I sigh at the dilemma but I know what to say.

"I could never hate you," I admit and she puts her small hands atop mine and strokes them with relief, "Just please. Never lie to me again."

"I promise." I touch my forehead to hers and I want to cherish this moment forever.

I never even dreamed of having children. My lifestyle would never allow it. But as I share this moment with Maer, I cannot help but marvel at the maternal instinct blooming inside me. I never imagined what being a parent would feel like and now I never want to let it go. This girl stumbled into my life as a soul to save and I believe that she has saved mine from the very institution we were running away from. We saved each other. And now I have a daughter.

I have a daught—

I hear a rush of air before a sharp crack.

I instantly look up and scan for the source of the noise but Breccan and Elijah stare wide-eyed and open-mouthed in horror.

With furrowed brows, I look to Maer.

Everything becomes a blur.

Trickles of blood fall from her mouth and her body starts to quiver violently in my hands as I secure her waist in my arms. Her eyes plead with mine in fear.

"What is happening?" I choke out but the dread closes my throat.

I can faintly hear a commotion in the background but I dismiss it.

Maer is turning whiter by the second.

I frantically search her body for the cause of this and when I look around her, I find a small black knife embedded in her back.

I do not have time to see where it came from; all I know is that it is there.

And my Maer is dying before my eyes.

"Lenny—" she tries speaking but blood spurts from her mouth and lands on my neck.

"No, no, no, no…" I lay her down in my arms and cradle her to me. I cannot take the knife out for fear of major blood loss. "Maer, stay with me. Someone find a healer!" I scream to whoever will listen.

Someone runs up the stairs.

I stroke the hair away from Maer's face and kiss her forehead. Her body continues to shake and I can feel her getting cold.

"Come on, Maer. Take my strength, you can do it." My tears fall upon her face in large droplets and I try to wipe them away so as not to hurt her further.

"It—it's—n—not… so easy t—this t—time," she answers and I sob.

"Please. I know you have it in you," I plead with her. "Where is that healer?" I shout again but to no avail.

"Y—you g—gave… me a h—home," she manages to say through a sob and I hold her tighter as if it would somehow keep her spirit with me.

"Maer, please. Just hold on. Someone will come. Someone will—" Her small hand touches my cheek and I hold it there, letting my wild tears run carefree.

"I… l—love you, Lenny."

"I love you too." She coughs up more blood and her tiny body convulses against me.

"Please, someone!" I scream at the top of my lungs. "Anyone, please, *help me*!"

As I look at Maer once more, her blood-coated mouth curves upwards into the smallest of smiles. I return that smile for her benefit as I hold her hand tighter to my face. With the smile still on her lips, she opens her mouth.

"M—mother…"

I hear footsteps tumbling down the stairwell but do not bother looking up.

Not now.

Not as I watch the light leave Maer's eyes.

"Maer?" I whimper. "Maer?" I hope to hear her kind voice but she does not answer me.

She will never answer me.

An inhuman noise escapes my mouth as I realise that my Maer is gone. I put my arms around her small lifeless body and lift her so that I can hold all of her to me. As if holding her tightly enough will bring her back.

I weep into her neck.

I weep like I never have before.

I glance at who ran down the stairs and Elijah has brought everyone he could back and all are distraught. Brogan, Roran, Alanaat... Ayla.

I focus on her completely.

"There must be something you can do." I get out, trying to swallow the ever-growing lump in my throat.

"I... I don't think that—"

"Please!" I shout at her, tears falling aimlessly. "*Please!*" I beg but she bites down her lip as it quivers. "My baby..." my face scrunches in a way only a grieving mother will understand.

I hug Maer.

I hug her as if my own life depended on it.

I kiss her cheeks fruitlessly and clutch her head to my shoulder.

She is dead.

Maer is dead.

And there is nothing I can do about it.

Nothing but scream away my grief.

My friends watch helplessly as the Warrior's soul shatters before them in a storm of angst and grief, wondering if it can ever be restored.